Once Upon a Lie

Other Books by Ellen Frazer-Jameson

The Love Trilogy:

Love Mother Love Daughter

Love Refuses to Die

Love Kills with a Kiss

———

Flame Island
(originally released as *Dark Hole in My Soul*)

Seven Steps to Fabulous

Slim with the Stars

Travels with Otto

ELLEN FRAZER-JAMESON

FOURTH DIMENSION
of South Beach

Published by
Fourth Dimension of South Beach

© 2019 Ellen Frazer-Jameson

The right of Ellen Frazer-Jameson to be identified as author of
this Work has been asserted by her in accordance with sections
77 and 78 of the Copyright, Designs and Patents Act 1988

ISBN: 978-0-578-42678-5

Cover design and typesetting: Gary A. Rosenberg
www.thebookcouple.com

In memory of
Salvatore's Eternal Flame.

Free to love again.
Time to believe that broken tears are
melting the ice that encases your heart.
Embrace the eternal flames that light
the path to the future.

Prologue

The ivory-handled penknife sliced with vicious intent through the shiny red masking tape that sealed the gift-wrapped cardboard box and offered a veneer of perceived privacy. The hand that wielded the blade disregarded the handwritten warning on the side of the box, *Personal—in the event of my death—destroy unopened.*

Two floors below and a world away, the mood of the funeral party escalated from somber to jovial and teetered on the verge of the macabre. Jokes, memories and anecdotes, revealed and fueled by an ocean of alcohol and accompanied by raucous laughter, joyously unveiled the deceased as a beautiful, untamed and unpredictable character. A rule-breaker and risk-taker. A pleasure-seeker.

Alone in the attic, shadowy figures, oblivious to the funeral party downstairs, slashed at the container with the knife. Refusing to be denied entry, they became ever more determined to uncover the secret of the sealed, bright-red cardboard box. The air filled with the sound of labored breathing that endowed the atmosphere with anticipation and desperation.

The seal held and issuing an ominous silent warning,

the very air, loyal to the recently departed Antoinette, threatened, "You will live to regret this."

* * *

Mediterranean sunshine demanded entry through the free-floating, full-length, pure white net curtains. Playfully it flickered on Antoinette's closed eyelids; the day called out for attention. Early warmth invited her to unwrap the silk brocade bed coverings and reveal her naked body.

Too late she prayed her mantra: "Please God have mercy on me. Don't make me wake up today."

The heartfelt prayer was repeated over and over again in the unforgiving blackness of the hours as her soul made its tortured journey through the unlit night.

Even the bright sunlight struggled to eliminate the saturation of dark despair left by the nighttime journey. Forced to accept that her desire was denied, she raised her weary body, eyes still tightly closed in defiance, and refused to acknowledge the light streaming into her opulently furnished bedroom.

A cruel joke that she should have to face yet another day.

Her back to the offending source of radiance that flooded the room with joy, she sat, unmoved, in silence and questioned an unseen Deity. "Tell me, when do grief, pain and humiliation win the battle and kill a barely alive human being?"

The answer, as always, eluded her.

"Damn you," she spoke out loud.

Wraith-like she rose from her eerily deserted king-size bed, once the luxurious resting place of two fully present human beings. The golden brocade outer covering, which matched the ornate ceiling-to-floor drapes, was disheveled on one side only. The other half, perfectly undisturbed, accused like an empty tomb. Half a life, she was condemned to live half a life.

Antoinette averted her eyes from the ornate gilt-framed mirror that reflected her solitary boudoir. Her reflection in the mirror too awful to contemplate, she made her way barefoot across the room.

"Promise me," she challenged the invisible presence, "that today you will give me the courage to take my own life."

Chapter One

Pounding waves crashed over white rock, and the surf rushed to the shore. A sparkling aquamarine sea reflected the painted blue sky with wispy clouds drifting in a tranquil landscape.

God was in His heaven and *elsewhere*; all may have been well with the world. Alone on a jagged outcrop, a forlorn figure, Antoinette Anderson fixed her gaze on the dark underbelly of the treacherous sea. She watched angry waves crash on black carbon rocks that sparkled with silver in the sunlight, and she remained steadfast as the salt spray seasoned her tears.

Reflecting the black hole that poured into her and overpowered her heart, she craved the moment when she would submerge herself in the inky black water as it splurged over the rocks and foamed with rage. She wanted to feel her body crushed by the excesses of the raging sea.

She knew this isolated place as though she owned every rock and boulder, but though it stirred deep, painful memories, she refused to stay away. The torment was sweet torture, precious moments when she felt real, engaged, strangely alive.

Amidst the misery, a light-filled memory of laughter, a protective hand caressing hers and an all-encompassing feeling of being loved fought to be acknowledged. She denied their existence.

"Love is for the living," she consoled herself. "I no longer have to believe the lie. I have lost the will to live. I am dead."

Chapter Two

White roses were Olivia Rose's favorite. Of all the thousands of perfect blooms at the Chelsea Flower Show, she never lost her love for the virginal white blossoms that held the promise of purity and innocence and offered a corsage of fresh petals on which to write a vision of the future.

There was no need of a reminder in her diary. For as long as she could remember, the five days in May and the months leading up to it were dedicated to the Royal Horticultural Society's showcase event held at the Royal Hospital Chelsea.

Rose Cottage Nurseries had been in her family for three generations. Her father and his father and his father before him had been competing at Chelsea for over sixty years and all were proud recipients of Gold Medals at the famous flower show that was attended by the British Royal family and visitors from every continent.

Silver was an indignation, less than a poor second best.

Champions' trophies, cups, medals and ribbons lined the shelves of the spacious lounge at the homely farmhouse in the small Surrey village designated by the

National Trust as an area of "Outstanding National Beauty," where her father tended his prize roses and exported new varieties all over the world.

Olivia Rose Anderson used seed catalogs as picture books before she could read.

Olivia Rose's father, Jason, a tall, handsome man with curly sand-colored hair and a permanent smile, acceded to his Italian wife's wishes to name their baby daughter Olivia, but he insisted that she be given the second name, Rose.

Jason rarely called Olivia Rose by her first name; her mother called her Olivia Rose when she was in one of her bad moods. Which was often.

Antoinette Anderson returned Jason's open smile with an uncompromising frown. Her husband was a disappointment to her and as a daddy's girl, Olivia Rose was cast as the enemy.

Father and daughter referred to Antoinette as the Red Queen and under their breaths whispered to each other, "Off with their heads."

Olivia Rose took particular pleasure in marching through Jason's immaculately tended greenhouses deadheading the roses. "Here comes the Red Queen," warned Olivia Rose, as she watched her mother leave the farmhouse and march down the garden path toward the temperature controlled area filled with fragrant Olivia Rose bushes.

"She's on the warpath," said Jason, not losing his grin but the smile did not reach his eyes.

"Hello, my dear," he said amiably as Antoinette,

who once answered to the nickname Twon but now preferred the full version of her name, flung open the glasshouse door. "What can I do for you?"

Olivia Rose had never dared question her father about when her parents' relationship had gone so wrong, but it appeared to be beyond repair. As Olivia Rose entered her teenage years, her mother regularly threatened to leave. Jason always talked her out of it. His contrition was accompanied by lavish gifts. Antoinette expected to be treated like a Queen.

Growing up she had been a beloved only daughter and her parents and their extended family loved to indulge their beautiful offspring. Antoinette was spoiled and no one denied her that privilege, for it had not turned her head, only confirmed her sense that she was entitled. Culturally, Italian girls were represented as precious objects, Madonna-like, feminine, delicate and worthy of respect and adoration.

To repay the privileged upbringing that was her birthright, Antoinette was dignified, charming, vivacious and a loving daughter. She was also a caring mother, though her isolation in a country where she did not speak the language and whose traditions and fashions were foreign to her often made her seem aloof. In her new surroundings, Antoinette's self-composure was perceived as superiority.

Jason was no match for Antoinette. Truth was, he had long ago accepted that she was out of his league. She intimidated him. He always felt wanting in her presence. A modest English rose grower was no match for a Roman Goddess. An Italian Count would have been more her style. He had plucked her from an elegant classical garden and transplanted her among his boring flower beds.

Olivia Rose feared another row between the two and attempted to leave the greenhouse. "Shall I come and help you make lunch?"

Her reply suggested that help around the house was not what was on Antoinette's mind. "No, darling, I have already made your favorite, Thai shrimp salad, and to follow, lemon sorbet." She flashed a dazzling smile that reminded Jason of the reason he fell in love with her. On a Royal Horticultural Society visit to Italy, Antoinette had shown the group around her family's olive farm in the Tuscany region.

A refined, statuesque redhead, she was almost as tall as Jason, who stood at 5 feet 11 inches. Over the years she had put on a few pounds, in all the right places.

"I've decided to go and visit my family in Italy," she said without preamble. "Will you two be alright home alone for a few days?"

Olivia Rose looked at her father. His smile had faded.

"When did you decide this?" he asked.

His wife maintained a pleasant demeanor, seeking approval for her plan. "I could take Olivia with me if you like," she said. "The family loves to see her. They make such a fuss of her."

Olivia Rose's eyes pleaded with her father, and she shook her head imperceptibly. She felt embarrassed that she had never learned to speak her mother's native tongue, and she found all the attention from aunts and uncles and cousins overwhelming. Not to mention that she got the uneasy feeling she was an object of curiosity to the whole village.

To her relief, Jason picked up the message. "No, leave Olivia Rose here with me. She's a good help; she loves the flowers." He avoided adding, "Unlike you."

Halfway out of the door, Antoinette issued orders. "Olivia, look after your father. Make sure you both eat.

"The housekeeper will be here the day after tomorrow; she'll make sure the house is cleaned up before I get back."

The panes of glass rattled as she made her exit, but she wasn't quite finished. "I'm leaving tomorrow," she fired a parting shot. "You know where I am if you need me."

Jason's body slumped as the roaring force that was his wife departed the premises. He sat down on one of his upturned giant plant pots and put his head in his hands. "Yes, I know where you will be," he said through gritted teeth.

Olivia Rose realized that she was not meant to hear that remark and did not ask for an explanation. Instead, she made light of the situation. "Yippee, we're off the reins for a few days. Tell me something fun you'd like to do. And don't dare suggest a game of croquet."

They laughed together, and Jason pasted his grin back in place.

Chapter Three

Olivia Rose heard first the sound of raised voices and then the crash of breaking glass. It was the middle of the night. She leaped from her bed and peered out of the window into the garden. She could see nothing through the pitch dark.

The angry voices continued; they were coming from the greenhouse and then there was the sound of more breaking glass. "What's going to go wrong, now?" she mumbled. It had not been a good day. Everything started to go wrong as the judging panel for Florist of the Year deliberated.

Jason had tensed and waited for the result. "That Gold medal has got my name on it," he had reminded Olivia Rose earlier as they drove to the Royal Hospital, home of the Chelsea Flower Show in London. "I've won it for the last five years, and before me, your grandfather and great-grandfather claimed the top prize."

The journey from their Surrey home was less than an hour, but for Olivia Rose, it was a most uncomfortable trip. "Yes, I know, I know; I'm sure you will win," she agreed, eager to reassure her father that she did understand how important his reputation and that of the nursery were.

"But can we please open the window to let out the smell of manure. Don't know why I bothered to dress up when I'm sitting with an open bag of s-h-i-t on the back seat."

Her father glared at her. "It's not manure, it's mulch," he said, displaying the irritation that worry over the Best in Show prize had brought up in him. This year in particular.

"I need to give the Olivia Rose bushes a cool drink of water and a little feed before the judges give them the final once-over. We want our prize roses to look their best, don't we?"

Nodding her head, Olivia Rose held her nose.

Later, as they stood with the other contenders in front of the judges' table, Olivia Rose squeezed her father's hand. "Of course you'll win, silly," she reassured him.

The judges did not keep the competitors in suspense. "Congratulations to our Gold Medal winner and Florist of the Year," said the Chairman in an even tone that belied the importance of the award, "Gianni Almora, a first-time contender from Italy."

No one was more shocked than Olivia Rose that her father had been denied the treasured first prize. Without waiting to hear the runner-up results, Jason stormed off, his face black as thunder. All trace of his trademark smile gone.

In all her sixteen years, Olivia Rose had never seen

her father so consumed with anger. But then he had never needed to be a good loser.

"I don't do Runner Up," he shouted over his shoulder when she caught up with him in the crowded pavilion. "Silver is for losers."

"We're going home," he said, "I'll get one of the local members to collect my exhibits and bring them home. The Show is over." With bitter irony, he added, "In more ways than one."

She tried to make conversation on the way home, but her father refused to respond. He didn't even laugh when she made a joke about the smell of manure. "I knew it was going to be a shitty day," she said.

"You don't know the half of it," he brooded.

By the gate at the bottom of the lane that led to their farmhouse, he dropped her off. "Where are you going?" Olivia Rose's voice was full of concern. "Can I come with you?"

"I'm going to get drunk," he admitted. "Don't wait up."

This was so not like her father. He never drank more than the odd glass of wine with dinner.

Olivia Rose endured a night at home alone. Her mother was off somewhere and hadn't even bothered to leave a message. Increasingly the married couple led separate lives, and Olivia Rose felt like she lived in a single parent household with her dad. She realized she could be accused of being a daddy's girl and always taking his side, but the fact was, Antoinette was a hard act to follow. Olivia Rose never quite felt up to the competition. She wished she could be more like her mother, but in reality her personality was more like her father's.

Olivia Rose watched television, microwaved a pizza and ate indecent amounts of chocolate ice cream. She contemplated phoning friends but knew that none of them would want to hear about second prize in a flower growing competition. Even a prestigious event such as the Chelsea Flower Show. "Get a life," was their response whenever she tried to talk about her father's award-winning roses. Not even for the sake of their friendship did her supposed best friend attempt to spare her feelings. "The only roses that interest me are red ones in a great big ribbon tied with a bow sent by a gorgeous guy on Valentine's Day," one of her friends enlightened her.

Olivia Rose gave in to the emotional and exhausting events of the day and went to bed early. Her mother had texted, Out with a friend. Are you okay? Let me know if you want me to come home.

She texted her father several times and received short shrift in reply to each message. I'm fine. Be home soon. Don't wait up. GO TO BED.

Down on her knees, she searched under the bed for her over sized animal head slippers, carelessly kicked off when she climbed into her comfy feather bed several hours earlier. Exiting the bedroom, she grabbed a towelling bathrobe from the back of the door and put it on.

She pulled the bathrobe bottom up to her waist to avoid tripping down the stairs and clenched her toes to keep on the animal slippers. Olivia Rose could see through the open plan farmhouse kitchen with its pine dining table and heat-giving Aga oven and noticed that the back door was wide open.

In the dark, it was impossible to keep up her fast pace. Despite the fact that she knew every paving stone in the moss-covered path that led down to the greenhouse, Olivia Rose checked every step and trod carefully.

Silhouetted against the all-glass greenhouse windowpanes, illuminated by low-level lighting and heaters warming the beds where the Olivia Rose bushes took root and flourished, Antoinette and Jason were locked in verbal battle.

The words were indistinguishable, but their fury was undeniable. Olivia Rose hesitated. She did not want to intrude, but neither did she care to witness her parents engaged in such fury. Her father was seriously drunk; her mother looked at him with disgust.

Heart pounding and having no idea of what she might be able to do to make the situation better, she crept closer to the greenhouse. The shouting grew louder, and she watched in horror as her father picked up one of his beloved Olivia Rose bushes, a special variety he had spent years breeding to perfection.

He balanced it above his head like a javelin thrower and then let go as he launched it at high speed toward one of the plate glass windows. The window shattered, and the whole greenhouse threatened to come crashing down.

Face contorted with rage, he picked up an even larger potted Olivia Rose bush. Olivia Rose feared for her life if she tried to walk toward the missile and enter the greenhouse. Frightened to stay and scared to go, she stared at the shattered glass that glinted viciously on the dark ground and tried to sidestep it.

Jason held the plant as he screamed at Antoinette, who appeared transfixed by the spectacle as her drunk husband wreaked havoc on his life's work.

"Your sordid little affair was not enough for you. How much do you think you hurt me over all the years? I forgave and turned a blind eye for the sake of our family, our daughter, our home, the business I put my heart and soul into."

The bottled up humiliation and pain of years poured out and he trembled with rage. "As if that wasn't enough, you stole the thing you knew I valued above everything else. My reputation. You destroyed my life and handed me a Runner-Up ribbon. You knew he was going to compete against me.

"God, how you two must have laughed at me. You may as well have put a knife through my heart as take away my Best in Show. Your lover. How dare he steal my Florist of the Year award?"

Antoinette flinched visibly but never took her eyes from the weapon in her frenzied husband's hand.

"I could kill you," he screamed as he used both hands to throw the Olivia Rose bush in its terracotta pot across the room, which was filled with row upon row of roses in various stages of growth, from baby seedlings all spindly and bare to luxuriant full-grown bushes. Inside him something snapped that night. Torn apart and broken, his spirit never recovered.

Cold night air from the shattered window rushed into the greenhouse. Jason broke down in tears and fell to his knees, all rage spent. Antoinette looked on with disdain. Her arrogance intact. Jason had yet again fallen short of her standards. How long could she tolerate knowing her marriage was a sham? She had been given an ultimate; she needed to follow her heart.

Olivia Rose could stand no more. Leaving her place of safety, she picked her way through the river of broken glass. Opening the half-timbered door to the greenhouse, which still shook and rattled at the outrages imposed upon it, she made her way to her father. Knees bent, she reached down and cradled him in her arms. She wiped the sweat from his forehead with her bare hand and fixed unforgiving eyes on her mother. Her eyes burned with hatred and loathing as she looked at the woman who had inflicted so much damage.

Unflinching, her mother returned her steadfast gaze and, with only the barest sign of regret, made a weak apology, "I'm sorry, Olivia. I'm not leaving you. You can come to me anytime."

Her composure barely shattered, still Antoinette taunted her husband. Now that all the fight had gone from him, she retaliated. She used no weapons, only words. Words that cut into his flesh like the sharpest of rose thorns. "You always cared more about those stupid bloody roses than about me. I never wanted to be the wife of a small-town florist. Gianni is independently wealthy. He can give me the life I desire. He owns a vast estate of olive groves; his family and mine have been neighbors for generations."

She laughed at a private joke and informed her husband, "Growing roses is a hobby for Gianni. It amused him to compete against you. Italian men love to beat their rivals. Gianni was my first love. I should never have left him."

Her strappy red high-heeled shoes were covered in debris from the damaged building, but Antoinette seemed oblivious as she stepped through the wreckage, head held high. One final insult filled the shattered air. "People who live in glass houses shouldn't throw stones—or flower pots."

* * *

The broken glass in the greenhouse was repaired and looked good as new. The roses, hardy specimens that they were, survived. Jason did not. He was never the same again.

Much as Olivia Rose cajoled, he refused to enter his blooms into the showcase Flower Show. Working together, pruning roses at a bench in the greenhouse that forever would hold the memories of that fateful night, Olivia Rose tried again. She handed him a pamphlet with an application form from the Royal Horticultural Society. "There's still time to qualify for entry into Chelsea," she pleaded. "Let's put the trophies back on display and remind ourselves of your glory days. You can do it again. It's not too late."

"Don't keep on at me. It's over," Jason replied. "I've nothing left to prove. What a fool I was. Can you believe, I thought your mother would be proud of me? Of the fine tradition of our family? She broke my heart, and I don't choose to endure the pain of failure again. You'll understand when you get your heart broken."

Olivia Rose despaired. She knew of no way to heal her fractured family and had taken a vow not to talk to her mother since the day she walked out several years before. It felt disloyal to her father.

"This is not about me," he tried to reason with her. "She's your mother. You'll regret your decision one day." Olivia Rose felt an overwhelming sense of abandonment. Since the night of the breaking glass, Jason had found solace in a bottle.

Olivia Rose lived with the pain of the betrayal they had both endured and, in her darkest moments, challenged herself to find an escape from the despair that hung on her like a black cloud.

The way out of her dilemma came in a flash. "I need to prove to myself that love, marriage and happiness do exist," she told Jason. "Your beloved roses inspired me. I'm going to open my own wedding planning business.

"I already have the name. It's to be called White Roses Wedding Services, Pure Romance."

Chapter Four

Gold boots, once the trademark of a soccer God, were now a forlorn symbol of his fall from Grace. Callum Lavelle knew how amazing it felt to live life at the top of his profession, applauded, revered, entitled. On the field of battle in Premier League matches and Internationals all over the world, his gold boots dazzled and showed off his exceptional footwork, skill and ball control. Corporate sponsors fought bidding wars to sign him for exclusive multimillion-pound contracts.

Thanks to the gold boots and his attention-grabbing fashion statements, the press conferred on him a nick-name: Callum Cool. A statue of the gold boots held pride of place on the trophy shelf in his man cave. Before it all crumbled to dust.

Like a Cinderella whose clothes turned to rags at midnight, Callum Cool was no more. Kicked off Mount Olympus. "I feel like I've become the invisible man," he confided to his mother. "The Club doesn't want to know me. My teammates are scared their reputations will suffer if they hang out with me and the fans have made me a scapegoat for all that's wrong with the team."

"Why don't you go to the press?" asked his mother. She still burned with indignation that her son, the soccer star, the shining light of her life, had been brought down to earth. "You did nothing wrong," she told him over and over again, ignoring the facts of the case.

"I took a banned substance," he reminded her. "No one believes that the coaches handed them out and claimed they were performance enhancers, not illegal substances. Mind you, they did stress that they were undetectable in drug tests so they knew they were not on the approved list. How many athletes do you think have been banned for taking drugs that they didn't know were banned in professional competition? Whole countries of professional athletes are taking these products."

"Go to the press," she said again.

Holding on to his temper, Callum tried once more to explain. "I signed a Non-Disclosure Agreement with the Club. If I make any comments publicly, they can sue me. As if I'm not in enough trouble already."

Callum was tired of the conversation but acutely aware that his mother was one of the few people who still answered his calls. "I've got to go," he said. "I'm moving to a new hotel tonight. I'll be in touch."

"Remember what I told you," she replied. "Don't come home. The police are still looking for you. They come round here every couple of days. That bitch, your ex-wife, is determined to press charges."

Callum disconnected the call, threw money on the bar to pay his bill and walked out of the nondescript Spanish seafront hotel. At the first rubbish bin, he jettisoned the cell phone. Every few days he bought a new pay-as-you-go. Untraceable. His fancy iPhone was in a storage locker at the airport along with his wallet and credit cards. In his pocket, he carried a large wad of cash, and he concealed his passport in the lining of the baseball cap he wore all the time. It offered anonymity and shielded him from prying eyes.

If it weren't so scary, it would be funny, he told himself. *I've become a fugitive, a man with no name. Thank God for all those detective stories I read and watched on TV and video as a kid because I learned what to do. A man on the run from justice. Or so the ex-wife would have everyone believe.*

What else could she expect?

After the call from the Chairman that had shattered him and delivered the devastating news that he was banned from his sport —and any other—for life, Callum drove straight to the home of his ex-wife. A fancy modern house in a gated community on England's South Coast that he had bought for her after the divorce. A property for her and his young daughter to keep them in the manner to which they had become accustomed. The Judge was very clear about that.

Despite the divorce and continuing acrimony between the warring couple, now and then they kissed and made up—and ended up in bed. A truce was in operation, and they spent a loving few days together on the weekend of Callum's fateful drug test.

Samantha answered the door and was not happy to see her ex-husband. He soon realized why. She had another visitor. Callum asked no questions. He was filled with rage at the news he had received from the Chairman; he was ready to fight anyone. Samantha's male visitor made a bolt for the back door when Callum angrily forced his way into the lounge, grabbed him by the throat and proceeded to pummel him with his mighty fists.

Leaving the visitor bloodied and bruised, Callum threw the guy onto the floor and pushed Samantha aside as she screamed, "I've called the police."

"Wouldn't be the first time," said Callum as he stormed down the hallway and out of the house. "You always think they can protect you when you're the one in the wrong."

With no intention of hanging around to await their arrival, Callum jumped into the SUV and drove straight to the airport one hour away. He parked in the long-term car park and took the shuttle to the terminal.

At the British Airways desk, he threw down his limitless Black American Express card and asked, "I need some sunshine. When's the next plane leaving for Spain? I'll have a First Class ticket."

Forty minutes later he was settled in a window seat on his way to Barcelona, drinking champagne. On arrival three hours later, Callum Googled a hotel in the city center and booked a luxury room for two nights. Checking in at reception, he ordered a bottle of champagne for his room. The mini bar would take care of the rest of his needs. Given enough alcohol he hoped to at least sleep through to the next morning, then he'd come up with a plan.

Falling into unconsciousness several hours later, he remembered, *I promised myself I wouldn't drink today. Too late now. Perhaps a drink would make it all better. It could hardly make it worse.*

Chapter Five

"Another cancellation," said Olivia Rose, as she pressed the red disconnect button on her cell phone. "The third this week. Our business is in ruins. What's happening? What did we do wrong?" Olivia Rose addressed the question to her assistant, who shrugged. She had no answers but could see where this was heading. She would soon be out of a job.

White Roses Wedding Services had enjoyed an excellent reputation since Olivia Rose started the business from a small office crammed in the back of her father's nursery garden. After moving flower pots, trays and bags of earth, her father painted the walls white, cleaned the tiny window and made the small room habitable.

"Soon as you turn a profit, you can get yourself proper premises," he said, "but for now, marketing and building up a reputation is more important."

In no time at all, Olivia Rose outgrew the potting shed and moved her business into a fancy high street office she shared with a wedding dress shop. Perfect partners, the two businesses grew and flourished. Olivia Rose was in her element. She had found her passion and even if she had not yet found her own happy ever after, she was inspired to make sure that other brides experienced their unforgettable dream wedding.

Olivia Rose loved discovering all about the bride and her husband-to-be and helping to plan every detail of the wedding. Every bride was treated as a VIP and encouraged to spend as much time as she needed to discuss her wedding requirements and to work her way through the mountain of books, photographs, catalogs and brochures Olivia Rose had collected in her journey through the wonderful world of weddings.

Sharing the vision of the bride and gently guiding her to possibilities she had not been aware of, Olivia Rose delighted in the adventure as well as the opportunity to use her expertise and experience. In a beautifully furnished white room, hung with white tulle curtains and decorated with enormous vases of white roses, Olivia Rose guided and encouraged the eager brides.

Even when she had an army of assistants working for her, she went out of her way to welcome every bride. "What's your vision?" she asked. "This extraordinary day will live on in your memory for the rest of your life; nothing is too good for you. It's my job to help you make it happen. Let's not even consider the cost at this stage. Don't limit your imagination. Tell me your dream."

At ease and confident that no request would be too extreme or outlandish, the brides opened up. Often even their mothers or friends who accompanied them to the consultation had no idea of the fantasies that filled their wedding dreams. "Think of me like a fairy godmother," said Olivia Rose. "Together we can make this happen."

Venues, catering, music, transport and, of course, the most exotic floral arrangements, Olivia Rose knew about them all. "The perfect wedding takes a year to plan," she told her clients, "don't rush the process.

"Allowing yourself time will ensure less disappointment when places or people or cars or the wedding photographers or caterers of your choice are booked up. Enjoy every day of the journey. And be prepared for tears.

"Your groom may not always see the event the same way as you do. Use these opportunities to see how you as a couple manage your expectations and how well you negotiate and compromise. Planning the wedding will tell you a lot about how your groom expects you to manage your married life. Is he accommodating or demanding, are you able to accept the difference maturely or do you burst into tears and threaten to call off the wedding at every sign of disagreement."

Olivia Rose relished her role as an advisor, counselor, mother of the bride, best friend and, on occasion, an arbitrator in disputes. Constant attention to detail and the bulging file of letters from satisfied customers ensured recommendations and even repeat business. Not all marriages last forever, but hope springs eternal and some brides needed to give romance a second chance.

"So, where did we go wrong?" Olivia Rose repeated the question to her assistant. "Our business has attracted more blight than a barrel of dead roses."

She looked out from the sanctuary of her specially designed salon at the rear of the store into the wedding dress shop at the front. "Judging by the number of starry-eyed young ladies who gaze with longing at the wedding dresses, I can't believe that hearts and flowers or romance have gone out of fashion.

"Why are people canceling their wedding with White Rose?" She was seriously worried.

Her assistant Maria was flicking through a wedding magazine, her head already filled with thoughts of where she would get another job. Maria hated to admit it, even to herself, but she had come to work at *White Rose* in the hope of finding a husband. The logic somehow made sense to her, as if she expected men to come into the store looking for a bride along with other wedding services. Sadly the image she held in her mind of herself as the perfect bride did not necessarily correspond with what any potential bridegroom might see.

Maria was shorter than she imagined herself to be, she was less slim than her ideal image, and her curly black hair enjoyed more bad hair days than the average great hair day goddess. She dressed flamboyantly but not necessarily to best effect.

The secret of her real worth, if only she could embrace it, was her enduring enthusiasm. Her belief that any and every bride deserved to be the most beautiful woman in the world on her wedding day. She encouraged brides to see their own best potential and to develop confidence that would shine through when the special day arrived.

Over time Maria had transitioned from working in the wedding store to being Olivia Rose's assistant. She was efficient, knowledgeable and had a massive network of wedding professionals. There was not a significant wedding show anywhere in the British Isles that she had not attended. She stuffed her show bag full of business cards, and her Rolodex contact file could have made a perfect confetti shower.

Olivia Rose depended on and trusted her right-hand woman and would do anything to ensure that the cohesive team they had developed would not fall apart. Always immaculately dressed, Olivia Rose favored Dior style suits, and today she was wearing a sky-blue two-piece with a pale pink blouse and navy stilettos.

Her father often teased her, "I should have known I wouldn't be able to keep you down on the farm in jeans and Wellington boots up to your eyes in the mud. You're the image of your mother, always turned out like a *Vogue* fashion model."

Olivia Rose was tall and elegant, and her hair was a striking combination of her mother's vibrant red tresses and her father's curly sand color—a burnished copper. Her hair fell in waves past her shoulders, and she wore a half fringe almost covering one eye, adding to the glamour of her overall look. Old-style Hollywood, like the legendary Veronica Lake. She had not yet filled out enough to acquire her mother's voluptuous figure. Instead, she was slim with curves on her hips and breasts.

"Pass me the order book, Maria," Olivia Rose said, "I'm going to get to the bottom of this. Three weddings canceled. I don't like the smell of it. I've got to find out what is happening."

Standing in the middle of the room and giving herself plenty of space and air, she planted her feet firmly on the ground. She knew from all her years of living and working in the nursery; plants only grow when they are firmly embedded in the earth. She took a deep breath and dialed the number of the first client who had canceled the White Roses Wedding Services. *Had they canceled the wedding or only her services?*

"It's Olivia Rose Anderson here from White Roses Wedding Services," she introduced herself. "Am I speaking to Amy Carter?" she asked when a woman answered the phone. "I hope you don't mind me calling, but I need to ask you a personal question. You have canceled the White Roses Wedding Services . . . "

Before she could go any further, the woman interrupted her. "Is this about the deposit? I know the contract said it was non-refundable but we were hoping you might agree to return at least fifty percent."

"I'll do better than that; you can have one hundred percent of your deposit back if you will tell me honestly the reason you canceled the service. Is the wedding off?"

"Oh no," said Amy, "thank goodness. My daughter is thrilled about the prospect of getting married to her boyfriend. They make a lovely couple."

"So why did you cancel our wedding services? We already had an initial consultation and looked at lots of exciting ideas for your daughter's wedding next year. She seemed particularly taken with the idea of a Scottish castle for the reception."

"I know, she came home with her head full of ideas

and plans. That's why we paid the deposit and hired your company."

Olivia Rose tried not to sound irritated. "So why did you cancel?"

Amy seemed reluctant to answer. "We had some information," she hesitated, "confidential information that your company was in financial trouble and might be out of business before the wedding next year."

Olivia Rose caught her breath. "Who told you that?" she demanded.

"Like I said, it was confidential."

"If you want your deposit refunded in full, I need to know where you got your information."

Amy still hesitated, and then the thought of the extra money coming back her way persuaded her. "Promise you won't tell her I told you," she pleaded.

"Please, I need to know," said Olivia Rose. Now she was agitated. "Of course I'm sad to lose the chance to arrange your daughter's wedding, but more important, I need to know who is spreading these rumors about my company."

Amy blurted it out. "Maria. It was Maria. Your assistant."

Olivia Rose almost dropped the phone. Surely this was not true. "Thank you, Amy. Thank you for telling me. I'll make sure your deposit is refunded. And please give your daughter all my best wishes for a wonderful wedding. Bye."

The silence in the office was deafening.

Olivia Rose looked toward Maria's desk. The jacket

that had previously hung on the back of her chair had gone. A noise from the ladies room made Olivia Rose turn around. Maria had not quite made her escape. She stood before Olivia Rose, defiant.

"Why?" asked Olivia Rose, and her voice threatened to break. "We're a team."

"Yes, but you get all the glory. You think I'm happy being your back-room girl. I'm not. I want to be part of the glamour for once."

Olivia Rose stared at her. She wasn't sure where this was leading, but she had an inkling. "Is this about the Tuscany wedding? The villa where George Clooney almost got married? We're hosting a wedding there next month."

Maria was close to tears. "It was my dream," she admitted. "That was my perfect wedding."

"But it's not your wedding," said Olivia Rose. "And he never even got married there. That was a rumor. He got married in Venice. We're doing a job. Overseeing a wedding of these proportions is hard work and a lot of stress."

"Yes, and you get to swan around dressed like a glamorous guest while I'm back here tied to my desk taking care of all the arrangements. On the phone, while you're in the wedding photographs."

Olivia Rose knew better than to hurt Maria's feelings further by laughing, but she did see the funny side of the situation. "I'm so sorry, Maria," she said, "I never meant to hurt or overlook you. I would have hoped you knew me better than that. Did you call the other two people who canceled and tell them the business was in trouble?"

Maria nodded her head. She looked as if she might be about to apologize, and Olivia Rose was keen to discourage her. "Obviously we can't work together anymore. You're dismissed and please don't ask for a reference. I know this was personal, and you are still perfectly capable of doing a first class job for someone else, but I won't be recommending you."

Maria now offered her apology. "I shouldn't have done it. I shouldn't have tried to destroy your business. I'm sorry."

Olivia Rose fought back the nausea and sick feeling that arose in the pit of her stomach. All that she had built up, undermined by resentment and jealousy. She turned her back on Maria who had now begun to sob. "Good-bye, Maria. I hope your dream comes true. Take your belongings. I'll pay you until the end of the month."

With dignity, Olivia Rose walked across the room to her desk. She sat down and opened her computer. She did not look up as Maria said, "Good-bye."

Betrayal was becoming a habit in her life, she realized. She opened the folder containing all the information about the Italian palazzo wedding. She took a moment to give thanks that Maria had not corrupted or destroyed the files.

Olivia Rose smiled despite herself. The truth was, she was looking forward to experiencing a slice of La Dolce Vita.

Chapter Six

"Shoot me if I fall in love with an Italian Stallion," Olivia Rose told her father, Jason, as he saw her off at the Departures Gate and waved good-bye to her at London's Heathrow airport.

It worried him that his beloved daughter had never fallen in love and he blamed himself. Her first trip to Italy filled him with anticipation and a strange foreboding. Olivia Rose, he never called her just Olivia, was half Italian on her mother's side and he regretted that up to now she had had no opportunity to explore her heritage and the glorious Iberian culture. "I fell in love with a beautiful Italian," he reminded her.

Olivia Rose knew perfectly well that the region of Italy she was to visit was not far from her mother's, Antoinette's, home, but she had no intention of making contact. Olivia Rose was adamant, "Not so long as I live will I forgive her, but that's not to stop me from exploring my Italian roots."

From her window seat, Olivia Rose delighted at the first sight of her mother's homeland. Lakes and mountains and vast fields of lavender were visible as the plane made its descent into Florence airport.

She checked off instructions in a large folder open on her lap. Every detail had to be reviewed and confirmed. Wedding guests were booked to arrive on this flight on this day next week. Up to now, all arrangements had been made on the internet and the telephone; many of the preparations had been organized by Maria. Now the real groundwork began. The map is not the country Olivia Rose reminded herself. She lived by the motto, "Every day brings a new challenge. It is our job to find solutions."

In the Arrivals lounge, she quickly identified the chauffeur holding a sign, *White Roses Wedding Services*, and followed him to a waiting limousine.

"No luggage?" he asked.

"Only hand luggage. I travel light," Olivia Rose responded but realized that even this brief exchange was beyond his understanding of the English language. "No luggage," she repeated and added a smile. The universal language.

Settled in the back seat of the eight-seater luxury limousine, Olivia Rose stretched out and allowed herself to relax and enjoy the ride. She kicked off her towering high heels and sunk her stockinged feet into the plush white carpet.

Glorious sunshine illuminated the landscape, and the constantly changing images of the fast-moving country-side filled her with a sense of wonder and delight. Her soul leaped with joy to return to a place she knew so well, even though she had never been there before.

She opened the window and filled her lungs with

life-enhancing breath as smells and sights and sounds resonated throughout her whole body. Cities, towns and hamlets receded into the past, and Olivia Rose focused her attention on the future and the wide-open spaces.

Guests would be driven along the route using the Florence Executive car service as they arrived for the upcoming wedding, and Olivia Rose made a note to request that, in each vehicle, fresh flower decorations, chilled champagne and a selection of chocolates be available.

Olivia Rose closed her eyes and endeavored to bring to mind any added luxury that would make this entry to the wedding event more perfect. The meditative technique of creative visualization allowed her to imagine herself into the place and time as she walked through the future scenarios.

Her dream-like state gave rise to a vivid hallucination. Olivia Rose immersed herself in the vision. She was traveling to her wedding in a pearl-encrusted white gown, carrying a bouquet of white roses tied with satin ribbons. *Perfect Romance*. Peering more closely into the frame of the picture, Olivia Rose recoiled; her tears were not of joy. There was no denying the sadness in her eyes. The veil she wore was torn.

Snapped back to reality, Olivia Rose shook the disturbing vision from her mind. Romance, for her, was always interlinked with pain. She had hoped that real-life experience in the wedding planning business would prove to her that love was real and would endure, but, though she kept her hope alive, some profound dark force insisted on showing up and raining on her parade.

The Palazzo La Grande where the wedding was to be held came into view. The thirteenth-century castle, built on the ruins of an ancient Roman villa, dominated the skyline and its panoramic views remained undiminished by time or advances of civilization. In a medieval courtyard, resplendent with fountains and marble statues, the timeless grandeur of the building never failed to impress. Landscaped gardens were framed with statuesque centuries-old trees, and cascading flower-filled urns lined the grand entrance.

The limousine glided to a halt. The Palazzo, straight out of a fairy tale, was breathtaking and the best-composed photographs and videos could not express the sense of awe inspired by its classic beauty. Flags fluttered in the soft breeze atop decorated turrets and towers and columns, the perfection of classical architecture.

At the pinnacle of a marble staircase, a liveried footman awaited guests. "Welcome, madam. You are expected," he said with a smile. Despite protests that she had only one small carry-on, he insisted on relieving her of her Louis Vuitton travel case and her laptop bag.

Nothing could have prepared Olivia Rose for the breathtaking magnificence of the Palazzo. She anticipated that each guest would have the same reaction as she did. One of awe and wonder and delight. A visit to the Palace of Versailles might invoke a similar response, but the Palazzo La Grande was not a museum piece. Here guests became royalty.

Honored guests slept in bed chambers built of marble and illuminated by glittering chandeliers, where every inch of wall space proudly displayed centuries-old works of art and exquisite rococo furnishings. Extravagance and grandeur cocooned guests in a rarefied world of luxury and elegance. The Palazzo was rightly proud of its reputation as one of the top ten luxury hotels in the world.

The floral decorations took Olivia Rose's breath away.

The manager of the six-star hotel came forward to greet her. "Mademoiselle Anderson, my pleasure." He bowed. The name badge identified him as Signor Manuel Devine. He was immaculately attired, at noon, in a three-piece black evening suit. "Please allow me to show you to your room before I introduce you to our Executive Events team. No doubt you will be eager to check all the arrangements for your company's wedding next week?"

Olivia Rose was enchanted. This wedding was the most significant her company had undertaken, and she was determined not to feel undermined because she was flying solo. *Maria is history*, she reminded herself. *You're on your own now.*

The groom, who had indicated that no expense was to be spared, insisted that Olivia Rose stay at the same hotel as his guests though she had offered to stay somewhere more modest. "I want you right there on the premises at all times," he insisted. "You will be my go-to woman throughout this event."

Olivia Rose changed her clothes at lightning speed. She didn't intend to waste a minute of this valuable reconnaissance time. Her minimal baggage left few wardrobe choices. Black/white and a splash of red. She had never agreed with the fashion myth that redheads should not wear scarlet. "It's my favorite color," she declared. "It complements my hair beautifully."

She chose a business-like, plain black D&G fitted dress, white jacket, red high-heeled shoes and gold jewelry and clipped her long, flowing hair with a jeweled clasp. She reapplied lipstick and perfume. A quick check in the mirror and she was ready.

The vision from the car threatened to derail her good intentions, but Olivia Rose made herself a vow: *The wedding of my clients, Johnathan, a city banker, and his much younger bride, Jennifer, will exceed all expectations. It will be spectacular.*

Johnathan was wealthy, and Jennifer was a television soap opera actress. Best-selling wedding magazines planned full-page picture spreads, and the publicity from the event promised to take Olivia Rose's business to a new level.

Olivia Rose was lost in thought as she glided down the Palazzo's magnificent staircase. Manuel approached, caught up with her and, with one hand on the small of her back, guided her to the bottom of the stairs. She was caught by surprise as he asked, "You are not married?"

Olivia Rose had been asked the question hundreds of times. She relied on a handful of standard answers that she offered depending on the circumstances: *I haven't found the right man. I'm too busy with my work. I'm too young.*

Making eye contact with Manuel, she decided to ignore the standard polite answers. "If I tell you the truth, do you promise to keep my secret?" she asked.

He was intrigued.

"I don't believe in happy ever after," she admitted. "Hopefully one day someone or something will prove me wrong. In the meantime, all my energy goes into providing the best starting point for my clients. I plan perfect weddings, after that it is up to them to make it last."

Manuel laughed, and he had a twinkle in his eyes as he told her, "Maybe here in Florence at the Palazzo La Grande, we can make you a believer."

Olivia Rose smiled. "I would love that to happen, but I won't hold my breath.""

Co-conspirators, they made their way to the meeting room where Olivia Rose was to be introduced to the Events team. "Forgive me. I almost forgot to pass on a message," said Manuel, once again all business. "Your mother is on her way to the Palazzo; she hopes you will be free to join her for lunch."

Olivia Rose saw no escape. She was furious. *How dare she?*

Here in the center of the most idyllic wedding fairy tale, she was to be forced to confront the woman who had stolen her dream of true love. *Perfect Romance—* Happy Ever After. Not a chance.

Chapter Seven

Olivia Rose failed to anticipate the wave of emotion she experienced as she caught sight of her mother, who sat alone in a window seat in the sumptuous dining room of the Palazzo La Grande. Perched on a gilt chair at a table set for two with a white tablecloth, silver cutlery, sparkling crystal and a delicate white floral centerpiece, Antoinette commanded the attention of the room. She possessed a stillness and composure that made her look as though she were settled and posed in whatever setting she found herself.

She wore a sky-blue dress, which crept up above the knee, exposing her thigh and showing off her shapely legs, and navy stilettos with a trademark red sole. Her white and navy Gucci clutch bag, with the intertwined gold G's visible, was on the table in front of her. Brushed loose and worn in a page boy style, her titian red hair framed her face and caught the sunlight as it streamed through barely there window coverings.

The maître d' smiled and nodded toward the table where Antoinette sat as soon as Olivia Rose entered the dining room. His intuition was well tuned for identifying which guest was joining which, but he needed no special skills to match Olivia Rose with Antoinette. Olivia Rose was a mirror image of her mother.

Having outgrown her teenaged-girl, slightly gangly, casual phase, Olivia Rose now dressed with the elegance of her mother and carried herself with her poise. She might not have been happy to know that she also exuded the veneer of superiority that led her father and Olivia Rose to call Antoinette the Red Queen. In repose Olivia Rose's face was unreadable.

Smiles had to be earned, but they were worth the wait.

Antoinette was smiling now as she watched Olivia Rose from the table and waited for her to make her way across the vast dining salon. She stretched out her arms as she willed her daughter to return the embrace. "Olivia, my darling girl, you look so beautiful," she said. "So grown up. Come here, let me look at you. Please, I have missed you so much."

Olivia Rose stiffened, not yet ready to give up her prideful resistance, but then she relented. "Hello, mother," she said and allowed herself to be hugged.

The waiter hovered but did not interrupt as he observed mother and daughter deep in conversation. He was ready to serve when they needed him.

Antoinette sat back down and gestured for Olivia Rose to do the same. There was an awkward silence, filled by the waiter offering outsized menus. "What can I get you to drink?" he asked, notebook at the ready.

"Agua," said Antoinette.

"Same," said Olivia, "con gas."

Olivia Rose was anxious to ensure her objections

were heard. "This is unacceptable," she said, straightening her shoulders and sitting upright in her straightbacked chair. "I've been hijacked. I made my feelings very clear to my father. Though I was visiting Italy, I had no intention of meeting with you. He had no right to tell you I would be here. I'm working, and that's what I intend to focus on during my visit.

"Not mending fences with you. As far as I am concerned, there's nothing to say."

Antoinette avoided Olivia Rose's gaze and focused on the menu, a foot-square, tasseled, leather-bound booklet, gold embossed on the cover. "The menu can be overwhelming, especially at lunchtime," Antoinette explained. "I invariably choose fish of the day with seasonal vegetables."

It came as a surprise that Antoinette was familiar with the hotel as it was some two hours' drive from her own home in Siena, but she explained, "Gianni does business here."

"I'll be guided by you," Olivia Rose conceded. "Fish is fine." Forgetting for a moment, her anger toward her mother, she admitted, "I'm starving. I had coffee and a croissant on the plane, but that was hours ago."

Antoinette's parenting skills left much to be desired, but like a good Italian mama, she could be relied upon to feed her offspring. "You're very slim," she said. "Doesn't your father feed you?"

Olivia Rose was not prepared to hear any criticism of her father. "I'm a grown woman," she said. "We share a house. We look after each other."

"I'm sorry," said Antoinette, and she did look genuinely remorseful. "I'm so nervous. I don't know what to say. I know you didn't want to see me. But I couldn't bear it any longer. I've asked your father so many times over the years to plead my case to you and persuade you to talk to me."

Olivia Rose hid her surprise; she hadn't realized the two were in contact. She felt annoyed that things had happened behind her back. She was being excluded and treated like a child.

Antoinette was quick to explain. "At first he was resistant," she said. "Only to be expected. He had no interest in talking to me, but he did agree that I could phone and find out how you were getting on."

Olivia Rose bit the inside of her cheek. "He did suggest that I should talk to you," she felt forced to admit. "I said, 'no.' He was convinced I would regret it one day."

"I understand why you made that decision," Antoinette sympathized. "I don't blame you."

Neither knew where the conversation should go next. Fortunately, they were spared their discomfort. The smiling waiter appeared carrying an elaborate oblong silver tray. He pulled open a ledge on the table and balanced the tray as he placed two silver covers and a serving dish of vegetables in front of the diners. With a flourish he simultaneously removed the covers to reveal salmon steaks garnished with giant prawns, capers and muslin-wrapped lemon wedges on the side.

Antoinette smiled her approval, and the waiter

refilled their crystal glasses with sparkling water. She shook her head to indicate there was nothing else they required.

"*Godere*. Enjoy," he said as he backed away.

"Godere," Antoinette encouraged Olivia Rose.

Olivia Rose fought to hold on to her resentment, but she was pleased and relieved to see her mother. The two did get on well and were at ease in each others company, especially when Jason was not present. Divided loyalties drove a wedge between them.

Enjoying their meal in companionable silence, the two were mirror images of each other. Self-composed, unhurried, lady-like. From time to time, they smiled shyly at each other.

"I missed you," said Antoinette as they finished their main course. "Please, will you let me explain my side of the story?"

Olivia Rose looked as if she might refuse, then she laughed. "On one condition," she said, "that while you're talking, we share an enormous slice of chocolate cake."

Antoinette squeezed her daughter's hand. "Of course, nothing I'd like better. You are a lovely girl, I'm so happy to see you," she told her. "My heart can now mend."

To the waiter, she gave her order and made it clear "ONE plate. TWO forks."

Sharing an indulgence they had relished so many times before, mother and daughter united. Antoinette was grateful for the opportunity to explain her side of the breakup to Olivia Rose. Fork in midair, she looked off into the distance and recalled her life with Jason.

"I was eighteen, younger than you are now. To say my life was sheltered is an understatement. I lived on the olive farm with my parents, an only child. Life was simple, rural, uncomplicated. The biggest excitement was the annual olive harvest in November when we joined with other villagers in our community to press the olive oil. We lit bonfires in the empty barrels and enjoyed music and dancing all night long.

"Even a trip to any of the nearby towns was a major event. I'd only been to Rome once, with the local church. Italian girls were chaperoned everywhere at that time—many still are—and I'd never had a boyfriend. But I did have a dream. I dreamt that one day I would marry Gianni, the son of the family on the next olive farm.

"He was a catch. All the village girls were in love with him. Once a year he and I danced at the olive harvest. We would sneak off into the orchard and kiss. Can you believe I waited all year for that kiss?"

Olivia Rose laughed and was enchanted by the image of her mother, the young farm girl, dancing and dreaming of her Prince Charming. "Did you think you would marry him?" she asked.

"Yes, of course. Isn't that the dream of every young girl? You should know, Miss Wedding Planner."

"What happened?"

"He went off to help his uncle on his farm in Spain. By the way, did you know, Spain, not Italy, is the number one world producer of olive oil?

"His family owned vast estates and a multi-million-euro olive oil business. His company was quick to realize the sales potential of the internet, and they exported olive oil all over the globe. Gianni was the right age to seize the opportunities. He knew about technology and also about olive growing. He was so busy on his uncle's farm in Spain, building an empire, he hardly ever came home."

From her handbag, she took a photograph of herself, a fresh-faced teenage girl in a summer dress, hand in hand with a smiling young man, Gianni. "I'm trying to make you understand. Gianni was everything I ever wanted. A good-looking, successful Italian man bought up in the same village. We spoke the same language. We shared a heritage, a culture, tradition. Our families had known each other for generations."

Olivia Rose finished the chocolate cake and pushed the empty plate across the table. As usual, Antoinette had eaten two mouthfuls, and she had consumed the rest. "So where did my father come into the picture?" she asked her mother, and wiped her lips with a linen napkin as she waited for an answer.

The dining room was empty, lunch was over and the staff was setting up for dinner. No one disturbed the two women engrossed in conversation.

Antoinette gestured to a passing waiter. "Coffee please."

"Your father toured our farm with a delegation from the Royal Horticultural Society—it sounded so grand and romantic. I suppose you could say he swept me off my feet. We only knew each other for a few days, but he wrote to me and then made a special visit to ask my father for my hand in marriage.

"He was a real gentleman. He respected the fact that a nice girl like me would not go to bed with a man until married, so," she shrugged, "he married me."

"It wasn't a fancy wedding but it was romantic. The ceremony was held in the garden by the local church, in a field of one hundred olive trees. The whole village came out. All my family and friends. Gianni was still in Spain. I'd given up on him. Jason and I left for England a couple of days later. The flower growing business was run like a hobby, and he also worked at a large house in one of the Surrey villages as a gardener.

"I was homesick. Jason and I didn't have anything in common. I was lonely. Alone in a small English village, I couldn't even speak the language. The best thing that happened was when I gave birth to you. Then I had a purpose, a real job. A baby to love."

Olivia Rose reached out and took her mother's hand. "I'm sorry you were so lonely," she told her. "Why didn't you explain any of this to me before?"

Antoinette sighed. "What would I have told you?—I don't love your father? He doesn't know how to make me happy? He has nothing I want?"

"I did leave a few times when you were little. I took you home to my village. I lived with my parents."

She gathered her thoughts and breathed deeply. "Gianni visited his family, and we started a love affair. A love affair that lasted all through your childhood. As the years went on, you were in school, so I left you with your father. He insisted on it.

"You obviously liked him better than me. Gianni and I lived together as man and wife. It suited our purpose because it was less of a scandal if I didn't flaunt the fact that I had a child and a husband in England."

Olivia Rose listened intently and declared herself willing to forgive her mother, but she had one burning question. "Why did you let Gianni compete against Dad at the Chelsea Flower Show?"

"That was wrong of me," her mother admitted. "I should have stopped it, but I guess I wanted to punish Jason. I blamed him for ruining my life. I waited sixteen years to get the life I wanted with Gianni. In the early days, he begged me to leave your father and go and live with him in Spain. Your father wouldn't let me take you, so I lived a lie. A double life, with Gianni in Italy and your father in England.

"As you can imagine, I was desperately unhappy. Then when Gianni won the Gold Medal for Florist of the Year I knew it was all over. I chose him instead of your father. Apart from the pain of missing you, my only daughter, I'm content now."

Olivia Rose reached across and hugged her mother. "I'm so glad to know the story," she said. "Thank you for sharing it with me."

Antoinette was in tears. "Olivia," she asked, "can you find it in your heat to grant me one wish? Will you come and let me introduce you to Gianni?"

"I'll need notice of that question," Olivia Rose responded.

"I know you're here in Florence to work, but, please, let me collect you and bring you to my village this weekend? It's only a couple of hours away. Your family—our family—is longing to see you again."

Olivia Rose felt her heart melt. How could she deny her mother the enduring love affair and the happy ever after that she hoped she would one day be granted?

Chapter Eight

A fiesta was in full swing early Sunday morning when Olivia Rose arrived at the charming Italian village that was her mother's home.

Antoinette collected Olivia Rose from the Palazzo and drove her in a red convertible Alpha Romeo sports car through fields of lavender and lemon and orange groves that climbed high into the rolling hills.

On a high-speed journey, they whizzed through the countryside past churches and monuments, villas and country homes and hamlets filled with traditional white-washed cottages with painted shutters and a profusion of flowers and stately trees. Children and pets played in the gardens and bedclothes fluttering in the breeze hung out of windows and on clotheslines to air.

For the first time, Olivia Rose observed her mother in her own environment. She laughed and chatted and seemed filled with a spirit that had failed to blossom in the sedate English countryside. Antoinette wore a wide-brimmed hat and encouraged Olivia Rose to tie back her hair with a brightly colored Pucci silk head scarf. "The wind will play havoc with your hairstyle," she said. "When we arrive, you will be the center of attention in the village. You want to look your best."

Olivia Rose experienced a flash of insight into the fact that what she perceived as her mother's bossiness when she was growing up was a desire for her daughter to look her best, be the best and have the best.

"Your father saw beauty in his roses," Antoinette explained, "but he didn't place much value on girly dressing up. His attitude made me feel shallow, unnecessary. I couldn't be one of those hearty country women, all Wellies, and anoraks with a little string of pearls poking out of their woolly jumpers. Truth to tell, I thought he was stuffy and so British. For him, I was too Latin."

Olivia Rose laughed at her mother's description of the women who ruled the Surrey village where she had grown up. She could see that Antoinette would have been way too hot to handle at meetings of the Women's Institute.

"Do you feel the Latin blood coursing through your veins?" her mother challenged.

"I'm getting there." Olivia Rose felt a rush of affection for her mother and wished they had developed an understanding of each other years before because they could have been good friends, and allies, instead of enemies.

"You're fortunate," her mother continued, "you are blended Italian/English. Like strong coffee served in a china cup—with a saucer, of course. You have British reserve sewn into your bones, but your blood boils from your Latin roots. We'll make an Italian of you yet."

Antoinette was bubbling over with excitement. "Almost there." She pointed with her elegantly manicured index finger. "Up ahead that farmland belongs to my family. And to you."

The piazza in the center of the village was festooned with flags and banners. Villagers hurried to and fro setting up tables and chairs in the center of the town square. In trucks, vans and on handcarts, scaffolding, wooden flooring and waterproof tarpaulin were delivered to erect the small stage.

Without words or the need for instructions, men built the stage in the same place and same manner as they and their fore-bearers had been doing for centuries.

Dressed head to foot in black, the oldest surviving parishioner in the village arrived. She leaned heavily on her brass-topped cane and walked head held high, escorted by her entourage of two daughters, three granddaughters, and six great-granddaughters. Her daily mass attendance completed, she had come to inspect the preparations.

"Mama, sit here." Her eldest daughter commandeered a table in the center of the proceedings, and the all-girl family group took their seats. The menfolk were busy with their manual work. The men would later join their friends at their exclusively all-male tables. Leaving the women to talk about what they perceived to be the only subject of conversation—their menfolk.

Mama graciously responded to the friendly greetings and nods of acknowledgment from every person who passed her. At ninety-eight years of age, she had earned her position of respect, and her presence was a reassurance that all was being conducted in a time-honored fashion.

Ladies delivered their lovingly prepared dishes of traditional food behind the covered stalls that lined three sides of the square. The catering stalls had been erected early that morning. "Buono, buono." Madame Albertini nodded her approval and took small sips as dishes were presented to her.

A band of traditional local musicians warmed up in one of the moss-covered arches that lined the walls of the square and backed up to the church. Discordant sounds of trumpets and high pitched horns filled the air. The arches—makeshift rehearsal rooms—acted as storage for the floats and statues and costumes used in the annual religious processions.

Every villager had a part to play and proudly followed the traditions of previous generations of their family. Musicians, flag bearers, costume-makers, float builders, flower arrangers, banner carriers, they learned their craft at the knee of mothers and fathers and uncles and cousins. No one was too rich or too important to be assigned a role in the festivals.

Antoinette parked in the church parking lot and took Olivia Rose's arm as she walked her around the square. "First we have to go and pay our respects to Madame Albertini," she explained. "The husband she buried fifty years ago and three of her sons were mayors of this town. She is a person of great influence, and, even at her advanced age, her mind is razor sharp. No decisions are made in the village without her approval. She has many fascinating stories to tell. Pity you don't speak Italian."

Olivia Rose had taken Italian in high school for a couple of semesters, but apart from a few words of greeting, she hadn't retained much of the language. At home, they spoke English and Jason had been keen that Antoinette learn to communicate more effectively. "You will be less lonely if you have some friends," he had told her, "but first you will have to learn to speak English."

Olivia Rose found another regret arise inside her. She and her mother would have had a stronger bond if she had persevered with her Italian and helped her mother learn English. Instead of joining her father in his irritation at her lack of progress. "No wonder you felt so isolated," said Olivia Rose, aware that her empathy for her mother's situation had come decades too late.

"Well, at least we now understand each other," her mother assured her.

Having proudly presented her daughter to Madame Albertini, Antoinette urged, "Let's go to the farm, and I can show you around. It'll be a couple of hours before the fiesta gets into full swing. You will stay all day, won't you?"

Olivia Rose waited for an appropriate moment to explain that she needed to leave early. "I've got a mountain of work to do back at the hotel. It's only four days till the wedding and three days till the guests arrive."

Her mother looked disappointed. "Sunday is a day of rest," she said. "But I won't put you under pressure. I know you have an important job to do. I'm grateful we can spend this time together. Whatever you want, I'll go along with it. But I really hoped you would stay for the dance this evening. The whole village comes out to celebrate."

"Celebrate what?" asked Olivia Rose.

"The Feast day of our village saint. The religious procession of the statues through the village was yesterday. Today is the fun day."

The road to the farm led up hills and down valleys, and each turn in the track showed an even more breathtaking view.

Antoinette's farmhouse was straight out of a picture book. An Italianate pastoral scene. A barking black-and-white dog ran out to greet them, but he didn't keep up the guard dog pretense for long. His tail wagged as he followed them into the white-washed house.

"It's small but comfortable," Antoinette said modestly. "When I was growing up, it was smaller than this, but over the years we expanded and renovated."

The front door was open.

"Is someone at home?" asked Olivia Rose.

"No, there's only me, and I'm not here often. Gianni and I travel a lot. Our base is his home in Spain." Antoinette laughed. "We don't lock doors, we know all our neighbors. I understand it does sound like we live in the last century and most of us are keen to keep it that way. We're old-fashioned." The downstairs lounge was an open plan leading into a small kitchen. Antoinette was right; it was old-fashioned. The furniture was almost antique and hardly had signs of wear and tear. It looked like it would endure forever. Window shutters were tightly closed against the hot sun.

Landscapes and family portraits adorned the brightly painted walls. Embossed high-backed love seats with carved legs were covered in elaborately embroidered throws and jewel-colored cushions. Faded silk rugs were spread on cool tiled floors, and immovable black consoles provided a home for gilt clocks, religious statues, family photographs, mostly old black and whites, and bowls of fresh flowers.

"I love it," said Olivia Rose.

"Good, because one day it will be yours. "

"Can I see upstairs?" asked Olivia Rose, giving only a passing glance to the outdated kitchen and downstairs cloakroom. Two small bedrooms with painted red walls contained far too much furniture, but the feather beds looked inviting. Antoinette's clothes, shoes and accessories spilled out of wardrobes and drawers. No doubt about it, her mother was a fashionista.

Through leaded windows, Olivia Rose gazed in awe at the rolling countryside and, as far as the eye could see, olive trees and lavender fields. She had found her idea of heaven.

"Come, let's go walk in the orchard," urged Antoinette.

As they walked and talked, Olivia Rose bubbled over with excitement and asked questions. All trace of resentment dissipated. "Did you pick the olives when you were young?"

"It wasn't my favorite job," Antoinette admitted. "The harvest took about three weeks, and my arms ached from being stuck up in the trees. My main memory is of slipping and sliding on the stones on the path. Thank goodness, we always had plenty of villagers to help us pick. Then it was our turn to go and help them."

"And now?" asked Olivia Rose.

"We have a team of workers. They prepare the harvest for the village cooperative to sell."

"I kind of feel that with a name like Olivia, I should have an affinity for picking olives."

"Come back at harvest time," said Antoinette, "we'll be glad for your help."

Olivia Rose accepted the invitation and made a promise that she would come back, but for now, she had other things on her mind. She reminded her mother, "No wonder you couldn't keep your mind on picking olives, you told me that you lived for the celebration dancing and a romantic visit to the orchard with Gianni."

"After all these years, I still insist on that kiss in the orchard at harvest time," a laughing Antoinette confided. "You've reminded me. He'll be waiting for us in the town square."

At high speed, Antoinette drove to the town square. The church parking lot was full, and she parked in a space at the back of the local bar under an ancient spreading tree. In a quick change back at the house she had dressed for the fiesta in a short, red ruffled dress and sparkling dancing shoes. Anxious to protect her heels, she stepped on tiptoes carefully across the gravel parking lot. Olivia Rose had chosen to wear a pair of tight-fitting black trousers, a red jacket and ballet pumps. Mother and daughter complemented each other but did not match.

"Remember how we used to wear matching outfits when I was a little girl?" asked Olivia Rose. "I loved looking like you even though I complained at the time."

As they made their way into the crowded fiesta, all eyes were on the glamorous pair. In a small village, most knew at least part of Antoinette's history, but few of them could recall ever having seen her with her daughter. Except maybe the all-knowing Madame Albertini.

However, the handsome, smiling man who now approached needed no introduction. Her mother's smile said it all. "May I escort you ladies?" he asked as he stepped forward and linked arms with Antoinette.

Antoinette beamed. "Gianni meet my daughter, Olivia Rose."

"Enchanted. Beautiful as her mother," he said, and his eyes crinkled in a smile. "May I?" he asked Olivia Rose, as he held out his arm and waited for her to accept the invitation.

Antoinette beamed. "Olivia, this is Gianni."

Olivia Rose hesitated for a moment, then took his arm. "Yes, I know who he is. He hasn't changed much since the Chelsea Flower Show." The atmosphere turned to frost. For a moment, memories of the past threatened to ruin the festivities and the happy reunion of mother and daughter.

Olivia Rose considered her position and then brightened. She looked directly at her mother and smiled. "Your childhood sweetheart is even more handsome than I remembered." With a wink, she teased her mother, "No wonder you left home for him."

The ice well and truly broken, arm in arm, step-by-step, the trio walked to a table by the front of the stage. All three enjoyed their evening of music, dancing and home-cooked bite-size tapas dishes and fish stew followed by almond pastries.

Despite Olivia Rose's protests, her mother and Gianni insisted that she join them and the rest of the village in the skirt swirling, fast-paced traditional dances.

"I don't know the steps," Olivia Rose protested.

"Follow us," they laughed, "no one cares if you get it wrong. Keep moving and keep changing partners."

Old and young danced together, and Olivia Rose soon picked up the pace and became familiar with the set steps of the dance thanks to help from a fan club of enthusiastic village menfolk.

"That certainly gets the adrenalin going. I'm exhausted," she admitted as she returned to the table after what felt like hours of dancing.

"You're a natural," Gianni complimented her. "It's in the blood. Like mother, like daughter."

"Do you mind?" asked Antoinette, as the band played a final love song, "if I dance with Gianni to our special favorite? It's our song. Then I'll drive you home."

Olivia Rose watched and waited as her mother and Gianni danced, cheek-to-cheek. So in love after all this time.

She drifted off to sleep in the front seat as her mother drove her through the warm, starry night back to Florence. In the depths of her slumbers, she was visited by the wedding vision. The bride's pure white dress was perfect, perfume from the bouquet of roses she held in her lap filled the small space of the speeding car. The bridal veil was tattered and torn. But the bride was not Olivia Rose; it was her mother.

Chapter Nine

"White Roses Wedding Service," said Olivia Rose to the unknown caller as she answered her cell phone. She did not recognize the UK number.

"It's me, Jennifer Morrow," said the voice at the other end of the line. "I'm using a phone in the production office at the studio." Jennifer, the bride-to-be, was not the easiest person to deal with. A self-admitted Bridezilla, she displayed numerous signs of being spoiled and entitled, and in the long months of planning the wedding, there had been many tantrums. Olivia Rose allowed for that, every bride wanted to make their day perfect, and the many decisions that had to be made caused stress.

As the wedding planner, Olivia Rose did everything possible to relieve the bride's anxiety and guide her to make decisions that pleased her and her groom. Jennifer had the added anxiety of a publicity machine blatantly exploiting the wedding to increase her profile and draw attention to her starring role in a television series.

In Olivia Rose's experience, most grooms took the view, "It's the bride's day, and I'll go along with what makes her happy." Jennifer's groom, Johnathan, was more demanding. Marrying a famous actress was good for his professional reputation, and the brokers' office in the city where he worked loved the attention their high profile account executive was generating.

Jennifer checked every decision with Johnathan, but today she had a special request. She wanted to surprise him on the wedding day. "A black hawk," stated Jennifer. "I want a black hawk to fly through the wedding chapel with the wedding rings in a velvet pouch around his neck. The guests will love it.

"And this is the best bit. Johnathan's company is called Black Hawk. Isn't that amazing? I don't know why I didn't think of it before. Well, I don't think I'd heard about the ring carrying hawk before. I saw it on the news. A hawk got out of control and attacked the best man who had the rings in his pocket. That's why I want our rings in a velvet pouch."

Olivia Rose was puzzled by the reasoning that because a hawk had got out of control, Jennifer would want it as part of the ceremony. Jennifer explained, "The video went viral. Millions of hits on YouTube and it was on the news. Great publicity."

"I'm sure it will be spectacular," Olivia Rose agreed. Fortunately the bride was unable to see the look of doubt that clouded Olivia Rose's features. Lucky they were not using Facetime.

With the wedding three days away, Olivia Rose kept her fingers crossed that she would be able to find a hawk and handler who were available on the day. In her experience, the adage, "Never work with children and animals" was true. Both were highly unpredictable.

"Okay, let me see what I can do," she assured Jennifer. "Was there anything else on your mind?"

"Did you pass on the photographs I sent for the makeup artists and hairdresser?" asked Jennifer.

"All done," said Olivia Rose, "and the team will come to the hotel in time for the rehearsal dinner the night before the wedding to check any last minute instructions. They are also booked to do your hair and glam you up after your flight from London."

Jennifer remembered her manners and thanked her. "Everything else going to plan?" she asked.

"Of course you know the venue is perfect," said Olivia Rose. The three of them had made a trip to the hotel a few months before the wedding date. Unlike couples who confidently booked online, Jennifer and Johnathan insisted on visiting several hotels in the region before making their choice. "The weather is almost guaranteed, and the team at the hotel are super professional."

Stroking her ego, she also informed Jennifer, "Everyone is very excited to be hosting the wedding of a top actress and celebrity. Since George Clooney married in Italy, all the hotels have been competing for spreads in the glossy wedding magazines and videos of the wedding on the entertainment shows."

Jennifer's pre-wedding nerves that had consistently made an appearance every hour on the hour these last few weeks were soothed, and she returned to the television studio confident that all was under control.

Olivia Rose exercised her usual rule of only passing

on to the bride information on a "need to know basis."
She saw no need to tell her about the mix-up with the
wedding flowers. At a meeting that morning, the hotel
team and Olivia Rose had again checked and rechecked
every detail of the upcoming event. On a large time
planner calendar, the date for the wedding of Johnathan Farmsworth and Jennifer Morrow was highlighted.
A six-foot by three-foot wide sheet of rolled paper
stretched across two desks. Photographs and designs
lined up with the headings: *Contact, Booked, Confirmed,
Paid, Arrival Time and Date.*

"Belt and braces," explained Olivia Rose, passing
round photocopies of the sheets. "To be double and
triple sure," she said as she took a marker and wrote on
a whiteboard:

- Venue—Palazzo La Grande, Florence. CHECK

- Ceremony—Garden of Hotel. Red carpet/Floral
  arch. CHECK.

- Sit down meal for 200—catered by Hotel. Table
  decorations—supplied by Hotel. CHECK

- Reception—wines and glasses supplied by Hotel.
  CHECK

- Music—string quartet—locally sourced and recommended. CHECK

- Local band for the evening—hotel nightclub. CHECK

- 5-tier Cake—locally sourced and recommended (and
  tasted). CHECK

- Hotel rooms for 50 guests (billed to groom). CHECK

- Makeup/Hair Team—from Hotel Salon. CHECK

- Bridal Outfits—wedding guests own. CHECK

- Car service from the airport to hotel—and return. CHECK

Olivia Rose had completed her checklist.

"Keeping services in-house is always a bonus," she commented. "Especially when the hotel is as well run as this one. Tell me if I have overlooked anything."

The Events team looked well pleased with the acknowledgment. "Only one item is missing from the list," said the leader.

"And that is?" asked Olivia Rose.

"Bride's bouquet," came the reply, "bridesmaids' bouquets and two hundred boutonnieres for the guests."

Olivia Rose struggled to understand. Her head began to spin and she had a sickening sensation of impending doom in her stomach. "Bouquets?" she repeated, as if she'd never heard the word. "Bride's bouquet? Boutonnieres?" Her voice was raised. "Tell me, tell me what you mean."

The team leader, a young but highly efficient event organizer, looked embarrassed. "White Roses Wedding Services was our supplier. They were to deliver by DHL air freight the evening before the wedding. A white bouquet for the bride, pink for the bridesmaids and one hundred each of white and red boutonnieres."

"We were notified that they canceled a few days

ago. They are unable to complete the order. We never received an invoice, so no money was paid to them. Your office assured us that they had another supplier able to fulfill the order. We have not been able to contact them."

Olivia Rose hoped she was wrong, but she had a sickening feeling that she knew what had happened. "White Roses Wedding Services don't supply flowers," she said trying to keep the panic out of her voice.

"We were informed that your father ran the company," explained Santos, the hotel representative and youngest member of the team. "It didn't seem appropriate to question you."

Olivia Rose prayed the ground would open up and swallow her. True, her father's company often did supply flowers for the weddings she planned. She trusted him to provide a first class job but to fly flowers out of the country presented too many opportunities for things to go wrong. She looked around at the faces of the team who previously seemed so impressed by her organizational skills. "Any ideas?" she asked. "Where am I going to get this flower order filled on such short notice?"

With no resources or contacts to fall on back on, she took the only option possible and left the problem in the team's capable hands. Following the phone call from Jennifer, she returned to the office. Leaning against the door, she grimaced as she caught Santos's attention, "By the way, do you know where I can get a trained black hawk to fly down and deliver the wedding rings?"

Chapter Ten

Olivia Rose made a frantic phone call to her father.

"I've got a problem," she told him.

"Par for the course when planning a wedding," he attempted to make a joke of her predicament. "But you know what you signed up for, the sign on your desk says, 'The Buck Stops Here.'"

Olivia Rose sighed. "Dad, this is serious. I think it's a case of corporate espionage."

"Now that is serious," he agreed. "What's the problem?"

"White roses," she said. "Not my company but the actual flowers. Did you have an order to supply the personal bouquets for the wedding in Florence? The one that is taking place in forty-eight hours' time?"

Jason did not hesitate. "Yes, and I was none too pleased when they canceled the order at the last minute. I'd gone to a great deal of trouble to make sure I would have all the blooms at the peak of freshness for the event. Also I took great care to arrange flights and transportation to ensure the flowers arrived in the best possible condition. I paid a high price for insurance, but

I wanted to make sure everything was perfect. I know how much this wedding means to you."

"Stop there," said Olivia Rose. "Who placed the order and who canceled?"

"Maria, your assistant," he said, "sent me an email. She said the wedding party—namely a somewhat difficult bride—changed her mind about certain decisions. I was annoyed, of course, but when you said you had dismissed Maria, there seemed no point in complaining about something that I couldn't see had been her fault. Lucky for me, the insurance company have agreed to pay out for loss of business and my expenses."

"Her cell phone is disconnected, and she ignores emails," sighed Olivia Rose. "How could my judgment about someone I worked with have been so wrong?"

Jason listened but dreaded Olivia Rose's next question.

"Dad," she asked in her pleading little girl voice. "Is there any way you could get those flowers to me tomorrow?"

"Olivia Rose, darling," he replied. "If there were any way I could help, you know I would, but I don't even have the flowers. I made a deal and sold them off to the local flower shop. The lovely lady who runs the shop was delighted to have them."

"Okay, thanks," said Olivia Rose. "Don't worry; I'll find a way to solve the problem. But Maria won't get away with this. I'm going to consult a lawyer about her industrial sabotage."

"By the way, how are you enjoying your trip?" asked her father. "I thought you were calling to tell me off for letting your mother know you were at the hotel in Italy."

"No, that's okay," she assured him. "She appeared and took me by surprise, but I was glad to see her. Even if I was forced into the situation. I'll tell you all about it when I get home. Now I need to go and raid a flower stall. Love you."

Easier said, than done, Olivia Rose thought as she hung up the phone.

* * *

Laptop open and ready for heavy duty surfing, she settled in a comfortable, secluded spot in the ornate marble and gilded reception area of the Palazzo. Opulence and luxury surrounded her, but Olivia Rose could not afford to be diverted.

Immediately she was forced to face the enormity of the task in front of her. Not least because of the language barrier. Not able to differentiate growers from sellers from retail stores, she did not know where to start. She had no local knowledge of the area and no idea how to communicate with anyone who might be able to offer guidance.

The hotel events' team was her best resource. Pride made her want to deliver at least part of the solution, but she had no resources or connections and time was fast running out. Not only did she need roses for the bouquets, but she also required people who could tie them and prepare two hundred boutonnieres. *Ask the questions*, she reminded herself of the processes she had successfully used so many times before when searching for answers. *Who do I know? What do I need? When is the deadline? Where? Why would they help me?* Olivia Rose felt a warm glow as she realized that here in a strange country a thousand miles from home, she was not alone. She did know someone who would be more than willing to help. Her mother, Antoinette. She called her mother's cell phone.

Gianni answered. "Hello, lovely girl," he said with a smile in his voice. "Good to hear from you. How's the wedding?"

Olivia Rose was reluctant to admit her problem to her mother's boyfriend. The man who for so many years had been the enemy. "Fine, thank you," said Olivia Rose abruptly. "Is my mother there? I thought this was her number."

"It is, but we kind of share. We use this number for business, and I answer if she's not around. Today she's not around here. She's gone to our house in Spain. She'll be back on the weekend."

"Okay, thank you, I'll catch up with her then." Olivia Rose could hardly hide her disappointment. She saw her best chance of solving her problem disappear.

Reluctant to let her go, especially when she sounded so upset, Gianni asked, "Can I help?"

Olivia Rose had no other options. Surely it could do no harm to at least explain her dilemma. Gianni did not interrupt. *Keep it brief. The facts, give him the facts*, Olivia Rose warned herself. It wouldn't help to blame

Maria, and she was determined not to bring her father's name into the conversation. Olivia Rose knew she was on the verge of tears. "This is my biggest wedding yet. It's very high profile. The British press is full of the story. I can't bear to let them down. And it doesn't help that I don't speak Italian."

Gianni laughed. "Well, I do speak Italian," he said, "so we are now ahead of the game."

Olivia Rose felt a massive burden lift from her shoulders. "Will you help me?" she asked, trying not to sound too female and needy.

"Of course, I'd like to, but I'm not sure we will have much success," he said. Her hopes were dashed. "How long did you say we have, twenty-four hours? White roses for a bridal bouquet."

"Don't forget the boutonnieres," interjected Olivia Rose.

In desperation, Olivia Rose clutched at straws. "Do you still grow roses?"

Gianni had the grace to sound embarrassed. "I hoped you wouldn't mention the competition between your father and myself at the Chelsea Flower Show. I behaved badly. One day I may get the opportunity to apologize to him. For now, I can apologize to you."

Olivia Rose was impressed by the gesture, but not sure she would pass on the message to her father.

"In answer to your question, no, I no longer grow roses. All my time is taken up with olives. That doesn't mean I don't have some contacts. I do not promise anything, but I'll make a few phone calls."

"Thank you, I appreciate that," said Olivia Rose. "When can I follow up with you? I'll also text you my email. Thank you, again."

Olivia Rose relaxed enough to allow herself some lunch, a delicious salad on ciabatta out on the Palazzo terrace. She also put her head into the door of the Events team and asked if they had any news. "Still tracking down florists," they informed her, "but I think we may have a breakthrough on the black hawk. The handler is checking his diary. As long as he keeps us guessing, he can raise his price."

Olivia Rose laughed. "I've got a few feelers out on the flower issue," she said, happy to report that she had been on the case but not giving so much hope that they would stop working on delivering a floral supplier.

"I'm off for a walk around town," she explained. "I'd like to see the sights and have information on hand when wedding guests want to explore. If I find a flower stall piled high with beautiful roses, I'll buy every bloom and tie the bouquets myself."

Olivia Rose set off to explore the city and with the help of a guidebook, excitedly marked off the awesome collection of places of interest. Most of the wedding guests had not visited Florence previously and to enhance their enjoyment of the stunning wedding venue, during their visit, everyone was to receive an information folder and entrance tickets to the city land-marks. Olivia Rose set off to walk the route that she would recommend as a sightseeing itinerary.

Ranked one of the most beautiful cities in the world,

Florence surpassed all expectations. Olivia Rose was excited to put together a guide and introduce Johnathan and Jennifer's guests to the stunning array of art, culture and architecture on show.

Without doubt, the city's most iconic landmark is the Duomo, the Cathedral on which construction started in 1296 and was completed 150 years later in 1436. Capped by a red tiled cupola, it is a breathtaking structure of pink, white and green marble. The magnificent building dominates the skyscape and the interior glories in forty-four stained glass windows.

Olivia Rose had done her research and knew that the most viewed statue in the Piazza della Signoria was a copy, erected in 1910. The original work of art was moved by the Italian government to ensure their ownership of the masterpiece.

She intended to see Michelangelo's statue of David in all its naked and original glory at the Galleria dell' Accademia. Transfixed, like many millions of tourists before her, by the most famous statue in Florence and probably the world, Michelangelo's David, Olivia Rose felt overwhelmed and wiped away a tear as she gazed on the perfection of the fourteen-foot-high gleaming white marble statue.

Michelangelo was twenty-six years old in 1501 and one of the most famous artists in the Renaissance world when he accepted the commission to sculpt a religious statue to depict the bible story of David. A shepherd boy, David defeated Goliath, the champion of the Philistine's, with a single shot from his slingshot. To show the triumph of mind over might, David was armed with only his sling, a rock and his faith in God.

Other highlights of her proposed tour included the statues and fountains of Piazza della Signoria and the Ponte Vecchio, the oldest bridge in the city under which the craft shops have traded since ancient times.

She made a mental note to include in her exploration of the city the Dantesque district; she was reliably informed that traces of Dante's life and his works were still visible.

Olivia Rose set out full of anticipation. First stop, the Boboli Gardens, designed for the Medici family, is one of the earliest examples of the Italian Garden that later inspired those of many European Courts. She walked in wonder through the open-air museum with its Renaissance statues, grottoes and large fountains. The serene setting invoked images of life at court, and she imagined herself a grand lady strolling with her companions, gossiping, sharing intrigues and catching the eye of passing noblemen.

Olivia Rose visited Florence's Rose Garden where she took photographs of some of the hundreds of varieties to send to her father. *No chance to pick any of them, more's the pity,* she thought. In the Horticultural Park, she sipped tea with butterflies fluttering all around.

She toured the Cathedral, churches, art galleries and palazzos and she lingered as she sat down to write up her notes in parks and gardens where the formal, structured landscapes were replicated in magnificent gardens all over the world. The architecture and artistic heritage enthralled her, and everywhere grandeur and beauty were celebrated.

One of Italy's fashion capitals, Firenze style existed not only on the catwalks and in the exclusive designer boutiques but was paraded on the streets and sidewalks and worn with panache by elegant ladies as they strode purposefully, heads held high.

Olivia Rose felt her spirit rejoice and respond to the displays of confidence, and deep inside she was proud to be reminded she was indeed one of them. An Italian. Funny she always identified herself as British, not wishing to be associated with all the hurt and pain that had been inflicted by her mother. In her mind, her mother had been airbrushed out of her life. Jason and Olivia Rose closed ranks against the outsider who destroyed their lives.

In this city of dreams, Olivia Rose gave herself permission to celebrate her European roots. She treated herself to gelato from a passing vendor and licked at the delicious pistachio-filled cornetto with a new sense of adventure. She resisted the urge to hum the theme song of a well-known British advertising campaign, "Just one Cornetto," to the tune of "O, Sole Mio."

With a vibrant rush of spontaneity and spirit-filled enthusiasm, she embraced her heritage. "Anything is possible," she told herself. Refusing to feel intimidated, even though the prices were higher than she would generally contemplate paying, Olivia Rose sailed through the marble entrance way, pushed opened the gilt and glass door and entered one of the grand boutiques by the piazza.

Without having had any prior intention, carried away with the moment, she bought a hat. A magnificent, outrageous, glorious hat. An ivory wide-brimmed hat with gold studs on the rim and one discreet rose strategically placed more visible from the back than the front.

"Bella, Bella." The sales assistant encouraged her, holding up a mirror. "This hat is made for you."

Olivia Rose agreed. It made her feel like a starlet in a Fellini film. "No need to wrap it," she told the smiling saleswoman. "I will wear it. Be sure to remove the price tag. My new life starts right now."

A well-practiced smile and a few words of English were the sales tools the woman possessed. Conversation was beyond her, but she knew a happy customer when she saw one.

Olivia Rose almost skipped down the street. She refused to allow unresolved problems of bouquets, boutonnieres and black hawks to cast a shadow on her joyful afternoon, but truly they were never far from her mind. Everywhere a flower bloomed, she stopped and checked out the potential to fulfill her floral wedding requirements. If necessary, she would gather the Events team and march them from flower shop to market stall to gather blooms.

The single white rose on her hat was a symbol of faith. *The universe will provide*, she repeated her mantra. *The flowers will be delivered. I will not fail. I embrace a new life. A new me. Failure is not an option. I will succeed.*

Face held up to the sun, Olivia Rose sat alongside

the towering Fountain of Neptune in the piazza as the spray playfully splashed her face. All thoughts of disloyalty to her father set aside, she saw with a new pair of eyes. She was thankful to be reunited with her mother. *No wonder my mother Antoinette had to be faithful to her Latin roots; no way could she be expected to stay bottled up in a small Surrey town forever. I can't blame her for choosing to come home to Italy and Gianni. From now on, I dedicate myself to La Dolce Vita.*

Chapter Eleven

"Miss Anderson, you have a visitor," the reception informed Olivia Rose. "He is waiting for you in the garden. Cara and Rudi from the events' team are already there."

Olivia Rose hurried outside to the landscaped garden where the wedding ceremony would take place. She had not been expecting visitors and hoped it did not indicate trouble. No wedding guests were scheduled to arrive until the next day.

Cara and Rudi stood by the flower arch that carpenters had already started erecting in front of a small raised dais. A red carpet protected by waterproofing was rolled up under a pile of gilt chairs. Rudi shaded his eyes from the sun, and beside him Cara craned her neck to see up beyond the symmetrical ball of the most massive tree in the immaculately manicured garden.

A towering figure, tall and as impressive as a superhero, claimed his space in the center of the lawn. Dressed head to toe in black, he wore a black visor and black leather gauntlets. Attached to his right wrist, he held a thick coil of rope and this he wound and rewound through his fingers as if plaiting it. He did not look up but gazed straight ahead and made a strange clicking sound with his teeth. From his buckled belt, embellished with wings, hung a silver whistle and a small silver bell.

Rudi indicated the masked figure. "He insisted on checking out the venue and showing us what he can do. Meet the Prey Man, Alphonso, and one of the stars of his show, the black hawk, Pepe. Alphonso's birds of prey are part of a medieval display at one of the local villas. They take part in aerial performances, and brave visitors even feed them from their hands. Alphonso comes highly recommended for entertainment value, and as far as we could establish, there have never been any issues of safety regarding his shows."

Olivia Rose looked to the sky as she heard a *whooshing* sound and steeled herself not to cover her head and protect her new hat, as a black hawk swooped down and landed on the outstretched arm of his handler. Olivia Rose was reluctant to go too close, but Rudi insisted on introducing her to Alphonso.

"Thank you for agreeing to be part of the wedding ceremony," Olivia Rose said, as she raised her voice and hoped her words could be heard through the tight fitting bird-like helmet. "I can assure you Pepe will be a star attraction at our upcoming wedding. Rudi will explain what needs to happen and the timing of the day."

There was no response from Alphonso nor had Olivia Rose expected one, but Rudi had taken charge and reassured her. "Cara will provide a red velvet pouch that contains the wedding rings, and Alphonso will control the hawk at all times. Pepe will fly free and follow a food trail to his landing place on a velvet cushion perched on a column on the stage. Alphonso knows that he is to remove the pouch and hand it to the best man. Then he and Pepe are welcome to fly off."

Olivia Rose smiled her thanks to Rudi and Cara and left them to make final arrangements with Alphonso. "You did a great job," she told them, "it's great to be working with you."

Alphonso was keen to put on another display, and Olivia Rose excused herself. Walking away she called over her shoulder, "Any news on the flowers?"

Cara walked with her and answered. "Yes, but it means getting up at 4 a.m. tomorrow to go to the flower market. Rudi and I are up for it."

"I love your problem-solving abilities," said Olivia Rose. "I'll text you. But if that's what it takes, I'm game. You two are stars." *The universe will provide,* she confirmed, and, with any luck, she may not need to get up at that ridiculous hour.

It was time to see if Gianni had a rescue plan in place.

Chapter Twelve

Gianni showed no signs of false modesty about his achievements. "I am your hero," he declared, full of bravado. "I have saved the day."

Olivia Rose recalled the look of triumph on his face as he beat her father to Best of Show at Chelsea all those years ago. For a moment she regretted having asked for his help on this occasion. If only she'd spoken to her mother directly.

"You are staying at Palazzo La Grande? I'll come to the hotel and collect you. You will be ready in one hour?" Gianni issued his instructions and answered his own questions. "I will need a list of all the floral arrangements you require. We may need to make some substitutions, but you will not be disappointed. Trust me. Ciao."

Olivia Rose checked the time and put in a call to Cara. "Do you have the original order of the personal flowers we need?" Cara confirmed it was in her file. "Please leave a copy of it for me at reception. You can also email it, but I'd like a hard copy in hand. Do it straight away; I am leaving the hotel in an hour. I'm not promising, but we may be spared a dawn raid on the flower market."

Olivia Rose took a quick shower, reapplied her makeup and considered what she should wear, given her limited choices. Not knowing where she was headed, she chose a smart black trouser suit, red silk blouse, and red high heels. Her new hat would make its official public appearance on the day of the wedding.

Gianni was prompt, and as she stepped into the car, Olivia Rose commented on the fact that he was driving her mother's red convertible. The sporty Italian model.

"We are partners," he shrugged. "We share everything."

"May I ask where we are going?" Olivia Rose questioned him.

"In this country, we always rely on a friend to do a favor," explained Gianni. "I have a friend for you."

Italian opera played on the radio, the night air was warm and Olivia Rose settled in to enjoy a magical mystery tour. The presence of a handsome Italian male was a bonus. There was no denying; her mother had good taste. Even in a country known for its good-looking men, Gianni's dark eyes, jet black hair and impeccable grooming marked him as extra special. Everything about him signaled wealth and privilege, and his casual arrogance added to the attraction.

Gianni said little, but from time to time he turned to face Olivia Rose and gave her the benefit of his winning smile. "Up ahead, you see the villa," he pointed out. "This is the home of my friend."

Black ironwork gates swung open as Gianni leaned from the car and pressed an entry button. The ancient ivy-clad villa was constructed of a mellow sunshine-yellow sandstone with sky-blue shutters. Close-up signs of deterioration showed and in places the walls and balustrades crumbled. A small ornamental pool with floating water lilies looked in need of attention, and a fountain of the Water Bearer was covered in rust and bore no water.

Gianni gestured to the distressed building. "This all belongs to my friend, Tiberius; his family was Italian aristocracy. Now he is impoverished, but he refuses to give up the villa. He pays the expenses by renting the place out as an events venue and having rich Americans stay. They love the fact that he is a Count."

Olivia Rose did not admit that she, too, was impressed by his lineage, even though Tiberius, a man of mature years, appeared dressed in frayed denims and an old working shirt. Barefoot.

He greeted Gianni with three kisses, one on each cheek and one for luck, and clasped Olivia Rose to his bosom. "You are every bit as beautiful as I was informed." He smiled as he took her hand and kissed it.

She also received triple kisses. Gianni looked on approvingly. "Tibi is the man to solve your problem," said Gianni. "Come, let him show you."

Tibi led the way, and Gianni took her arm as they walked around the side of the once grand house. A terrace led down to the overgrown gardens, and here Tibi stopped and pointed to an outbuilding in the near distance. A glass greenhouse. "My pride and joy," he exclaimed.

Olivia Rose smiled. She had spent most of her childhood believing that everyone had a greenhouse in the garden. People who did spoke her language.

The door to the greenhouse jammed, then reluctantly creaked open. The three of them squeezed through the narrow gap into a glorious wonderland of plants, flowers and bushes.

"My collection is at your disposal," said Tibi graciously. "I have many fine specimens of roses. When is your wedding?"

Olivia Rose laughed and looked at Gianni. "It's not my wedding. I'm a wedding planner. The flowers are for a client."

Tibi nodded. "Good," he pronounced, "you are much too young to get married. In fact, if I weren't so old, I would consider marrying you myself."

"You wouldn't need to ask twice," said Olivia Rose and smiled, contemplating herself as a Countess.

"Okay," ordered Gianni, "let's get to work before it gets dark. Which flowers do you require for the wedding? Do you have your list?"

Olivia Rose pulled the list from her shiny red tote bag and handed it to Gianni, who in turn passed it to Tibi. For a few moments, he stared at it, then, without admitting that he could not read it, said, "Where do we start?"

"White roses," proclaimed Olivia Rose, "for the bride's bouquet and enough pink roses for six bridesmaids."

Tibi produced raffia baskets, plus three sets of

mismatched garden gloves, and all three of them walked the aisles of the greenhouse selecting roses, ferns and greenery.

"Next," called Gianni from the far end of the building.

"This might be tricky," admitted Olivia Rose. "I need two hundred single stems for boutonnieres and corsages. A combination of red and white would be ideal."

Tibi walked her to the last row of flowers. "Will these be suitable?" he asked. "They are still in bud, not quite fully grown. What do you think?"

"I'll take them," Olivia Rose decided. "Nested inside wispy green ferns, they will be perfect."

The sun set while they worked. By the light of heating lamps and candles, Tibi, Gianni and Olivia Rose sat and drank wine from Tibi's vineyard. "I can't thank you enough," said Olivia. "Now I have to figure out how to get all of this back to the hotel."

Gianni was not fazed. "It will all go in the car." He had no doubt.

Olivia Rose looked skeptical.

"Bring the baskets," he ordered.

Tibi led the way down the unlit paths and around the side of the house as the trio made their way to the car, hardly able to see over the piles of blooms. Gianni placed each basket with care on the small back seat of the car. The pots of greenery fit on the floor.

Tibi held the door for Olivia Rose to get into the car, and she held up the collar of her jacket, as thorns and spiky leaves threatened to pierce her skin.

Gianni noticed and voiced his concern. "Are you going to be alright?" Gianni asked.

"Am I the daughter of a champion rose grower?" she replied. "I'm used to sharing my transport with plants and trees. They always get a better seat than the human beings."

Gianni was amused. "You are quite a girl," he told her. He was about to drive away when Olivia Rose stopped him. "Wait a minute," she said, "I haven't paid for the flowers.

"That's not a problem," he reassured her. "We can sort it out later. I'll take care of Tibi. He was glad to help. That's what friends are for."

On the ride back to the hotel, Olivia Rose and Gianni laughed and teased each other as they dodged a wall of rose bushes and picked leaves out of each others hair.

Gianni directed the whole operation. At the hotel, he summoned a porter and instructed him to take the contents of the car up to Olivia Rose's room. The porter did not bat an eyelid. He had seen stranger things in all his years in the hospitality business. One client had arrived carrying a goldfish in a bowl. "He gets lonely at home," the hotel guest had explained.

Olivia Rose looked puzzled as the porter loaded the roses onto a luggage cart. Gianni enlightened her. "You are to play host to several hundred prize-winning roses. They need to be put in water in your bath. Tomorrow you can ask the hotel to move them, and you will be able to have a bath."

"Are you kidding me?" asked Olivia Rose.

"How else are you going to keep them fresh until morning?" he demanded. "I'll come and help you put them to bed." Good as his word, Gianni ensured that every rose and plant was watered, bedded down for the night and treated with tender loving care.

"All sleeping peacefully," he said as he closed the bathroom door. "Crisis over."

Cara had been much relieved to receive Olivia Rose's earlier message confirming that they did not have to get up at dawn. She had organized assistance to tie bouquets and prepare the corsages and boutonnieres. So, yes, that particular crisis was over.

Olivia Rose walked Gianni to the door of her room. "I can't thank you enough," she said. "You are my hero."

Gianni leaned in to hug her and thinking he was about to kiss her on the cheek, Olivia Rose turned her face toward him. Their lips met, and Olivia Rose felt a surge of longing as they kissed. The moment lasted and neither moved to break away. After what seemed an eternity, Gianni took control. He held Olivia Rose at arm's length and told her, "That was not meant to happen. Please forgive me."

Olivia Rose, still stunned by the force of the physical contact, stepped away from the embrace, and Gianni exited without a backward glance. *That was most certainly not meant to happen.* Olivia Rose shook her head in disbelief when he had gone. *But I'm not sorry. I've never been rescued by my own real live hero before.*

Olivia Rose allowed herself the luxury of denial as she savored the sensation of her unexpected electrifying kiss. She secretly relished the knowledge of the devastation her mother would feel should the betrayal ever be revealed. In a moment of defiance, she hardened her heart. *I'm the one who was abandoned*, she affirmed. *No one will ever know how much it hurt to have my mother walk out on me. To leave a husband is personal, to leave a daughter unforgivable.*

The memory of a family holiday photograph taken on the beach at Brighton, one of the last times they were all together, flashed into her mind. Jason and Antoinette, arms around each other, smiled into each others eyes as they embraced their laughing teenage daughter.

Gianni had destroyed the sacred family circle and Antoinette chose him instead of her own flesh and blood. Somebody had to pay for leaving pain and despair in the place of love and happiness. Always conscious of her father's pain, for years, Olivia Rose hid her anguish, but the scars inflicted by separation from her mother festered inside.

Gianni was the key to her redemption.

Chapter Thirteen

The first wedding guests arrived before lunch at Palazzo La Grande. Bride and groom planned to come straight from the airport to the wedding rehearsal in the early evening.

Bridesmaids, with enough luggage for a month's stay rather than the three nights for which their rooms were reserved, jockeyed for position, each stating a particular need to be nearest the bride's room. Family members with children also demanded treatment special.

"I'm the mother of the bride, and these are her nieces, the youngest bridesmaids," an English voice boomed out across the hotel reception. If the imperious attitude was meant to show a familiarity with staying in such opulent surroundings, it instead showed the opposite and gave away the fact that nerves were already frayed.

Olivia Rose stood by the reception desk and introduced herself to each new arrival. Her calm manner and the fact that she spoke English were a welcome reassurance. "Let me know if you need anything," she said handing over her business card. Though, of course, the international hotel staff was multilingual, the comfort level of "someone from home" brought an added reassurance.

Olivia Rose had total confidence that the choice of the wedding venue and the six-star hotel could not possibly disappoint the most demanding guest. Each spacious luxury bedroom was individually decorated with a different classical theme, all illuminated with glittering chandeliers, colorful wall frescoes and antique paintings. King-size beds, piled high with plump cushions in satin and velvet and silks, complemented top quality embroidered coverlets matching the heavy brocade drapes.

In contrast to the traditional style of the bedrooms, the bathrooms had been renovated and were modern and stylish. Marble Jacuzzi and whirlpool baths were large enough to accommodate at least a couple or a few hundred roses.

The hotel staff was hard at work from early morning preparing the garden and outdoor areas. The hotel had achieved an excellent reputation as a wedding reception for local and international guests, and at least once a week the team swung into action and in a coordinated operation dressed the stage of the fairy tale setting for each wedding.

Olivia Rose allowed herself to relax a little, quietly confident that all arrangements were in place. She looked in on the Event's office hourly and checked that there were no last-minute dramas. "Remember," she told Cara and Rudi, "it ain't over till the fat lady sings."

Their puzzled looks indicated they had no idea what she meant, but they smiled. They, too, like the maintenance and setup staff, went through this procedure regularly.

"The bouquets are ready," Cara informed Olivia Rose on one of her tours of inspection. "They look beautiful and have been placed in cold storage."

"Very good, thank you," said Olivia Rose. "And confirm for me, Alphonso and his black hawk, Pepe, are NOT coming to the rehearsal tonight?"

"No," Rudi called across the room. "Alphonso loves an audience and every opportunity to perform, but we persuaded him it would spoil the surprise. He understood."

"The banquet manager will be here in a few minutes," said Cara, "he will confirm with you all the preparations that are in place for tonight's supper and tomorrow's main event."

Olivia Rose had only one engagement for the rest of the afternoon. She had promised to accompany some guests on a truffle hunt at the nearby Four Seasons Hotel. One man and his dog, both professional truffle hunters, awaited the small party, and they set off to look for truffles in a nearby woodland. A gourmet meal and lecture on how to cook truffles given by a top chef followed. Olivia Rose declined to join them for the meal and returned alone to the Palazzo.

Every time she checked her phone for messages or a text she convinced herself it was work related. She was reluctant to admit that she hoped for some communication from Gianni. Olivia Rose had little experience in the realm of romance. But she knew better than to make the first move. She was a late starter and now in her early twenties. At high school, there had been one steady boyfriend, but after a couple of years, even he got fed up waiting for Olivia Rose to make a commitment.

"You must be the only girl in school who doesn't put out sexually," he said. She refused to give him hope that the situation would change and eventually their relationship fizzled out. Olivia Rose could have blamed her reluctance on her father; he was strict and lectured her about "nice girls" and the fact that her mother had been a virgin when they married.

"That's hardly a great example of how to achieve a long and lasting relationship," Olivia Rose challenged him.

"No, and I have to admit," said Jason, "that if we'd lived together beforehand, we would probably never have married. I'm trying to protect you. I know I'm old-fashioned. You must do what feels right for you."

Olivia Rose went through college doing what she felt was right for her. Watching the hurt and pain suffered by her friends, who indulged in regular hookups and breakups, strengthened her resolve to wait. Not necessarily until she was married but certainly till she met the right man. They all only want one thing her father warned her over and over again.

Whenever she did go on a date, Olivia Rose dreaded the moment when she would be forced to take a stand and refuse to engage in physical activity. There seemed no easy way of letting down a man. Their egos would be bruised, and most did not know how to react. Usual responses were "Are you a religious nut?" "You're frigid" or "What are you saving yourself for?"

As she moved out of her teenage years and into her twenties, Olivia Rose had to accept that her many invitations to date came less and less. *Somewhere,* she reasoned, *there must be a man who is meant for me and understands. I have to be sure that he is the right one and that love will last.*

What had happened between her and Gianni last night rocked the foundation of everything she had believed up to then. So why was he on her mind? Why was she longing to hear from him?

⋆ ⋆ ⋆

Olivia Rose met the bridal couple when their plane from Heathrow landed. Johnathan and Jennifer came through the customs exit at Florence airport pushing two luggage carts piled high with Louis Vuitton luggage. Laid out on the top was a full-length gown carrier. The wedding dress. Jennifer refused to trust anyone but herself to deliver the precious gown safely to the wedding venue.

Jennifer was pretty in an actressy, rather obvious way, all big teeth and wide eyes. Petite with long blonde hair and lots of makeup, she teetered on five-inch Louboutin heels. At her neck, earrings and wrists, she wore gold jewelry plus a white-gold Rolex watch, and even she pushed a luggage cart, while making fluttery hand movements that drew attention to her long painted fingernails and the enormous, dazzling diamond engagement ring on her left hand.

Johnathan had an open, slightly pudgy face and a regulation, public school neat, unfussy haircut. He was stocky, dressed in casual Adidas brand workout gear and wearing sneakers. One small diamond stud glinted in his left earlobe.

J&J, the branding on all their wedding stationery and table decorations were stamped on Jennifer's LV tote.

The couple held hands even as they guided their luggage carts. The limousine driver stepped forward and took charge of the luggage. Olivia Rose stepped forward to greet the couple and was surprised also to be introduced to Johnathan's teenage son, who barely raised his eyes from his iPad to say "hello."

Johnathan and Jennifer stretched out in the back seat of the limousine and accepted a welcoming glass of champagne. Johnathan's son, Harry, chose to sit in the front beside the driver. His father refused the champagne on his behalf.

On the journey to the hotel, the couple talked excitedly about their upcoming nuptials and questioned Olivia Rose on various details. "You did confirm with the hotel that we require separate bedrooms for tonight?" Jennifer asked. "I'm so excited for us to start our married life in that fabulous four poster bed."

Olivia Rose had already meticulously checked out the bridal suite with its magnificent high ceilings, draped bed, ceiling frescoes, chandeliers, gold and red decorations and carved gilt furniture. In a palace overflowing with sumptuous bedrooms, the bridal suite was a masterpiece. The entire room was painted as a Garden of

Eden, placed somewhere between Heaven and earth. Cherubs, goddesses, trompe l'oeil—a super-size draped white satin four poster bed piled high with tasseled cushions and carved headrests was illuminated under a shining white globe chandelier.

"We'll move into the bridal suite after the wedding tomorrow. I don't want to sleep with Johnathan before we're married. We're traditional about things like that."

Harry looked up from his iPad long enough to make his only remark of the journey. "It's not like you haven't been shacked up together for the last year."

Johnathan and Jennifer shared a look and raised their eyebrows. They did not comment.

Olivia Rose felt a wave of sadness wash over her. Trouble in Paradise. Did every relationship have to come with complications and baggage, even if the luggage was Vuitton?

Back at the hotel, Olivia Rose confirmed that the hotel accommodated the separate room arrangements. Under the pretext of reporting back to Jennifer, Olivia Rose telephoned, checked that Johnathan was not in her room and gave an update about the black hawk.

"All is in order," she told Jennifer. "Handler and hawk will be here at noon tomorrow to await the signal to fly the rings to the best man. We have a red velvet pouch in case you didn't bring one.

"The best man needs to hand over the rings to my assistant Cara who will pass it to the hawk man to attach to the hawk's leg. I'll introduce all of them before the ceremony."

"Who knows about the Hawk?" asked Jennifer.

"Don't worry. Besides me, only members of the Events' team. The hawk will not be here tonight for the rehearsals; we don't want to spoil the surprise."

"It all sounds great, thank you," said Jennifer and clapped her hands with glee. "I love it when a plan works out."

"I've got a picture of Pepe, that's the hawk, on my phone; shall I send it to you?"

"Don't bother," said Jennifer, "I'm sure one hawk looks pretty much the same as another. It will to me anyway; I've never even seen one."

Olivia Rose laughed. "Take my word for it; he's a magnificent creature. Your guests and fans will be impressed."

* * *

The wedding scene was picture perfect as the bride posed on the red carpet under the flower arch, which was decorated with twenty-foot urns of cascading floral bouquets. Photographers from the press and a television camera crew competed with the couple's personal wedding photographer to capture the best pictures of the stunning bride.

Her white satin designer dress was strapless, with a mermaid style corset and long train. The dress sparkled in the sunlight with hundreds of hand-sewn silver sequins, and her white rose bouquet with long white ribbons was magnificent.

Six bridesmaids, two of whom were children, wore pink puffball dresses and glittering tiaras and proudly carried their pink bouquets with trailing ribbons.

Johnathan and his best man dressed in black evening suits with purple cummerbunds and bow ties, and white boutonnieres.

Young Harry followed his own dress code in denim jeans and a navy blue dinner jacket with one red and one white boutonniere on each lapel.

The officiating magistrate waited with Johnathan and the best man on the flower-filled raised stage for the bride. Eager not to give the game away but anxious to check out the black hawk who would deliver the rings, the best man peered nervously into the sky.

Jennifer arrived at her place; she also tried to look up without Johnathan noticing. The moment arrived. The marriage official looked to the best man. "The couple will now exchange rings as a token of their love and devotion."

Pepe's big moment had arrived. Here he would swoop down over the wedding party and land on the white column set off to the side of the stage. The wedding party waited. And waited. The best man made gestures indicating, "It's not my fault."

Silence descended as guests wondered what was going on.

Olivia Rose rushed to the back of the garden where she had last seen Alphonso stationed, hawk in hand. Now his thick rope coil was stretched to its fullest extent, and at the end of it, Pepe performed his aerial display. He flew ever faster over the crowd, round and round, wheeling, dipping and sweeping over the wedding party, wings outstretched.

Alphonso blew his whistle, rang his bell and made his clicking sounds. Still, Pepe flew on, refusing to relinquish his position as the center of attention. He saw his audience way down below and he enthusiastically entertained them with his whole routine. Alphonso strode down the aisle, a man in black, covered in embarrassment. He tried to bring Pepe's performance to an end with a ring on his bell, a blow on the whistle and a click of his teeth.

The wedding party, surprised at the interruption of the ceremony, nevertheless enjoyed the display. Alphonso took up his place beside the white column and tidbit of food in hand, willed Pepe to stop flying and land. Suddenly, without warning, Pepe remembered his training and obeying instructions, flew down, snatched the food from Alphonso's outstretched hand and flew off again. By accident or on purpose, he shook the velvet pouch from his claw as he exited and wheeled off swiftly to reclaim his freedom in the wide blue skies.

The crowd erupted with delight and reacted to the black hawk performance with loud cheering and noisy clapping. Alphonso left the stage, and Olivia Rose stepped forward to pick up the pouch and hand it over to the best man. She endeavored to make it all look as if it had been planned.

Pepe had stolen the show, and the crowd loved it.

Jennifer confided to Olivia Rose later. "The camera

crew filmed the whole thing. We're putting it on You-Tube. I'm hoping it will go viral. The Black Hawk Wedding Show."

Johnathan was full of praise for his new bride. "Congratulations to my highly imaginative wife. It's a great publicity stunt for Black Hawk Investments."

Olivia Rose enjoyed a celebratory glass of champagne with the happy couple at the reception and accepted compliments for her white rose hat, which she had teamed with a pastel-flowered shift dress and blush pink strappy sandals. She resisted the happy couple's invitations to stay longer. Slipping away quietly from the formal celebrations, she made her way to the Events office with a bottle of champagne to thank Cara and Rudi for their superb organization.

The three of them drank champagne and had fits of the giggles as they recalled the afternoon's entertainment. Cara and Rudi toasted her. "You are the best wedding planner ever," they said. "Pepe's performance was priceless! Here's to White Roses Wedding Service —and the black hawk."

* * *

Olivia Rose kicked off her high-heeled shoes, changed her dress for a silk robe and lay back on the outsize bed. She checked her phone. There were three texts from Gianni: How was the wedding? Do you have plans for this evening? Can I come to see you?

Perhaps it was the effects of the champagne or the

euphoria of the wedding, but she did not hesitate or consider the consequences. She answered him: The wedding was memorable. I have no plans. Of course, you can come to see me. Love Olivia Rose x

Chapter Fourteen

An ominous black cloud hung over the towering peaks of the Montgo National Park and threatened to fulfill the weather prediction for long and lasting rain showers. The mountain range rises as an impressive backdrop on the mainland of the Costa Blanca opposite the Balearic Islands, and overlooks the port of Denia, halfway between Alicante and Valencia. An eleventh-century castle takes a commanding position surveying the sea from a prominent place on the cliffs.

Denia claims to host a more significant number of festivals than any other town on the mainland and is most proud of its summer event, and popular tourist attraction, running with the bulls. Replicating in many ways the world famous Paloma showcase, in Denia, young men chase the bulls through the streets and, in a finish with no obvious winners, men and beasts rush across the sands into the sea. Bathing bulls aside, Trans Mediterranean ferries sail daily services from the port to the islands of Ibiza and Palma, Mallorca.

With no plans and nowhere to go, Callum Lavelle had driven from his hotel in Valencia, an hour away, to Denia. The reward for two days of solitary drinking was a monumental hangover and a total blackout of where he had gone and what he had done. Reluctant to hang around and find out, he checked out of his hotel and left town.

Without a good-bye or backward glance, he also left a young naked lady sleeping in his bed. With no idea of how she had gotten there, he didn't need to be drawn a diagram of what she had been doing there. He hung a *Do Not Disturb* sign on the door and asked reception to make a wake-up call to his unknown guest at check-out time. Aware that his attitude to women was far from gentlemanly, he blamed the women who threw themselves at men like him who had status and were wealthy.

He craved one glass of beer to combat a raging hangover that made him feel as if he had been run over by a truck. To spend another day in his room where he would drink the mini bar dry and venture out at night to goodness knows where was not an option.

Callum had a better idea. Ibiza was a favorite place of his for rest and recreation. Whenever he needed downtime, he and his teammates headed for the wild party island where discos, nightclubs, sun-kissed girls and wall-to-wall booze restored their spirits.

Thanks to his sporting fame, he was known in all the hip places, *Privilege,* which claims to be the largest nightclub in the world, *Space, Particular, Jockey Club, Amnesia;* friends ran exclusive beach restaurants and boutique hotels in secluded coves for the rich and famous, far from the tourist resorts.

The irony that the small car he had rented at the airport was the Ibiza model did not escape him. Ibiza called to him like an alluring siren. A line of slow moving vehicles snaked their way into the belly of the brightly colored aquamarine ferry that would take them on a two-hour sea journey to Ibiza. As instructed, he parked in the underground area of the ferry and turned off the alarm. He read the signs that stated all passengers are required to travel in the main decks during the voyage and are not permitted to return to the car decks.

The first Estrella beer was wearing off, and he needed another hit of alcohol. "A beer," he told the pretty young girl behind the food counter. She held up two bottles of Spanish beer and asked him to make a selection; he resisted the urge to take both.

The early evening fast ferry was on time and left port in Denia at 5 pm, due to arrive in Ibiza at 7 p.m.

The wide-open seating areas offered choices on several levels, and he walked through the cabin avoiding family groups and looked for a quiet space. Settling in a blue plastic reclining seat by the window, Callum stretched out, rested his feet on his backpack and stared into the distance as land faded. Waves lashed the windows as a watery combination of sea and rain foretold early indications of a rough crossing.

He was not keen to address the pressing matters that insisted on disturbing his peace of mind: how had his life had gotten out of control and how had he become a fugitive on the run. From what he hardly knew. Feelings of impending doom flooded through him, and he felt the world tighten its grip. Without warning, he felt himself under attack. His long legs were stretched across an aisle, and an unknown force fastened itself on his ankle.

First, he felt a sharp pain and then he heard a growl. He looked down and saw a white Highland terrier gnawing on his ankle. The cheek of the animal amused him, and Callum laughed.

"Harry, stop that. Stop that this minute," exclaimed the dog's owner while pulling him away. "I'm so sorry," she said as she held tightly to the dog's leash. "Are you hurt? What can I do to help? I'm so sorry."

Callum registered the genuine concern in her bright green eyes. "You should keep that wild animal under control," he told her, not laughing now. "How do I know he hasn't got rabies?"

"We're on our way upstairs to the kennels," said the owner by way of explanation. "Pets have to travel on the top deck. They're not allowed in the main cabin. I think something spooked him. Probably that black bulldog. He looked a bit fierce even with a muzzle on. Harry is a softie. He doesn't usually attack strangers."

Callum checked his ankle, a nip from a pint-size dog hardly registered compared with the kind of injuries he suffered for years in training and on the football field. "No harm done," he said. "Don't worry about it."

Harry still strained at his leash, and his owner was keen to continue her journey up to the pet deck with him. "Thank you," she said. "I'm sorry. Let me know if there is anything I can do. He usually plays nice, and his rabies shots are all up to date."

To show Harry there were no hard feelings, Callum bent down to pat him. Harry growled. His owner burst out laughing, and her smile lit up her beautiful features. "He's not ready to be friends," she said. "I better get him into that cage upstairs."

Callum was willing to forgive, but there was a condition.

"Harry might not want to be friends, but that doesn't stop us. There is something you can do. Will you have a coffee with me, once he is safely under lock and key?"

"Yes, okay," she said, eager to divert what could have developed into an awkward situation. "But I drink tea. Like you I'm British."

Quickly dispelling that misconception, Callum corrected her. "You've got the wrong man. I'm not British. I'm Irish."

"Sorry." She smiled. "What do I know? I'm Italian."

Callum nodded as if that explained everything and locked his eyes onto her as she made her way out of the cabin and up the metal staircase to the outside pet area. Her long auburn hair bobbed in a high ponytail, and she wore skinny white jeans and a red leather jacket with white boots. He usually preferred blondes, but when they looked like the one whose dog had bitten him, Callum was prepared to make an exception for a gorgeous redhead.

At every minute throughout the two-hour voyage, he expected her to return; however, she failed to show up. With Ibiza in sight, Callum made his way to the rear of the cabin and spied her come down the steep metal staircase; she carried Harry in her arms.

Callum waved, and she joined him as he waited for the all clear to go downstairs to the car deck. "Sorry, again," she said, "the only available cage was next to the black bulldog. I couldn't leave him up there alone. We missed our coffee."

"Maybe not," he said, anxious not to let her slip away as soon as they disembarked. "I know a place where they make a great cup of coffee and a decent cup of tea. It's right beside the port."

"Okay, as long as they allow dogs. I have to wait for my friend to collect me. She's running a little late."

A service announcement advised drivers to go below and collect their vehicles. "Passengers leave by the entryway, and meet your drivers at the car park."

"See you there, Harry," said, Callum. As an afterthought, he added, "By the way, I'm Callum. Cal for short. What's your name? I can't keep calling you Harry's mum."

With a smooth laugh, she answered him. "Antoinette, like the French Queen who said, 'Let them eat cake.'"

Chapter Fifteen

Callum and Antoinette were the only customers in the small family run bar. "This place has an amazing reputation," he told her. "Customers line up around the block for a table. Honest. But seven o'clock is very early in Ibiza and Spain in general. The Spanish eat late. Only Brits and Americans go for the early bird menu."

Antoinette nodded. "I know, I live in Spain," she replied.

Callum looked embarrassed. "Didn't mean to teach my grandmother to suck eggs."

It was Antoinette's turn to frown with incomprehension.

"I'm not familiar with that expression," she told him, "but I did live in England for many years. A little village in Surrey."

"I've got a place on the South Coast," he said. "Almost neighbors. And I'm guessing, Harry, being a Highland terrier, is Scottish."

Harry, settled under the table at Antoinette's feet, barked at the mention of his name. "I've got a confession to make," said Antoinette. "Harry is not my dog.

He belongs to my friend; she left him with me when she went on a trip. I'm returning him."

Callum was amused. "That reminds me of a joke. There's a dog in the park, and a man asks the person with him, 'Does your dog bite?' 'No,' says the man, and at that, the dog takes a lump out of his leg. Like Harry did with me. 'I thought you said your dog doesn't bite,' he said. The man replied, 'That's not my dog.'" They both laughed and, not to be left out, Harry joined in with a good-matured bark.

Antoinette sipped her tea and smiled across the table at Callum. She noticed that he hesitated when he ordered his drink. "Coffee and a brandy," he told the waiter, then corrected himself. "Coffee, espresso, double shot. No brandy."

"What are you doing in Ibiza?" she asked.

"Last minute decision," said Callum. "I fancied some chill-out time. I have friends here."

Antoinette nodded. "Ibiza does have a reputation as party central, but it's also a beautiful island with lots of history, culture and medieval architecture."

"You'll need to give me a guided tour," said Callum. "I've been here stacks of times but only seen the inside of nightclubs and bars."

Antoinette felt a pang of sadness. For all his charm and overt good looks, there was something about the young man that concerned her. She was wondering why she had agreed to have tea with him and how to extricate herself from his company when her phoned beeped.

"My friend is here," she said. "I've got to go. Thank you for the tea. I hope you find what you're looking for here in Ibiza."

From the car park, Antoinette's friend beeped her horn. Harry recognized the sound of his owner's car and started to bark wildly. "Okay, okay, we're going," she assured him. "There's a good boy."

Callum watched and waited. "Can I see you again?" he asked.

Antoinette was taken by surprise, not quite sure what she and the young man could possibly have in common. It was on the tip of her tongue to say, "My daughter is a better match for you. She's more your age," but she resisted. "You won't find me in any of your fancy nightclubs," she said.

"I thought you could take me sightseeing," he replied.

"Show me around the island."

Antoinette's friend was getting restless and so, too, was her dog. The car horn sounded again, and Harry pulled on his leash.

"Okay. If you're serious. Meet me here at noon tomorrow."

Callum extended his strong right hand and shook hers. "I could use a cultural tour with an elegant lady. I'll be here tomorrow. Promise."

The two exchanged phone numbers. "In case you want to cancel," said Antoinette. "I'm sure there are many attractions on the island that will divert your attention."

"You have my full attention," said Callum, looking directly into her eyes. "Don't you be letting me down now."

The restaurant door opened and Antoinette's friend called, "Are you ready?" Harry needed no persuading. Antoinette dropped the lead, and he rushed to his owner, jumped up to paw at her knees and licked her hands.

"Be right there," said Antoinette and followed her friend out to her car.

Callum watched her leave. He ordered another coffee and this time gratefully added a brandy. Unlike any of the other willing young women he dated, Antoinette had class, a quality that appealed.

Customers had begun to arrive while he and Antoinette talked. The clientele was mostly Spanish, and as he watched the families share their meals, chatter and laugh together, he missed his family and especially his daughter. Loneliness threatened to overwhelm him. The thought of the mess he had left behind at home made him sick, and he dreaded what he would face when he was finally brave enough to return.

He needed company. Female company. When he was alone in his head, he was in a dangerous neighborhood. He had a date for tomorrow, which he intended to keep, but for now, the night was still young—and full of potential. He took out his phone and scrolled through his contacts.

★ ★ ★

Antoinette arrived before noon at the café the next day. Her friend lost no time in telling her that she was mad. If she could have, she would have convinced her not to go at all. Antoinette and Claudia had been friends since school. They came from the same village, and Claudia now lived with her British husband in Ibiza and owned a small boutique.

"You don't know anything about him," she said. "He's a stranger you met on the ferry. You don't owe him anything, even if he was understanding about Harry nipping his ankle. Sounds like he was keen to get close to you and used Harry as a good excuse."

Antoinette could not dispute what she said, but she did not intend to stand Callum up. She had promised him a sightseeing tour. She would keep her word.

Claudia reluctantly agreed to drop her off at the same place she had collected her friend the previous day. She tapped Callum's number into her phone and made Antoinette promise she would call when she needed a ride home. Anytime. Anywhere. Claudia would collect her. And no doubt Harry would come along, too.

"Yes, Mum," said Antoinette, receiving her instructions as she stepped out of the car.

Callum pulled up in his car and pointed to the café. Antoinette was glad he had not come over to say hello. "Can't say I blame you," said Claudia relenting somewhat. "He is very handsome. What a great smile. Well turned out. And young."

Antoinette had left that detail out of her description when telling Claudia about her encounter. "It's not a date," she had insisted, "I'm showing him the sights."

Claudia smiled. Antoinette had arrived from her ferry trip returning Harry home with only a small overnight bag. Subsequently, she had raided Claudia's wardrobe to find something suitable to wear for her sightseeing tour. A floaty white lace dress, very Ibiza style, which showed off her tanned limbs and shapely legs with a matching ivory silk jacket and silver jeweled sandals completed the ensemble. Giant hooped silver earrings peeped through her long hair, which she wore down reaching beyond her shoulders.

Antoinette said good-bye to Claudia and Harry and followed Callum into the café. "Tea?" he asked her as he turned from the counter where the espresso machine gurgled and a hot stream of boiling water filled her cup.

"You look lovely," he said, as he set down the two cups and saucers he carried to the table, balancing milk, spoons and small packets of sugar.

"How was your evening?" asked Antoinette.

"Uneventful," he said and smiled. "I met friends at a chiriquitos down at Las Salinas, had dinner on the beach and an early night."

Antoinette wasn't sure she believed him, but it was none of her business.

"I was saving myself for today," he told her. "I'm looking forward to our cultural tour."

Antoinette reminded herself that this was not a date, but the cheeky wink of approval and huge grin Callum bestowed upon her set off a sensation of butterflies in her stomach. "Are you game to walk?" she asked him.

"Parking in the old town is a nightmare. Better to leave the car here."

"Yes, a walk sounds good," he said. "It's ages since I went to the gym. Normally I'm fanatically disciplined about my fitness routine. I like to keep myself in shape."

"I can see that," said Antoinette and regretted the personal remark as soon as it was out of her mouth.

Dressed in high-end designer casual smart black trousers and shirt, a toned physique was undeniable with his muscled arms and toned stomach muscles. He wore a man size multi-dial Tag Heuer watch. His sneakers were black with flashes of gold on the side, like Mercury's winged sandals.

"You don't look too bad yourself." He returned the compliment Antoinette had let escape.

He stood up, and she was reminded of how tall he was, six feet and change. He hoisted his backpack onto his broad shoulders. "Let's go," he said and walked in front of her to hold open the door. Callum had manners; she liked that.

They strolled through the port. The sky was cloudless, and the sun reflected off the shiny metal of the yachts and gleaming wood of the sailing boats in the busy harbor. Seagulls whirled overhead, and birds sang.

Callum took her arm, and she did not resist. He looked embarrassed when she raised her eyebrows at his habit of constantly chewing gum. "Nicotine gum," he admitted. "I'm trying to give up cigarettes. I know I shouldn't smoke, but every time I'm under pressure I go back to it. Then back to the nicotine gum."

Antoinette made a concerted effort to keep her mind on guiding Callum on a sightseeing tour, and off personal matters. She had visited Ibiza so often over the years that, like many residents of tourist destinations, she rarely spent time in the most picturesque parts of town. The picture-postcard views.

"We are now inside the ancient beating heart of the town," she told him as they climbed the steep hills up to D'Alt Villa, an area filled with a maze of narrow streets, which overlooks the port and the whole island of Ibiza.

They visited the Cathedral, checked out the arts and crafts in local shops and galleries and sat on a stone wall in the sunshine in the cannon-lined square, eating ice cream. "The view at night is spectacular," she told Callum. Antoinette was not prepared for his response.

"It's not night time, but the view from where I am sitting is spectacular," he told her.

Antoinette held her breath; she knew what was coming next. She longed to feel his arms around her. His lips on hers, but she could not allow this to happen. She'd led him on. She knew that, and it had been fun, but before this went any further, she must put a stop to it. "Let's go eat," she said as she jumped up. "There are so many award-winning restaurants up here; we should stop for lunch. Do you like Italian? I'm an expert. Follow me."

Callum did not show any sign of upset by her sudden change of heart. He knew what she tried to deny. He looked in her eyes and knew she wanted the embrace as much as he did. He liked a woman who played hard to get. So few of them did. But, he reminded himself, this was not some girl he had met in a nightclub. Antoinette was a woman, and she was apparently expecting to be wooed. He was up for the chase.

Escorted to the best table in the house, in her favorite Italian restaurant, after having been warmly welcomed by the owner and his wife who admonished her for not visiting more often, Antoinette excused herself to make a phone call.

Gianni did not answer; the call went to voicemail. "It's Saturday afternoon," she said. "I'm still in Ibiza. Dropped Harry off with Claudia, will get the ferry back to Denia Sunday morning. Be home by lunch-time. Hope you're having a successful business trip in Florence. Love you. Ciao."

Chapter Sixteen

"**Y**ou're dining with a wanted man," Callum revealed his secret to Antoinette as they waited for the main course to be served. "I'm on the run from the police back in England. There's a warrant out for my arrest."

Antoinette's intuition had told her there was a flaw in his story of arriving in Ibiza to party—alone. Claudia's warning came to mind as she realized that she could be in some kind of danger. "Do you want to tell me why?" she asked.

Callum signaled for the waiter. "Another beer," he told him. To Antoinette, he asked, "Are you sure you don't want anything to drink? Other than agua con gas, I mean."

Antoinette shook her head. The two enjoyed each others company and a top class meal in a small family run restaurant with red-and-white-checked tablecloths and personal photographs on the walls. The interior with a long polished wooden bar, creaky wood floors and shiny brass light fittings was dark and intimate. The owner insisted on choosing their menu selections and filled the table with the restaurant's speciality dishes of steaming homemade pasta, creamy sauces and hot bread served with olive oil.

"I'm fine, thanks," said Antoinette. "I need to let all that food settle. I didn't want to offend the hosts by refusing their delicious meals, but I may not need to eat for a week."

Callum eyed her with appreciation. "You don't look like you need to watch your figure. But you'll excuse me if I watch it."

"Let's not go there," said Antoinette, though she could not deny that she enjoyed his compliments, and the news that he was on the run had concentrated her mind. The last thing she wanted was to encourage familiarity that might later lead to trouble.

"Tell me the story," she said, judging that while she was in a public place, she was safe. As soon as lunch was over she would make her escape. Claudia was a phone call away. "Are you a bank robber, or did you fail to pay a parking ticket?" she asked.

Callum took a long swallow of his beer; she noticed that the golden liquid produced immediate results and he seemed more comfortable when he had a glass in his hand. "Do you want the long version or the edited highlights?" he asked.

"I'm not going anywhere," said Antoinette. "If it helps to tell me the whole story, you'll find I'm a good listener."

The owner of the restaurant's wife came to check that all had been satisfactory with their meal. "Excellent," Antoinette assured her. Callum flashed a grin and, to seal the deal, winked at her. Antoinette could see the question in her eyes, but diplomatically, she did not inquire about Gianni.

"We're going to sit on the terrace," Antoinette told her. "Will you bring the bill out there, please?"

"It's already taken care of," said her friend, as she nodded in Callum's direction. "He gave me his credit card—a no limit Black American Express—when you arrived."

Antoinette was impressed. "Thank you. You're a gentleman," she told him as they gathered their belongings and headed for a quiet spot on the terrace overlooking the harbor. A gypsy guitarist played, and a flower seller came by with arms full of roses.

Callum handed the lady a five euro note and took one red rose. This he passed to Antoinette. "No hidden motive," he joked. "I wanted to thank you for being such great company—and for looking so beautiful. Oh, yes, and for not freaking out when I told you I was on the run."

Antoinette could not deny she was flattered by his attention. He made her laugh, and for hours over lunch, they had talked and shared stories about their lives. Always stopping short of the reasons for his fugitive status.

"Time to come clean," she said. "Why are you on the run?"

Callum looked off into the distance. He let go of the glass and placed it on the table in front of him.

"I've made a total mess of my life," he told her. "I

was riding high. A professional athlete earning a small fortune, and in a moment of madness, I threw away my whole career. I took a banned substance and got caught." He shook his head as if to erase the memory.

"It's easy for me to want to blame other people. There are a hundred excuses, but I know that until I take responsibility for what happened, I won't be free. This anger bubbles up inside of me, and I hit out."

Antoinette listened but did not comment.

"I'd got the call saying that the banned substance was discovered in my blood sample. I wasn't the only one; a couple of my teammates also failed the drug test. My world was shattered. I phoned my now ex-wife and she blew me off. She'd heard about what had happened and she started yelling at me. There was no appeal. She should have cared; her extravagant lifestyle was about to be snatched away. I was raging.

"That rage got me where I am now. As if I wasn't in enough trouble. I went round to her house. She had a guy there. I wanted to lash out at someone. He got in the way."

Callum picked up his glass and drained it.

"The police were called. I panicked, and instead of staying around to face the music, I took off. Drove to the airport and left the country."

"I'm sorry," said Antoinette.

"What for?" he asked.

"For your loss. Losing your career must have been like losing a loved one. No wonder you were hurting."

Callum was thoughtful. "You're the first person to

say you're sorry," he told her. "Everyone else says I got what I deserved. Needed to be made an example of, a bad role model for young people. The bloody press had a field day. 'We expect higher standards of our sportsmen.'"

"I can imagine," said Antoinette. "Honestly. I feel your pain. You have my deepest sympathy. We all make mistakes in life, but we don't all have to pay such a high price." She reached out and took his hand. He clenched his palms together, and her hand felt tiny wrapped up in his fist.

"Sport was my life. My passion. Ever since I was a kid I'd been an athlete. I was good and knew I'd be able to make a living. Now I can only work for charity—if anyone wants me." He shrugged.

"I've been running scared ever since the assault happened," Callum admitted. "I'm supposed to be a tough guy. A warrior on the sports field but believe me, all that bravery has deserted me. I've wanted to cry my eyes out more than once."

"Go ahead, cry. It'll do you good," said Antoinette, and she moved nearer to him on the bench. She pressed her body up close and told him. "You don't have to be a tough guy for me. Crying is not a sign of weakness. It's authentic, an acknowledgment of your feelings."

Callum wrapped his arms around her shoulders and to avoid hiding behind his sunglasses; he took them off. "You don't know how good it feels to have someone understand. At least listen to me. I've felt like a total outcast. Are you a therapist?" he asked.

"No," she smiled. "I know pain when I see it. The world condemned you, and you've been punishing yourself."

Callum nodded. "It feels good to have told you the truth. I didn't want to; I thought I'd drive you away. That's not what I wanted. I'd rather have told you a story that made you stay."

For hours they talked, and when Antoinette felt the chill as the afternoon passed into nighttime, Callum wrapped her in his coat. And in his arms. They held hands as they walked back through the narrow alleyways down to the main town.

"I've never met anyone like you," Callum told Antoinette. "So easy to talk to, you make me so feel safe. I'm not ashamed to let you know who I am, or how scared I've been over this whole business. With someone like you at my side, I could start to get over what happened and figure out what to do with the rest of my life."

"Don't jump too far ahead," she warned him. "I'm flattered, but you don't know me or anything about me. For all you know, I might be on the run, too."

Callum played along with the game. "We could go on the run together," he said as he steered her into a wooden archway where a profusion of bright flowers cascaded down and hid them from view. "Like Bonnie and Clyde."

Antoinette was filled with excitement and antici-pation. The depth of their sharing opened a channel in her heart, and she had the strangest feeling that she belonged there and wanted to be close to him. She felt deep empathy and related to the frightened boy inside the man. His journey was not an easy one, but she wanted to be there beside him. A warning bell sounded in her head, and she felt a sense of foreboding as she asked Callum, "What did Harry get me into when he chose to bite you?"

Their first kiss was deep and passionate. The buzz of her phone broke into the moment. "It's Claudia. I need to answer this," she said.

"Yes. I'm fine," she assured Claudia. "I know it's late and I have an early ferry booked for the morning. You can pick me up in an hour at the harbor. Yes, where you dropped me."

Callum looked confused. "We're not going to spend the night together?"

"No," she said. "Much as I'd like to, believe me. I don't do one-night stands and come tomorrow, or someday soon, you are going to have to figure out what to do about your problems. I'm only a complication."

"What happens now?" he asked. "All I know is that you live somewhere close to the ferry port at Denia. On an olive farm."

"You'll find me when you need to," she insisted. "We can stay in touch but for now, I'm going back to my friend Claudia's, and I'll catch the ferry home tomorrow morning. She has plenty of room at her villa; I'm sure she would find you a spare couch for the night. Any friend of mine is a friend of hers."

Callum shook his head. "Thanks for the offer, but I

have plans for tomorrow. I'm meeting a few of the boys down at the beach. We're going to check out some extreme sports. Windsurfing, skydiving, jet-skiing. I need my fix of adrenaline."

Antoinette was relieved. The feelings he aroused were extreme sport enough for her. It was time to rein in this potentially explosive situation. Leave him to his boy toys; she needed to play the adult. But when he lifted her off her feet and carried her across a puddle of water that had formed on the harbor side, she felt giddy as a schoolgirl.

"You're an exceptional lady," he told her as they took their time over a lingering good-night kiss in the harbor car park. The ferry that Antoinette would take the next morning back to her real life was already docked.

"You made me feel very special," she agreed. "I know everything will work out. I'll be thinking about you. You've claimed a place in my heart."

Claudia pulled up and allowed Harry to jump out of the car. He ran as fast as his little legs would carry him and jumped up at Callum and licked his hands in greeting. "Harry won't forget me," said Callum, "will you, boy? Make sure you don't." He blew a kiss to Antoinette and waved as he climbed into his car and drove away.

Antoinette lifted Harry into her arms and kissed him. "Thank you for my adventure," she told the dog. "I feel like I got a new lease on life. For all our sakes, let's hope we have seen the last of Mr. Callum Lavelle. He's way too supercharged for me."

Chapter Seventeen

Olivia Rose ran down the hotel corridor to the reception desk. Hurriedly she had pulled on red Capri trousers and a T-shirt with a huge heart and *I Love Paris* embroidered on it. Her feet were bare, her hair flying loose and free. "I'm expecting a guest," she told the smiling clerk. "Please make my apologies and say I was called away unexpectedly. I'll reschedule."

Desperate in her disheveled state to avoid bumping into wedding guests, she had no idea where she was going. To avoid the elevators, she took the stairs and there the sign for the Hotel Thalasso Spa caught her attention. Perfect. She followed directions and breathed in the sensuous aromas as she stepped into a world of calm and luxury.

"Can I book a massage?" she asked the white-coated young woman behind the desk.

She consulted her computer screen. "Are you a hotel guest?" she asked Olivia Rose.

"Yes," Olivia Rose answered, "here's my room key."

"Thank you," said the young lady. "When do you require me to book your massage?"

"Now, please," said Olivia Rose. "Is that possible?

With a quick glance at the computer and the large gold-faced clock on the wall, the girl nodded. "Of course, Miss Anderson. The changing room is to your right; you will find towels and a robe. Please wait there, and the therapist will collect you."

Confident that she was in a safe place where Gianni would be unable to track her down, Olivia Rose relaxed. Wrapped head to toe in a fluffy white bathrobe, she poured a glass of iced water, stretched out in a recliner and picked up a copy of Italian *Vogue*.

A few minutes later, the masseuse appeared. "My name is Jasmine. Follow me, please," she indicated.

The lighting in the treatment room was subdued. Sweet smelling candles burned and birdsong played on the sound system. Olivia Rose lay face-down on the couch as instructed.

"Was there a particular massage you had in mind?" asked the masseuse.

"Yes, a de-stressor," said Olivia Rose.

"Fine. I have the perfect solution. A combination of aromatherapy oils to relax you and color crystals to revitalize the chakras."

"Thank you," said Olivia Rose. "I may also need something to bring down my heart rate. I think I'm hyperventilating."

"You will be good as new when you leave here," Jasmine assured her.

Olivia Rose coaxed herself into a state of mindfulness meditation designed to still her mind and relieve anxiety.

If a thought comes into your mind, let it drift off, she reminded herself. *Breathe deeply and let go of all everyday concerns.*

The sounds and smells and expert touch of the therapist lulled her into a gentle sleep. Jasmine was right, after her treatment, Olivia Rose was rejuvenated.

As she showered and covered her body in perfumed body lotion, she willed herself not to check her phone messages. Dressed and her hair clipped up into a bun, she thanked Jasmine and made her way back to her room. It had been almost two hours since Gianni was expected at the hotel, and she gave no thought to the fact that she would have to cross reception to get back to the elevators.

"Miss Anderson," the receptionist intercepted her. "Your visitor is waiting."

Olivia Rose glanced at the young lady with whom she had left the message that she had been called away. The girl nodded. "I passed on your message," she said.

Gianni rose from his cushioned armchair by the ornate marble fireplace. "Forgive me," he said. "I needed to speak to you."

Olivia Rose meant to transmit her displeasure. Instead, she smiled. "It was childish of me," she admitted, "to run away."

Gianni nodded his understanding. "It's complicated," he agreed. "Can we talk?"

"Yes, but I'm not fit to be seen in public," she said, gesturing to her hair and bare feet. "My reputation will be ruined. Let's go to my room. I'll order room service if you want a drink. As for me, I have already had too much champagne today. It goes to my head."

Gianni followed her down the richly carpeted corridor to her room. Italian landscape paintings lined the walls, and small console tables held antique statues and porcelain ornaments.

"No flowers in the bath today?" he inquired as she opened the door and stood back to let him in.

"I owe you my thanks," she said, "and the payment for Tiberius. The bouquets were a great success, but don't get me started on the story of the black hawk. I'll tell you some other time." In an effort to introduce a degree of protection against her feelings, she added, "It deserves a larger audience. Perhaps I'll wait till I can share it with mother, too."

Olivia Rose gestured Gianni to a seat by the window in a small dining alcove, and she sat opposite him, the round glass-topped table between them.

"Shall I order you a drink?" she asked. "Coffee maybe? Or there are soft drinks and wine in the mini bar."

"Nothing, thank you," he answered.

There was an awkward silence, and Olivia Rose tried to avoid looking directly at Gianni. Exuding Euro style, he wore it well, pressed navy denims and a striped blazer over a white shirt with Gucci loafers. He sat in the chair, one leg crossed over his knee, no socks, confidence personified.

Olivia Rose took up a defensive position. Regular yoga meant her limbs were flexible and she perched on the chair erect. Legs tucked up under her, arms crossed.

Gianni broke the silence. "My behavior was inappropriate," he said, "I hope you will accept my apology."

Olivia Rose relaxed. Maybe she had misunderstood his message. He had wanted to come and apologize; she had read more into it than intended. "I overreacted," she said. "Blame it on the wedding. I've been under a lot of stress. I was so grateful to you for rescuing the situation. My emotions were off-kilter."

"If there are no hard feelings, I will have that drink now," said Gianni, relieved that the matter had been put right and she had accepted his apology.

"What can I get you?" asked Olivia Rose.

"A glass of wine from the mini bar will be fine," he said. "I'll join you," said Olivia Rose.

"Great," said Gianni, "and perhaps you will relent and tell me the story of the black hawk."

Olivia Rose happily obliged, and the two of them laughed together as she shared the story of Alphonso and Pepe.

"Let me check it out on YouTube," said Gianni. "Yes, it's there. I must tell my friends. We all do business with this hotel. Congratulations to you for having White Roses Wedding Services go viral."

Olivia Rose chose to reserve judgment. "Maybe it will look as if I let things get out of control," she worried.

"Of course not. It's hilarious," said Gianni. "Look." He left his chair and knelt down beside Olivia Rose as they both watched the YouTube video on his iPhone. Each time they viewed the video of the bird winging and whirling high above the wedding guests and then dropping the pouch containing the rings, they laughed more.

Their heads were close together; they shared the moment.

Gradually the laughter stopped, the video ended but Olivia Rose and Gianni remained locked together. Their eyes asked the question. Neither looked away.

Holding her gaze, Gianni stood tall, took Olivia Rose's hand and watched as she untangled her limbs. They faced each other. "If you want me to leave, say so now," said Gianni. "If you let me stay, I can't be blamed for the outcome. You're working your magic on me all over again."

Olivia Rose made her decision. She had never felt before this desperate attraction to a man that Gianni aroused in her. It was as if he had lit the flames to a fire that had waited for so long to be ignited. She wished circumstances were different, but if happy ever after was to come only once in a lifetime, she was determined to seize the day. And if happy ever after lasted one day, so, too, did the lifetime of a butterfly; she was ready to fly.

Her whole body cried out to be loved by him, to be caressed, to be held in his strong embrace, to be awakened.

"Come," he enticed her, "The roses bloomed and so will you." He took her hand and led her to the bathroom. Hot taps gushed water into the marble Jacuzzi, and Gianni turned his back while she undressed.

Naked, the two of them slipped into the foaming water.

Under cover of bubbles and waves, the two kissed and explored each others bodies. Olivia Rose sighed with pleasure as Gianni introduced her to a kaleidoscope of sensual pleasures and became her lover.

From the bath to the bed, they made their way wrapped in the hotel's all-enveloping bathrobes. Slipping under the silky sheets of the huge double bed, they held each other close. Exhausted and satisfied, they drifted off to sleep in each others arms.

Hours later they awoke and loved each other all over again. Lost in their private world, neither chose to allow daylight to intrude upon their dreams.

Phone messages went unanswered and alarm clocks ignored.

Olivia Rose recalled that her mother, Antoinette, had once warned her: "For every moment of pleasure, we are called to suffer one moment of pain." Olivia Rose banished the thought from her mind, the knowledge that she had never before had so much pleasure with which to pay the price of pain.

Chapter Eighteen

Olivia Rose boarded the plane for her return to London. Gianni offered to drive her to the airport; she refused. "The last of the wedding guests are returning home on the flight," she explained. "I need to wear my wedding planner hat until they are all safely off the premises of Palazzo La Grande and delivered back to the airport. Then I can step down from my official duties."

The bride and groom hosted a casual Sunday brunch for those guests still at the hotel and then departed by stretch limousine for their honeymoon destination. Johnathan and Jennifer wasted no time to post Facebook and Instagram photos from their honeymoon hotel in Venice. "THIS is where George Clooney got married," they boasted.

Olivia Rose made a mental note that in future, whenever she wanted to impress a couple as they planned their wedding, she would invoke the words, "As recommended by George Clooney."

To her knowledge no celebrity wedding in recent time had attracted so much attention. It was undoubtedly a boon for the Italian wedding market. And why not, it was an idyllic place to be married.

I'll have an Italian wedding, she promised herself.

Heads turned as Olivia Rose strode through bustling Florence airport. Symbolically, she removed her wedding planner hat and replaced it with her new Italian rose picture hat.

She held her head high, an aura of assurance shone around her and she had a Mona Lisa smile on her lips. A lady with a secret. *I have finally come of age*, she congratulated herself. *I was filled with so many doubts and fears and uncertainties when I arrived in this magical country; now I feel ready to take on the world.*

Olivia Rose smiled at the message on her phone from Gianni: "To my English/Italian Rose, spread your wings and fly high. You are beautiful. G." She sent back a row of kisses and hearts.

She did not reply to the message from her mother: "Please don't be a stranger," wrote Antoinette. "Come back and see us soon."

Olivia Rose waved a farewell to wedding guests as they entered the plane and made their way to individual seats. She chose to sit alone. Duty done. "The party's over," she told herself.

The fairytale wedding was a memory. Come Monday morning, reality would intrude, and real life would return as if the magic had never happened. Except for the photographs and, of course, an enduring video of Pepe, the black hawk, flying free.

Light filled clouds outside the plane window reflected the feeling of freedom and joyous potential that radiated through Olivia Rose's body. Soft and weightless, she felt herself float above the ground and drift into a vast beyond. She would allow no thoughts of consequences to trouble her delicious bubble of pure happiness.

The plane prepared to land, and the shadow of the aircraft on the runway made her pause for a moment as she wondered, *Was the real world the one up there in the clouds or the dark shadow on the ground?*

* * *

Olivia Rose's father, Jason, insisted on meeting her at London's Gatwick airport. He stood behind the barrier as she walked through from the Nothing to Declare Customs channel.

"Don't you dare," she warned him when he suggested meeting her carrying a placard that read, *White Roses Wedding Services.*

"I like the hat," he commented, "let me know if you'd like a sign to stick in the back alongside the rose. Everything is marketing these days. You can't miss an opportunity."

"I'll be sure to let you know," Olivia Rose indulged him. Her father liked his little jokes.

They took the lift to the short-term parking lot, and Jason stowed Olivia Rose's luggage in the trunk. He thanked her for the duty-free carrier that contained a bottle of Italian cognac.

Navigating the roundabouts, he maneuvered out of an entrance ramp and entered the traffic lanes of the M23 motorway for the short journey home to their village.

Jason made polite comments about the wedding and congratulated Olivia Rose on her success. "You've become international," he told her with pride.

She shared a few highlights but could tell that there was only one question on his mind. "How's your mother?" he asked.

Olivia Rose planned to complain that he had told Antoinette about her trip and where to contact her, but instead she thanked him. "I don't think I would ever have relented," she admitted, "but you did the right thing. I had missed her, and it was good to see her again. She is quite a remarkable person. I'd forgotten how much she taught me. She and I used to have a good relationship before . . ." She stopped mid sentence.

Jason smiled, glad that he was not to be blamed for orchestrating an unwanted reunion. "I can see her influence on you already; the hat is very Antoinette. I always regretted that she wasn't there to guide you through your teenage years. You two would have had a lot of fun doing girly things, dressing up, going out and shopping."

Olivia Rose shared details about her stylish lunch with her mother and thanked her father. "She looked well," she told him, "and she asked after you."

"Antoinette was the most beautiful woman I ever met," Jason admitted and added with sadness in his voice. "There's never been anyone else. I was a fool; I didn't deserve her. A clash of two cultures. I didn't know how to give her what she wanted. But at least I did give her you," he said and reached over and patted Olivia Rose's cheek.

"I was pleased to see her again. We enjoyed each others company," she told him. "She collected me in a red convertible and drove me to her village. There was a fiesta."

Jason appeared to wipe away a tear but instead took a handkerchief from his trouser pocket. "Something in my eye," he said.

Olivia Rose nodded; she was not fooled.

He cleared his throat. "Did you meet *him*?" he asked through gritted teeth.

Olivia Rose contemplated playing dumb but instead asked, "Gianni?"

"Yes, bloody Gianni," he said, taking his eyes off the road and glaring at Olivia Rose.

"Yes," she said. "I saw him. I met him at the village with mother."

"Wife stealer," said Jason with emotion. "The man has no morals."

Olivia Rose was anxious to steer the conversation away from Gianni. Jason was not. Still smarting from years' old resentment, he declared, "Knows nothing about roses, he should never have won the Best in Show Trophy. He stole my wife, and he stole my trophy. Be warned; the man is not to be trusted."

Averting her eyes, she stared out the window at the familiar countryside as Jason drove through the lanes leading to their village. There was no contest. Her loyalty was to her father but still her fascination with Gianni made her reluctant to denounce him completely.

Instead Olivia Rose delivered a message from her mother. "Antoinette sent her love to you. I promised I'd pass it on."

Chapter Nineteen

Antoinette prided herself on knowing whenever Gianni started a new love affair. Throughout their twenty years of relationship, it was an all too common occurrence. For her betrayal in running away from the village and leaving him, Antoinette accepted the penance that she should never be totally convinced of his fidelity.

She was well aware of the widespread myth that Italian women willingly accept their husbands' right to have a mistress. The discreet afternoon visit men pay to the other woman during siesta time was considered, in some cultures, an open secret. An indication of the ego-driven Latin male passion that needed to be satisfied with extracurricular activity away from wife and home.

Antoinette had known but never accepted that she alone was not enough for the love of her life, Gianni. Over the years she contemplated taking a lover of her own. Then Gianni would have to face the fact that emotions cannot be put away in a box and denied their ability to cause pain. She had come close on some occasions, too close for comfort on others, but Antoinette had always pulled herself back from going too far. She flirted, she teased, she even enjoyed secret assignations with handsome men, but never had she been unfaithful. Not since the big betrayal when she had run away and married Olivia Rose's father over twenty years before.

All those years ago, Gianni was shocked when he discovered that the girl he loved and planned to marry had eloped with an Englishman. He was consumed with rage and swore vengeance, a vow of Latin retribution had burned in his heart.

Antoinette had been flattered, but it was no less than she would have expected. Olivia Rose was already at school before Antoinette and Gianni rekindled their love affair. Miles of countries between them and the distance of cultures between the two men allowed Antoinette to blind herself to her infidelity.

"Gianni was my destiny," she proclaimed.

The two had never formalized their relationship, though to all intents and purposes they were a married couple. Antoinette refused to relinquish her faith and, being a good Catholic girl, the question of divorce made her uncomfortable.

Gianni refused to acknowledge that the pain she felt when he took a new lover was comparable to that inflicted on him when she had married Jason. His affairs were thankfully brief. No more than a few weeks or months but so subtle were the changes in his behavior, she believed she knew as soon as his sights were set on a new conquest. And she sighed with relief when he returned to her. No words were spoken.

There was a new woman on the horizon; she felt it in her heart and prepared for the anguish that always accompanied the beginning of an affair. Was this the woman who would finally steal him from her? Would she be discarded this time? Punished for the fact that all those years ago she had broken a vow between her and Gianni?

* * *

Antoinette arrived back at their home in Spain from her brief trip to Ibiza. Gianni had not returned from Italy. A luxury villa perched high in the mountains on the coast road from Valencia to Alicante was Gianni's ancestral home; Gianni and Antoinette had made one wing of the magnificent property their home.

An incredible white Roman temple of porticoes, columns, arches and turrets, visible for miles around the surrounding countryside, oversaw his family's vast estates. From a position of power, the land at the pinnacle of the mountain peak dominated the countryside of farms, orchards, orange and lemon groves, fields of almonds and small holdings cultivated with Mediterranean vegetables. On the far horizon, a team of black bulls jousted each other as they awaited the call to their duties, either to stud to impregnate females or in the bullring to fight men.

Gianni was descended from one of the privileged families who had owned and controlled land across vast swathes of the countryside for generations. Gianni's father reveled in the story that his grandfather, being the youngest son, had drawn the short straw when he inherited the coastal land where crops refused to grow. No one foresaw the explosion in global tourism that guaranteed the coastal land would be developed as prime real estate. Gianni's great-grandfather had the last laugh; he surpassed the wealth of his brothers and became the richest member of the ruling family.

Gianni was proud of his family, his land and his landowner's home. Antoinette paid due respect to his heritage and considered it a privilege to share the home that stood as a testament to the Almora's enduring success and influence.

On her arrival back after the weekend, the grand house was empty. Only the housekeeping staff was there to welcome her. There was no comfort to be had there; she wandered aimlessly from room to room. She needed to clear her mind.

She left yet another message on Gianni's phone. For two days, he had failed to reply. How could he not know that this pattern of behavior signaled that he was feeling guilty but not about to confront the facts? He was off the radar, and when he resurfaced, vague excuses of "I got caught up with the business," were all she could expect.

Gone to my dressmaker and for some retail therapy, she texted him. I'll be home for dinner. Let me know if you want to meet somewhere. Love you, A x.

Antoinette drove Gianni's red Alfa Romeo convertible at high speed down the steep winding trail to the coast road, sheltered by mountains on one side and bordered by the sea on the other. The mountain range stretched for miles and offered an untamed landscape of rocks, boulders, chalk cliffs and impassable peaks.

Antoinette headed for her favorite coastal town, Altea, the Village of Artists. The name meant All Is Healed and acknowledged what she required. The pain deep inside had started, the inability to think or breathe properly threatened to overwhelm her as she recalled all the previous times she had felt her heart would break.

She drove the Italian sports car, top down, into the parking lot alongside the sea.

On a concrete bench, she observed two young girls, sitting cross-legged, one comforting the other. Head on her friend's shoulder, the attractive girl sobbed. Her friend held her and murmured like a mother to a baby, "There, there. It's not the end of the world. You'll get over him."

With the hindsight of her experience and accumulated years, Antoinette yearned to tell her the truth: "No, you won't get over him. Every hurt leaves a scar. The pain never goes away; it is reactivated every time another wound to the heart threatens to take away the desire to live. Love kills."

Altea Bay and its clear aquamarine waters sparkled in the sunshine. Distant mountains wrapped protectively around both outposts of the promenade. Off-shore, an outcrop of rocks added a feature to the bay and prevented easy navigation into the narrow waters. Palm trees stood sentinel all along the promenade, shade-giving squat varieties close to the water's edge and, along the promenade, tall, regal frond-waving specimens.

Antoinette approved of the palm trees and their innate disposition to bend with the wind. Offering no resistance, they allowed the wind to blow through their waving fingers. *What we resist, persists,* she reminded herself.

In the far distance, Ifach rock on the sands at Calpe marked the outer boundaries between coastal towns, and the mountain villages were visible as houses and villas challenged the terrain and climbed ever higher to the wooded peaks.

A line of man-made rocky outcrops reached out to sea and slowed the waves, forcing them around, over and through. Sandstone rocks embedded by the edge of the seawall, broken and scarred by the constant waves, held firm, and their scratched surfaces transformed shattered crevices into intricate patterns, reminiscent of ancient sea scrolls. Crafted white smooth stones stood sentinel by the more significant masterpieces and formed a patchwork border.

Antoinette's restless longing stilled beside the power of the ocean and the mountains. She felt small but not insignificant as she reminded herself, *Oceans and mountains don't care about your pain. Your fleeting existence. They have been here for millennia; they will be here for thousands of years to come.* The words of her long-dead grandmother echoed in her mind and soothed her, *Don't fret so, child. We will all be gone in the blink of an eye.*

Altea's rocky, pebble beach acted as a deterrent to

serious sun worshipers who preferred to lay their towels on soft sand. Young couples hand in hand, families with children in baby carriages and older couples with the aid of adapted hiking poles or in mobilized buggies strolled, marched and rode in a constant procession from one end of the promenade to the other, a distance of some two miles, but the beach was deserted.

Antoinette wore sneakers and stepped cautiously across the shifting pebbles and dried seaweed to the water's edge. Her eyes scanned and discarded thousands of pebbles. From experience, she knew that one would present itself to her as perfect for the task at hand. The chosen one she would hurl into the sea and ask that it carry away her pain and plead with whatever or who-ever in the universe heard the cries of people in distress.

Overlooked by the iconic blue dome of Altea's Church de Virgin Consuelo, Antoinette picked up and refused several stones until she stumbled upon the one she judged would most efficiently carry her prayer. She had selected a palm-size, smooth, blue-tinged pebble in a slightly off-center heart shape and hurled it with all her might into the farthest reaches of the sea. For a moment, a circle of seawater emanated from the pebble as it sank beneath the waves while Antoinette said her prayer aloud. "Dear God," she entreated. "Free me from my heartbreak. Return Gianni to me. Let me love and be loved."

Wryly, she observed, *your intervention has worked before. It works every time he tears my soul apart. It's only a matter of time before he comes back to me. Let me have faith.*

Antoinette made the sign of the cross as she stared up toward the blue-domed church. She checked her watch. She dared not be late for an appointment with her dressmaker, Tia.

The best and most sought-after dressmaker in town lived and worked in a narrow, whitewashed house on one of the cobbled alleyways leading up from the seafront. Behind a nondescript peeling wooden door, she worked her magic to design and sew exquisite gowns and formal dresses for the wealthy, stylish ladies of the area. A busy social life required repeated changes of outfit and a new wardrobe for each season.

Unlike many ladies her age, Antoinette had kept her slender figure. Her preferred style of dress changed little over the years—fitted bodice, a low but not too revealing V-neck, above the knee, straight skirt and bracelet sleeves. Tia used her dressmaking skills and the finest of materials in satin and silk to make every creation look unique.

Antoinette's high heels were in her handbag. They would be needed to ensure the correct dress length, but walking on uneven beach surfaces demanded a firm footing. When the ancient sea wall was covered during extensive construction work with a wooden boardwalk, a space of some three feet remained leading up to the invisible stone barrier. Here developed a wildflower garden. Plants and shrubs blown hither and yon by the wind, settled and grew. They embedded in the rocky shallow beachside and bloomed.

"Grow where you are planted," Antoinette observed.

One delicate blue flower caught her attention. She bent to admire it and alongside, as if placed to form a small shrine, was a sacred circle of tiny, shiny, blue shells. By no means expensive but precious. Antoinette took it to be a sign that a new bloom flowering beside the sea promised that she, too, would be granted a new lease on life.

Her mission complete, she climbed a small rickety set of steps up onto the promenade and crossed the one-way street in the Fisherman's or San Pere quarter, a reminder of Altea's fishing origins. An area of great demographic and economic importance during the eighteenth century, the cobbled alleyways led through the Plaza del Convento to the ruins of the ancient Moli de Bellaguarda watermill. The route marked the start of the well-trodden climb taken for hundreds of years by villagers following religious processions and ceremonial marches to the Place l'Esglesia, and the blue-domed Church de Virgin Consuelo.

Gates erected in 1617, still standing and in use, led to the fortress and the remains of the Renaissance era granting entry to magnificent buildings from the eighteenth and nineteenth centuries.

Lunch would have to wait, but she did have time for a thirst quenching soda. She headed for her favorite restaurant, but it was not open. The season had not yet started, and many restaurants kept their doors closed at lunchtime.

Antoinette sat on a wooden bench to change her shoes and noticed, not for the first time, an utterly derelict building right there amidst all the seafront eating establishments. The derelict building was partially covered with a faded canvas depicting an ambitious drawing of what a new and renovated structure might look like in the unlikely event that it would ever be undertaken.

The canvas, decades old, broken from its mooring, hung crazily half displayed, half caught on a jagged window frame attached to rusted rollers. A ghost town film set of a broken-down building erected to show extreme neglect and indicate that all human inhabitants were long gone could well use this building as a model of authenticity. Whitewashed walls with layers of peeling paint, coat upon coat of white, once-was-white and dirty whitish gray, with minimal brushstrokes, had been abandoned in a haphazard pattern of deterioration and defaced with graffiti. Each of the four floors of the once double-fronted building was scarred with broken black ironwork railings and cracked tiles. Wooden shutters hung from creaking hinges and failed to protect shattered glass windowpanes that left the interior rooms open to the elements. A blue metal door declared that once there had been comings and goings.

A flight of going-nowhere red-tiled steps led to a crumbling black ironwork balcony with room enough for one person to stand or sit or perhaps display a flowerpot. Four stories of long-forgotten hope and past glory. Memories of a once fine establishment in the center of town.

Signs of construction work started and abandoned indicated that once there was a desire to restore the building. An old-fashioned television aerial was attached to corroded power lines. Multistrand electric cable stretched across the adjoining alleyway and scarred the eyeline up the steep steps to the cobbled streets of the old town. At the top of the building, in another life, a roof terrace offered a prime location with views out over the promenade, the beach and across the sea. The original green glass-paneled door was still encircled by iron railings underneath a beige awning that rolled on metal holders. In the courtyard a bushy fern tree flourished.

Antoinette remembered times when red tablecloth tables and wooden chairs appeared from nowhere, a pop-up restaurant obscuring the broken-down building. Friendly waiters lit tea lights and brandished menus and served fresh pizza. *Was that a mirage? A foretelling of what could be?*

Antoinette studied the faded canvas. The vision was for apartments with wraparound terraces, a roof garden and a retail space on the ground floor. As if to keep the dream alive, two concrete flowerpots were planted with shrubs; they dressed the front of the building and undertook the brave job to brighten up the exterior.

An old tattered lace curtain fluttered from a barred window on the first floor beside a battered old carriage lamp. Antoinette strained her eyes as she tried to make out the outline of a stonework statue on a ledge, and in a pot beside it, a long-dead brown cactus. Modeling the Venus de Milo, the statue had no arms.

In a flash, Antoinette received a vision and saw her

future. The building deserved to be restored, and she was eager to undertake the job. The thrill of a new project coursed through her veins. With a burst of enthusiasm, she believed that the building and her love could rise phoenix-like from the ashes.

* * *

Retracing her steps along the promenade, Antoinette observed the profusion of retail spaces, clothes shops, jewelry stores, restaurants and ice cream parlors. The hardworking people who ran these stores would be her neighbors.

On the seafront, she stopped to catch her breath, and adrenaline pulsed through her. She rested on a circular stone terrace where the curved balustrades depicted the blue tiles of the church that attracted visitors, artists and designers. She trod the wooden walkway down to the sea and consulted her phone. She needed the services of a first class real estate agent, and she knew the man to recruit.

Her friend, Jan, owner of D&D Real Estate came to Altea almost twenty years ago from Holland; he had an enviable network of contacts. Also a track record of renovation and construction. She needed someone she could trust to handle such a massive project for her. "Hola, Jan," she said when he answered his cell phone on the first ring. "Do you know who owns the derelict building on the seafront, the one close to the tourist info office?"

"I can find out," he said without hesitation. "Why do you want to know?"

"I want to buy it," she said. "I plan to restore the building to its former glory. I'm going to need your help."

He asked no more questions but told her. "I'll get back to you."

"Oh, one thing," she stopped him before he hung up. "I don't want anyone to know that I am the buyer. Not even Gianni."

* * *

Tia welcomed Antoinette at the door to her home and kissed her on both cheeks. "Come, come." She took Antoinette's hands. "I can't wait to show you my new fabrics. I have been saving my favorites for you. The Queen of Spain, Letitia, has started a new fashion for a return to exquisitely embellished dresses. So feminine, so stylish. You will love the outfits I have in mind. Each one designed to make you look the most beautiful."

"I bet you say that to all your clients," laughed Antoinette.

"Yes," she admitted, with a twinkle in her eyes, "only, for you, it is true. I don't need to work so hard, but let us not forget, you are no longer that young girl who first came to me."

"Thanks, for reminding me," Antoinette called, as the older, and possibly wiser, woman left the room.

Tia disappeared into a back room and reappeared, her arms full of bundles of fabric in the richest of jewel colors with embroidered voile overdresses of flowers. "Time will have its way, whatever I do," she said, her tone serious, as she sorted the rolls and laid them on her large cutting table. "Women must be armed against other women. Never underestimate the competition. You have a handsome, wealthy husband; always, women will try to steal him from you."

Steeling herself for the battle ahead and determined not to lose her courage, Antoinette smiled and told her, "Make me a suit of armor in your finest silver silk."

Chapter Twenty

Jason slammed closed the laptop as Olivia Rose entered his office.

"Is everything alright?" she asked. "You look upset."

"Nothing to worry about," he said with forced cheerfulness. "Can I help you with something, or is this a purely social visit?"

"Thought I could buy you lunch. Take you to the Vineyard. You always enjoy the tour." She smiled with affection at her father. "And you like nothing better than a tasting session where you give the owners the benefit of your opinion on the contents of their latest wine list."

Olivia Rose knew that this unexpected invitation sprang from her guilt that she had neglected him of late. It was not difficult to trace her change of behavior to the time of the Italian wedding. The truth was that she was nervous her romantic encounter with Gianni would somehow be revealed. She felt desperately disloyal.

"We share a house, but I feel like I never see you," she tried to persuade her father. "You're up half the night on the internet. Please, say you'll come. I made a reservation; you know how busy the restaurant is on weekends."

Lunch with his daughter was a treat Jason cherished, but on this occasion, he did not feel like socializing. His mind was on other matters, and he was distracted. He was on the verge of saying, "No," outright when Olivia Rose gave him that please-daddy look he found so hard to avoid.

"You win," he said. "As usual. Give me ten minutes to change out of these old gardening trousers, and I'll be with you. Tell you what. Take your car, and I'll meet you there. I've business to do in town after lunch."

The arrangement suited Olivia Rose. It cut down on the time they spent together but allowed her to be seen to do the right thing. Sunday lunch together, a family tradition. Home-cooked food at the Vineyard was, Olivia Rose often said, actually even better than home-cooked food at home.

The outdoor tour was underway by the time Olivia met up with her father. They had visited many times before. "We're in time for the tasting," Olivia Rose offered as a consolation.

In the domed glass conservatory, Jason and Olivia Rose collected a wine list and made their way to the tasting table. Jason sampled and tasted and spat out the selections of red and white wines. Olivia Rose chose to sample the rosé but was reluctant to spit it out.

Jason marked the tasting cards with some of his favorite comments: woody, fruity, cheeky. "I never claimed to be a wine connoisseur," he admitted to

Olivia Rose. "It's a full-time job to become an expert. But, I am happy to drink the stuff. Before we leave, I'll order a mixed case to be delivered to the house."

Olivia Rose sipped her wine and risked her father's disapproval as she topped it off with water. "Wine goes to my head," she reminded him. "I really shouldn't drink at all. My decision-making faculties become seriously impaired."

Jason nodded. His daughter had never been a drinker, but on a few occasions, he had noticed her low tolerance level. On the other hand, he liked to believe that his tolerance was high, and he tested it by drinking far more than was good for him.

"Wine is fine for daytime," he was fond of saying, "but in the evening I need a proper drink. Whisky helps me sleep."

Olivia Rose nodded. She had heard all the arguments too many times before. She had given up trying to persuade her father to moderate his drinking. The wine she tolerated; when he opened the whiskey bottle, she made her excuses and left. At least he did all his drinking at home, so she didn't worry too much about his safety. Only his health.

Jason ordered a roast beef dinner with all the trimmings while Olivia Rose choose the salmon. He drank his wine and could not ignore the revelation that his drinking had undeniably been a contributing factor in his current troubles. His mind was miles away when he came back to the present and realized Olivia Rose was telling him about her latest business plans.

"This is a fabulous wedding venue," she explained, "and I have been offered the opportunity to set up an office here and act as an in-house wedding planner. It's exciting, but I'm reluctant to give up my own business. Obviously, I can't do both; there's a conflict of interests. What do you think?" she asked.

Jason was reluctant to admit that he was distracted and had missed half of what she said. He struggled to understand the concept. "You've worked so hard to establish your business," he said. "Do you want to become an employee?"

Olivia Rose showed her irritation. "That's what I'm explaining to you," she said. "I need an imaginative way to combine an in-house position without relinquishing my own wedding services. Do you have any suggestions?"

Jason looked blank. "Can't say I see the way through at the moment," he said, "but let me give it some thought."

Olivia Rose placed her hand over her wineglass by way of refusal, as the waiter offered her more wine. Jason accepted.

"I do have one idea," she said. "It's a whole new business model, but it will require some investment to get started. Will you provide the seed money for a start-up?"

Jason was not prepared for the question. "Olivia Rose, is that what this lunch was about? Butter me up and then ask for money?"

His daughter looked hurt. "First and foremost, I

wanted your opinion. Then if you think it is a workable idea, we can discuss your participation. I certainly don't want a reluctant partner. You haven't even listened to my idea yet."

Jason endeavored to rescue the situation. "I'm sorry, I don't mean to overreact, but you have to admit it was out of the blue. White Roses Wedding Services is doing so well. People still talk about the YouTube video of the black hawk. I saw it on a television clip the other day. I'm proud to see you stand on your own two feet."

Olivia Rose was in no mood to listen to his apology. She gathered her bag and phone. "I'll pay the bill on my way out." She added the warning, "You better not have any more wine; you're driving. I'll see you back at home."

"Thanks for lunch," Jason said, as he kissed her good-bye and promised, "we'll have this discussion again later."

Olivia Rose headed for her car and, once inside, wiped tears of frustration from her eyes. "It's not fair," she said out loud. "He's got plenty of money." She slammed the car into gear and headed for her office.

Father was right. Her own business was doing well, and she had several upcoming weddings in the order book. The proposed new business model would capitalize on what she had built, but she was keen to expand and take the company internationally.

Olivia Rose called the man who filled her head with dreams of ever grander business schemes and declarations of his love for her.

"He's mean," she said, as soon as Gianni answered the phone. "He doesn't want to give me the money. I'll work on him."

Olivia Rose knew Gianni preferred that he phone her but she wanted his reassurance. "I have complete faith in your persuasive powers," he said and laughed. "Love you. Ciao."

* * *

My fault, Olivia Rose texted her father. Lunch was a bit of a disaster. Peace offering: I'll come home early and cook dinner tonight.

He replied with a thumbs-up emoji.

Relieved that she had at least started to mend fences, Olivia Rose went about her business. The afternoon was filled with short trips to deliver and collect items. On her final trip of the day, keeping her promise to go home early, she drove past the local police station. Her father's car was in the parking lot.

Fear welled up inside her. She parked her vehicle in a visitor spot and rushed into the police station. The desk sergeant recognized her. She had planned his daughter's wedding. At the Vineyard, as it happened. "Hello, Miss Anderson," he said, all smiles. "Good to see you. I know why you're here."

"That's more than I do," said Olivia Rose.

"It's your father."

"Did something happen to him?" she asked.

"He's in a holding cell," said the sergeant. "We

refused to let him go until he had someone to drive him home."

Olivia Rose felt ashamed. Her father in a cell. "Has he been charged?" she asked.

"No, he's fortunate," said the sergeant kindly. "He came in here to complain about another matter. The young officer smelled alcohol on him. Here's the officer now; you can talk to him yourself."

"Can you tell me what happened, please officer?" asked Olivia Rose.

"Your father narrowly missed being charged with drunk driving," he told her. "I smelled the alcohol and asked if he had driven here and he said, 'Yes.' He parked his vehicle in our parking lot. We can't arrest someone unless they are in the vehicle or we catch them in the act of driving," he explained. "I warned him that if he attempted to drive the vehicle, I would arrest him. He refused a breath test, which was within his rights to do as he wasn't in the vehicle at the time."

Olivia Rose's face showed her confusion.

"Why was he here?" she asked.

"He came in to make a complaint about another matter."

"Can you tell me what that was?" she asked.

The desk sergeant intervened. "Not possible, Miss Anderson. It's confidential. All I can say is he must be extremely worried, or stupid, to come and make a report to the police in his state."

At that moment her father appeared from a door behind the sergeant's desk. He looked shaken but in control. "Thank you, officer," he said. "My daughter will drive me home, and I'll send for the car. I did try to order a taxi, but now that Olivia Rose is here she can escort me."

Olivia Rose pursed her lips. *How dare he make light of this serious situation?*

"Okay, sir, you're free to go, but let this be a warning to you," said the officer.

"Bye, Miss Anderson," said the sergeant. "I'll tell my daughter I saw you."

Olivia Rose attempted to cover her embarrassment by putting on her sunglasses, which had been on the top of her head. She walked ahead of her father to her car and slammed her door as she got in. He had not even had time to fasten his seat belt before she challenged him. "What the hell is all this about?" she raised her voice.

The bravado he displayed in the police station was gone. He hung his head like a naughty schoolboy called before the headmaster.

"Whatever possessed you to show your face at the police station when you'd been drinking? I hope you know how close you were to a conviction for drunk driving."

Olivia Rose drove and held up her fingers to demonstrate the foolishness of his actions. "One," she almost poked her finger in his face. "You could go to jail. Two, a driving suspension. Three, your name splashed all over the local paper as a convicted criminal. Four,

156

what kind of publicity is that for my business—and my reputation—and yours, if you still have one."

"I've been a fool. Believe me, I know that." He was anxious to calm her down. Bad as the situation was, there was more to come. "I'm well aware of the consequences. There's no fool like an old fool," he told her as he put his head in his hands and began to cry.

Olivia Rose was shocked. She could only recall seeing her father sob like that, once. That dreadful night when he wrecked the conservatory. The night her mother left home.

"Okay, okay." She reached over and patted his shoulder. "Whatever it is, we'll sort it out. Don't cry, please."

Jason pulled a handkerchief from his pant pocket and wiped his eyes. "Olivia Rose," he said, his voice trembling. "You're going to be so angry with me. I've lost all my money. I'm broke. All my savings are gone. I've let you down. I've been such a fool." He started to cry again.

"It will keep till we get home," she said, kindly. "We're a team. We'll work it out."

Chapter Twenty-One

"Engaged?" Olivia Rose was incensed. "Engaged?" she repeated. "What on earth are you talking about?"

Jason looked sheepish.

The two faced each other across the dining table in an alcove of the comfortable living room of their country cottage. The layout and decoration of the home were old-fashioned. Jason liked it that way. There had been no changes for over twenty years.

Good to her word, Olivia Rose made dinner in the compact kitchen, and when he tried to interrupt her in middle of her cooking, she refused to start a discussion with her father until they sat down to their meal.

The fork with which she was dishing up vegetables slipped from her hand and clattered onto the table. "I don't believe what I'm hearing," she said. "Who in heaven's name are you engaged to? You've never even had a girlfriend since Mum left."

"If you stop shouting, I could start explaining," said Jason. "It's complicated."

Olivia Rose put aside her cutlery and folded her

arms across her chest. "Okay, I'm listening. This had better be good," she said.

"I'm the innocent victim of an internet scam," he told her. Jason lowered his eyes. "A romance scam."

Olivia Rose was intrigued. "Tell me more—the full story."

Jason ignored Olivia Rose's disapproving look and topped off his glass of wine.

"It all started a few months ago when you came back from your Italian trip. You'd seen your mother, and that stirred up all kinds of memories for me. I felt so many regrets about my relationship with her. I can see now the reason the marriage failed was my fault. She was a young woman who'd lived a completely sheltered existence in her village in Italy and here she was in a new country, a different culture where she couldn't even speak the language. Instead of helping her to integrate, I isolated her even more. We lived out here in the house where my parents had lived all their lives. Antoinette craved more excitement than I could give her. She should never have agreed to marry an old stick in the mud, like me."

Olivia Rose interrupted, "What has all this to do with an internet scam and losing all your money?

"It is relevant," he replied. "I was full of regret and blamed myself for Antoinette's unhappiness and the fact that you lost your mother at a crucial time in your development. A teenage girl needs the guidance of her mother."

Olivia Rose reached out to stroke his hand. She

acknowledged that mistakes had been made and their lives could all have been so different. "I didn't turn out so bad, did I?" she asked.

He smiled at her fondly. "No, I'm very proud of you," he said. "The problem was with me. I tortured myself. All the hurt and regret I had pushed down for so long came back. If I hadn't been hurting so much and feeling so inadequate, I might have ignored the message I received from a young lady. She said she'd seen my photo on Facebook and thought I looked handsome and kind."

"On Facebook? I didn't know you were on Facebook," said Olivia Rose.

"It started with a site called Friends Reunited, or something like that. I got a message from an old friend. A flower grower, an exhibitor at Chelsea. We communicated from time to time. From there, various people, male and female, asked to 'Friend' me."

Olivia Rose laughed as her father made air sign quote marks.

"With nothing better to do, I replied to them. Usually late at night."

"When you'd had too much to drink," Olivia Rose remarked.

"I was lonely," Jason defended himself.

"Sorry," she said, "go on. Who was this woman?"

"Not anyone I knew," he said. "But she sent a photograph of herself. She was gorgeous. She looked like a model. She reminded me of Antoinette when she was younger."

Alarm bells rang in Olivia Rose's head. She couldn't understand why they hadn't rung in her father's head.

Jason was quick to defend himself. "It wasn't a romance at the start. We became friends. She claimed she wasn't looking for a relationship; she needed someone to befriend her. That's all there was to it. We became friends."

Olivia Rose heard the hope in his voice.

"We messaged each other practically every night. First through Facebook and then we exchanged personal emails. Natalie told me she was a student and lived in Moscow. Far away from her family and friends, she was lonely, too.

"We told each other about our lives. She had been let down by a boyfriend, and until she finished her studies had no intention of getting involved with anyone else. I told her about Antoinette. And my regrets about our marriage. I enjoyed having someone to talk to, and she valued my opinions on lots of life issues. I say talk, but I mean message. We always meant to set up a Skype connection, but she didn't have regular access to the internet. She lived in a student shared house, so it was difficult for her to get privacy."

Olivia Rose wanted to berate her father for his gullibility but sensed that he had beaten himself up enough.

"When did the friendship turn to romance?" she asked.

"Quite quickly," he admitted. "We discovered how much we had in common. We liked a lot of the same music, and she introduced me to albums I hadn't heard;

we loved many of the same films and had the same sense of humor.

"We went on virtual dates. Both of us would watch a film and then talk about it. Those shared experiences led to flirting and gradually we fell in love.

"Natalie was due to come and visit me, but it didn't work out. I sent her money for the fare from Moscow, but she had a family crisis. Her mother was very ill and needed an operation; I sent the money."

"Where did you send the money?" Olivia Rose asked.

"She has an aunt who lives in Amsterdam; I sent a money order via Western Union. Her aunt cashed the money order and sent the money to Natalie. Currency requirements are stringent; we had to follow a process."

Olivia Rose was becoming more agitated. She asked her father, "Why didn't you suspect it was a scam?"

For an answer, Jason pushed away his plate, left the table and crossed the room. Olivia Rose got up and cleared the table. Jason picked up his laptop from where it lay on the sofa and, returning to the table, opened up pages. He had not yet let go of the notion that Natalie was a genuine romantic prospect.

"Got her. Look, this is her," he said pointing to a photograph of a smiling, heavily made-up, young blonde woman. "You can see how beautiful she is, can't you?"

Olivia Rose noticed the thumbnails of several other photographs. Natalie in a bikini, Natalie in a pair of tight summer shorts and low-cut top, Natalie in a flimsy black dress that might have been a negligee.

Jason followed Olivia Rose's gaze and turned the laptop on the dining table to an angle where she could not view the photos. "I felt sorry for her," he admitted. "She kept apologizing for the fact that she couldn't come to visit. I promised that we'd make it happen.

"She took ages to tell me that she couldn't come without a visa and that cost money. Over the months I sent thousands to pay for a visa and taxes. Natalie always sent the documents and, after the payments were made, she mailed me receipts. It was an expensive business. Eventually, I told her that when she did manage to get to Britain, we should arrange to get married. Make her legal. She was delighted. So was I."

Olivia Rose waited expectantly. "When is she coming?"

Jason turned his back and stared at the screen. "Her mother had to go into a convalescence home and, as Natalie wasn't there to take care of her, I paid the fees."

In despair, Olivia Rose paced the floor. "I can't believe that an intelligent man like you would fall for this arrant nonsense. It's extortion."

Jason was embarrassed. "I know that now. When I refused to pay any more money, Natalie threatened to publicly post the intimate messages I sent her. She said all my friends and family would see that I had seduced a woman younger than my daughter. Each time she threatened, she revealed that her age was even younger than I realized. The blackmail and threats got more and more nasty. I couldn't believe how she'd turned from a loving, sweet woman into a criminal."

Olivia Rose was not surprised. "I suspect she was a criminal all along," she said. "That's if there ever was a Natalie. How much money did you give her?"

"I worked it out, almost eighty thousand pounds."

Olivia Rose gasped. "In a couple of months?"

"Yes," said Jason. "I've been such a fool. She's wiped out my savings. I don't suppose I'll ever get any of that money back."

"Don't hold your breath," said Olivia Rose. "Where do you go from here?"

"Natalie has disappeared." Jason brought Olivia Rose up to date. "Her email account is closed down and so is her Facebook. I went to the police station today to ask if I could prosecute for internet fraud. They didn't hold out much hope but did give me a telephone number for a police squad at Scotland Yard that specializes in these crimes.

"They also told me about a service on the internet where you can compare names and photographs of men and women who are known to operate Romance scams. It seems they steal other people's images and pretend to be them—they often use professional photos of models. The models don't even know."

"Does Natalie appear on the website?"

"I didn't want to find out," said Jason miserably.

Natalie reached over and took from his hand the slip of paper on which the policeman had written down a website address for her father. She pulled his laptop toward her and typed in www.Romancescammers.net.

Jason reluctantly helped her search. They checked

through dozens of photographs. "I'm relieved she's not a known scammer," said Jason.

"Sorry, dad," said Olivia Rose, "here's your new fiancé. It's the same picture she used to scam you, but you can take your pick of names: Natalya, Natalie, Nadia, Natasha. You can kiss your money good-bye."

"I won't let her get away with this," said Jason, as his pent-up anger rushed to the surface. "I'm going to pursue it. Perhaps I can stop other poor suckers from being taken in.

"You've got to promise me one thing," he told Olivia Rose. "I feel ashamed that I had to admit all this to you. Your mother and her fancy man must never know. I'll be a laughingstock."

"You've got my word," said Olivia Rose. "Remember, internet scamming is a multi-billion-pound business run by international criminals."

"Natalie was right about one thing," she soothed him. "You are handsome and kind."

Chapter Twenty-Two

Wind billowed in his bright yellow and blue glider as the parasailer flew in an ever higher arc over Altea Bay. Silhouetted against a cloudless sky, he swooped and swirled and joined in a joyous dance with the cackling seabirds.

Antoinette watched in fascination and recalled the only time she had jumped out of a perfectly good aeroplane. She was strapped to the back of an instructor, and a fellow jumper gave her an almost imperceptible push as she tumbled backward into the stillness of the morning skies. The full force of air and atmosphere and engine noise and the smell of aircraft fuel assaulted her senses. She prayed as hard as she ever had in her life, "Oh, my God. Oh, my God."

Her instructed warned her, "Even atheists become religious the first time they jump out of an airplane."

The sensory overload and sensation of falling terrified her, and she felt alone in the universe, though, unseen below her, she was strapped to the back of the instructor who was completing his two-thousandth jump. Without warning, he released his parachute as they somersaulted and reversed positions. She became fixated on the ground, hundreds of feet below.

Antoinette almost chickened out when presented with a thirty-page disclaimer that she was legally bound to sign before being led out to the aircraft. The document, which stated that she would not attempt to sue in the case of injury or death, did nothing to alleviate the blind panic that she would crash face-first into the grass landing field.

The exquisite torture lasted for no more than a few seconds before a feeling of total calm and serenity infused her whole being. "Oh, my God," she repeated, "I've waited all my life to experience this feeling. I'm flying. I'm free," she breathed. The ground rushed toward her, and she remembered to brace her legs before sinking into the impact.

"You landed like a ballet dancer, on tiptoes. Graceful and in control," the instructor complimented her and unclipped her from the bulky cables and jumping equipment.

Antoinette lay on the ground in a starburst position, laughing and crying. "Amazing," she repeated again and again. My first dive—and my last."

The professional instructor was perplexed. "If you enjoyed it so much, why wouldn't you want to do it again?"

Antoinette stared him down, "My whole life flashed before me on the jump. I don't intend to tempt fate by ever doing it again. I'm no daredevil."

Watching the parasailer fly hundreds of feet above

Altea Bay, she recalled second by second the roller coaster of ecstasy, pleasure, fear and terror. Deep inside she longed to experience the sensations again. To embrace the freedom.

The glider, which was hooked up by cables to the back of a powerboat, flew closer and closer to the water's edge, until the parasailer grabbed the frame and maneuvered the canopy as it slowed and began to descend. Antoinette stood on the promenade, gazing out over the ocean, and watched his every movement.

Avoiding the outcrop of T-shaped rocks close to the shore, the parasailer skimmed the surface of the water as the glider was released from the boat. His feet dipped into the blue sea. The glider followed him into the ocean. Waist-high in the clear waters, he waded through the waves and used his free arm to propel himself toward the shore. With the other arm, he pulled the trailing ropes attached to the specially designed overarching wing that looked like a parachute.

Dressed in a wetsuit and protective helmet, the figure strode with purpose onto the pebble beach. Right in front of where Antoinette stood. He removed his helmet and waved. Antoinette laughed in delight. Callum Lavelle had shared his paragliding experience with her and now stood yards from the restaurant where they were due to meet for lunch.

Antoinette recalled that there had once been a television advertisement in which a man in black went to extraordinary lengths, including climbing up buildings, to deliver a box of chocolates to his lady love. She was tempted to ask if he had brought her chocolate, but she was mindful that Callum was probably too young to have seen the advertisement. He wouldn't know what she was talking about.

She attempted to embrace him through the wet-suit and the dripping seawater. Like a shaggy dog, he shook his wet hair, and the spray went in all directions. Antoinette didn't mind that her carefully chosen outfit was splattered.

"Told you I'd surprise you." He looked pleased with himself.

"You certainly know how to achieve that adrenalin rush," she complimented him. "Are you dressed for lunch?" she asked.

He pointed out to sea and explained, "The speed-boat is waiting to pick me up. Their base is a few miles away; I'll shower and change at the Yacht Club. Give me half an hour; I'll meet you at the restaurant."

Antoinette climbed the narrow staircase up to the second floor of FranXerra, one of Altea's most prestigious restaurants in a prime seafront position overlooking the entire bay. She asked for a table outside on the terrace and ordered a jug of sangria, which came served with fresh strawberries.

Callum's unorthodox appearance was the second surprise of the day. She had not heard a word from him since their encounter in Ibiza almost a month before. Out of the blue, she received a text. A man of few words, it read, Lunch, today?

Her first reaction was to claim she was busy. "I'm

not jumping to his commands," she sulked. "Besides, I AM busy."

Have plans, she texted back. In Altea.

That works, he persisted. I'm along the coast in Calpe. What time? Where?

His cheek amused her. She responded to his text. 2 p.m. Meet me outside Hotel San Miguel.

Got it. Prepare to be surprised.

Antoinette sipped a goldfish bowl–size glass of sangria and waited for Callum. Good as his word, he arrived half an hour later dressed in black slacks, a crisp white shirt and wearing his black and gold sneakers. He accepted the outsize glass of sangria and touched his glass to hers.

"Cheers." They clinked glasses.

Antoinette decided she would not ask him where he had been or what he had been doing since they last met. Let him lead the conversation. *As if it matters to me,* she shrugged inwardly.

"I suppose you wondered why I haven't been in touch," he said.

"Not particularly," she played it cool. "There was no obligation on your part."

"You were on my mind," he said. "Several times I started to text, then deleted. I didn't want you to get mixed up with all the drama."

"Am I allowed to ask what drama?" she said.

"My usual downfalls," he admitted. "Drink, drugs and women."

"It starts with one, leads to the next and onto the

other and often ends up with an arrest. The club scene in Ibiza is pretty wild. The nightclubs are some of the best in the world. Mind-blowing music, fantastic light shows, futuristic venues. Pool parties. I know lots of people on the DJ circuit. I'm on all the VIP lists. It's easy for me to get led astray."

Antoinette was furious but determined not to show it. She adjusted her chair to increase the distance between them. In her mind's eye, she envisioned scantily clad girls, younger than her daughter, cavorting seductively on table tops and splashing in foam filled swimming pools all to the beat of pounding music and flashing lights.

"I'm glad you enjoyed yourself," she said. "You certainly weren't in a rush to extricate yourself."

Callum sensed her coldness and admitted, "I'm never good at keeping myself out of trouble." He shrugged. "Shall we order?"

"I'm in rather a hurry," she said pointedly. "I'll have a goat's cheese salad."

"I need fuel after all my morning activities," he told her, as he gestured for the waiter. "I'll have a fillet steak, medium, and a house salad."

Antoinette had no idea what to expect when he texted to suggest lunch. *It's just lunch,* she told herself. "Are you still in Ibiza?" she asked.

"No," he told her, "I'm on my way home, back to the UK. I wanted to see you before I left."

"Really, and why would that be?" she said, unable to keep the frostiness out of her tone.

"Because I keep thinking about you. It might not have meant anything to you," he challenged, "but our time in Ibiza was special to me. For the first time I can remember, I felt completely at ease with a woman. I could be myself. I didn't have to put on a show. You didn't want anything from me. No pressure."

"I suppose I should be flattered," said Antoinette.

"Women have always terrified me," he admitted. "They know so much better than men what they want, and they go all out to get it. I can't chat a girl up or go to bed with them until I've had a drink or am on drugs."

Antoinette felt herself slip again into the role of counselor/rescuer.

"You remind me of my mum," he said.

Antoinette wanted to slap him. She took a large gulp of air. "Well, thanks for that, young man," she almost spat out. Instead she retained her dignity and told him, "Look, I do have things to do. It was kind of you to 'drop in' and say 'good-bye.'"

Callum blushed. "That came out wrong. My mum is the most amazing woman I've ever known. No wonder I've never been able to find a woman who measures up to her."

Antoinette didn't know whether to be flattered or annoyed.

"My mum brought me up," he said. "She was a single parent. No one could get the better of her. She encouraged me to pursue my sporting ambitions. I know I've let her down, but I also know that doesn't stop her from being on my side. She'll fight for me like a tiger. She's dealing with the attorney back home about my legal problem. She's been telling me to stay away; now she's told me to come back. She thinks it can be sorted out."

The waiter set their food on the table. Callum and Antoinette were too engrossed in each other to take notice. He lowered his voice. "I feel I could trust you like that," he told her. "Unconditional love. We don't receive it often in our lives. I want you to know who I am, what I am. All the darkness and demons inside."

Antoinette was on the verge of tears. She didn't know how to respond. She was scared of the burden he had placed on her. *What if she let him down? What if she could not live up to his expectations?*

"I want to tell you my deep dark secret. The reason why I can't open up honestly to people." His directness compelled her to look him right in the eye.

"Is it about the arrest?" she asked.

"No," he said. "It's about my stepmother. The woman my dad ran off with when he left my mum. My dad made me go and stay with her and him. She ran a catering business. Very successful. Made a fortune. Except it's not a catering business. It's an escort agency. She's been running it since I was a kid. I found out years ago and her and my dad threatened me not to tell anyone. Especially my mum. That's my dirty little secret."

Shocked and intrigued, Antoinette saw precisely the dilemma that faced a young man whose stepmother was "in business."

"I've been running wild since I was a teenager," he admitted. "Drinking, partying. You name it; I've done it. I was already in that world. I knew all the party girls. A lot of it was covered up. My mum and dad didn't talk and she hated the stepmother. Mum tried to keep me out of trouble, but I was always terrified that the secret would come out."

"No wonder you were running scared," said Antoinette. "Thank you for telling me. I don't know what I can do about it, but at least I know what drives you."

"I've got a plan," said Callum. "I'm leaving to go back home today. I don't know how long it will take to sort out my problems. Jail, probation, house arrest. Who knows? But when I am free, I'm coming back here. There's nothing left for me at home. I don't have a future. The shame of my ban for drug-taking will always hang over me. I'm sick of being ashamed. I want to be able to hold my head up. When I come back, I want to come back to you."

Antoinette knew she should caution him not to say what she sensed was coming next. "Callum, think carefully," she said. "This might not work out. Don't I get any say?"

"I love you," he said. "I want you to give me a chance to prove it. Whatever happens from now on, I have a purpose, a plan. Believe me; the game is on, I don't give up til I win."

Chapter Twenty-Three

Callum Lavelle was arrested at the airport. Approached by two plainclothes officers at Passport Control, he considered for less than a second if there were any means of escape. The arrest was not unexpected. From the day he had flown out of the same airport in Southern England, more than a month before, he had known he was a wanted man.

Every day as he feigned freedom in a Spanish seaside town and on the island of Ibiza, he looked over his shoulder and made elaborate diversions on all journeys. The pilot had radioed ahead to confirm that the fugitive was on board.

"I'll come quietly," Callum told the escort officers, "don't cuff me in public." They didn't answer but walked him to a nearby wall and, as they stood on either side, boxed him in. He held out little hope that they would grant his request but it was worth try.

"Hands behind your back, please, sir. Legs apart," said the younger of the two, a well-built young man who looked like he could handle himself, but against the bulk and impressive physique of Callum, he would be forced to punch well above his weight.

Passengers from the flight slowed down as they passed the trio and craned their necks, as if by looking close enough they would be able to gauge what was going on.

Callum kept his eyes fixed on the wall and refused to react, even when the policeman caught the radial nerve on his wrist in the hinge of the closed handcuff. His face burned with shame, and he heard one woman exclaim, as she walked past, "He was sitting right behind me. Someone should have told me I was in danger. He could have turned violent. Started attacking innocent people." She had earned her fifteen minutes of drama and attention all on a two-hour flight back from a holiday destination.

Hands behind his back and cuffed with a chain to the wrist of one of the law enforcement officers, Callum was led through the airport. In a brief pat-down search, his phone and wallet were confiscated and his backpack was now carried by an officer.

Through the busy airport, they propelled him. Not knowing which way to look to hide his shame, Callum fixed his eyes on a spot somewhere in the far distance. One of the officers had done the decent thing and adjusted Callum's jacket so that it covered the handcuffs at the back. The sleeves hid the chain attached to the officer.

"Where you taking me?" he asked.

"We've got a car outside to take you back to your local police station. Shouldn't take an hour," was the reply.

"Squad car?" asked Callum.

"No," the officer laughed, "no blue flashing lights and sirens for you. We're escorts, not charge officers; you're not under arrest. You're wanted for questioning about an assault. They'll decide at the station what happens next."

"Can I call my lawyer?" asked Callum.

"Yea, when you get to the station."

The black unmarked police car was parked in a No Parking zone, patrolled by airport security. The officer released one cuff, giving him a free left hand with the restraining cuff still attached to their wrists. He nudged Callum into the back of the car and climbed in beside while his colleague took up his position in the driver's seat. The tension in the car eased as they drove fast along the M25 ring road around London.

"Been a naughty boy?" asked the policemen in the front seat.

"Ex-wife trouble," said Callum, chatting now to the policemen as if they were almost friends. "Bitch," he said, "I caught her with another bloke, gave him a hammering."

The policemen laughed and nodded acknowledgment that they would likely have done the same.

"Used to watch you play soccer. I support your old team," said the policeman at Callum's side. "You were good. Real professional. How come you got banned for life?"

"Long story," said Callum, as he turned his face to look out of the window of the speeding car. Being a well-known athlete and sometime television commentator was great when you were riding high. But it opened the door to too much familiarity, especially when it came to discussions you didn't want to have with anyone. Least of all two cops taking you into custody.

"Shot yourself in the foot, didn't you," said the policeman, "taking drugs. You're all the bloody same you celebrities. "Too much money, fame, fast cars and women throwing themselves at you. Must have been a great life. Now, look at you."

"Yea, thanks for reminding me," said Callum, and the three of them laughed. All blokes together.

Chapter Twenty-Four

The room was in darkness; no light penetrated the rusty, paint-cracked bars of the jail cell. Callum struggled to remember where he was; it was a luxury he allowed himself for the first few moments of another day. Soon he would be unable to ignore the incoherent yelling, angry banging and chaotic noise as the prison block awoke.

"Welcome to another day in bloody paradise," shouted an unseen voice. The daily attempt at humor still found an appreciative audience as several good-natured prisoners broke into laughter.

Callum did not laugh. Only in sleep was he relieved of the heartbreaking regrets and guilt that filled his days.

"Rise and shine, sweetheart," shouted the guard, as he unlocked and kicked open the cell door. Callum didn't react or respond. The first lesson he learned during his incarceration was *Keep your head down and obey orders.* It helped that most of the correctional officers and the other prisoners knew who he was—or who he had once been. An international cup–winning soccer player. "Man of the Match." A celebrity, rich, powerful, the world at his feet.

The glory days of glittering prizes and awards receded further from his memory every day. What did not was the devastating memory of the phone call that brought his world crashing down around him.

There were no preliminary niceties as the chairman of his league club called his landline on that Monday morning near the end of the last season. Callum could not remember receiving a telephone call from this illustrious person before, but the voice at the other end of the phone needed no introduction.

"Wainwright here," the chairman said in the booming voice that hardly needed a microphone as he made his feelings known on the loudspeaker system that reverberated around the soccer stadium after every game. "Remember, soccer is not a matter of life and death; it's more important than that. Well done, lads, see you all next week."

Without preamble, he dropped the bombshell. "You failed the drug test. Banned for life. Effective immediately. Your contract is terminated. Can't say I wish you luck because I don't approve of players like you bringing the game into disrepute, but you were a valuable team member. Sorry to lose you. Don't talk to the press."

Callum felt the blood drain from his face. His body shook, and the receiver felt like a foreign object. He dropped it as if it were red hot and it clattered into the cradle.

He had seen family members accept phone calls telling of sudden deaths, and they had been able to muster more presence of mind that he now felt. Rooted to the spot, he observed himself in the silver-framed mirror above the telephone.

His designer, geometrically patterned haircut, topped with a man bun that had so delighted the fans at that weekend's cup winning match now made him feel exposed and shamed. *Banned for life* repeated on a loop in his brain.

The intercom system beeped, and he feared the press was already on the story. "Where the fuck do I go from here?" he asked aloud.

The voice of his three-year-old daughter startled him. "What's the matter, daddy?" asked the toddler tugging at the bottoms of his jogging pants.

Callum had entirely forgotten that, unusually, he had been designated to babysit while his mother ran an errand. The girl had been asleep in her cot upstairs in the nursery.

"Where's nanny?" she asked and looked to be on the verge of tears.

Callum felt helpless. Much as he loved his only child, parenting skills eluded him. One thing that convinced him to buy his five-bedroom barn conversion on the outskirts of a South Coast town was that he did not have to entertain or socialize with other family members. While there was plenty of room for visitors—they especially enjoyed the indoor swimming pool—Callum lived the life of a bachelor in a separate wing of the house.

His mother, Greta, had almost moved in, and she lived at the house on grandma duty when it was his turn to have visiting rights every second weekend. She and his ex-wife worked it out among themselves; he took little interest in arrangements or the practicalities of childcare.

"Grandma will be back in a minute," he placated the child while simultaneously texting his mother, Get back here now.

Pulling into the garage, she returned the text.

Okay, I'll take your car. Leave the automatic door open and open the gates. Got to go—talk later. Carly is awake.

Always prepared for the unexpected, by the front door Callum's emergency kit in a black backpack contained everyday clothing, underwear and toiletries. Anything else could always be purchased at the destination, wherever in the world.

Callum rushed past his surprised mother, jumped in her car, reversed out of the garage and, like a bat out of hell, drove out of the main gates.

The young man in the navy-blue suit, standing with his neck craned by the cast-iron gates and ready to pounce, was not wearing a hat, but he did not need a sign saying *Press* tucked in his hatband for Callum to identify him. He was a member of the local press corps and often interviewed Callum and the rest of the team after matches. He tried hard not to be partisan, but the truth was, he was a supporter of their team. A loyal fan.

Callum had good reason to take his mother's SUV. Tinted windows meant he was not visible from the outside. His own black Porsche did not have tinted windows, and Callum liked to be seen as he drove around town. But not today.

He slammed on the accelerator and was halfway down the country lane before the reporter had time to shout out one single question. Callum knew the answer to the unasked question and all the others. "No Comment."

Sadly he did not even have an answer for himself. He could see the newspaper headlines now,

STAR SOCCER PLAYER BANNED FOR LIFE.

Chapter Twenty-Five

Olivia Rose accepted the invitation from a large hotel chain in the Dominican Republic to check out their facilities for an Indian-style wedding on the beach. The four-day familiarization trip would enable her to offer the wedding venue as an option for her clients. Bridal couples were becoming more and more adventurous in their choice of wedding locations, and this one promised to be super exotic.

Olivia Rose had first become aware of the venue at a wedding show she had attended. She wanted to check it out for herself. Everything about it sounded idyllic. Couples were able to choose backdrops such as Minitas Beach, the romantic sixteenth-century-style St. Stanislaus Church in Altos de Chavón overlooking the river valley, a luxurious beachfront villa or one of the many traditional ballrooms. Each location could be transformed to fit the couple's every wish, from Moroccan-themed festivities at the Safari Club and candlelit dining on the legendary golf courses to waterfront celebrations at the marina and cocktails in the gardens of Altos de Chavón.

Indian-themed weddings are held on the private

Minitas Beach. With a backdrop of golden sands and bright blue sea, the magical scene combines magnificent themed arches, swathes of luxurious silk in an array of vibrant colors and decorative ornaments to complete the Indian look. A beach wedding with all the sights and sounds and symbolism of a traditional Asian marriage.

"The trip will be a welcome break," she told her father. "It will give me space to think about what I want to do next."

She refused to lay a guilt trip on him by admitting that all her hopes had been pinned on him investing his money to take her wedding planning business to the next level. There was no way she could admit the real motivation behind her desires to move from a one-woman business to an international concern.

Gianni had planted the idea in her mind. He talked to her about the opportunity to expand her business on the internet and accept bridal commissions from all over the world. The trip to the Dominican Republic on which she was about to embark would allow her to make contacts and interchange business.

Instead of offering her wedding services to brides in her local area, she could bring international brides to Britain. The service would include bringing families and putting them up in hotels for the duration of the wedding, which these days was more often than not spread over several days.

The exclusive contract offered by the Vineyard to promote and market their wedding facilities was a start. There was one snag. She needed money to grow the business and did not want to go to an outside investor who might insist on managing the business.

Olivia Rose had her vision and was determined to pursue it according to her desires. She pushed to the back of her mind that the main reason for her ambition was to impress Gianni.

He offered to mentor her and recommend people who could help with the technical side of an expanded website and marketing concern. She was utterly baffled by talk of algorithms and funnels and front-loading in the growing of an internet business, but Gianni promised to introduce her to people who could bring her up to speed.

By agreeing to the business expansion, she had access to Gianni. She called to ask advice and discuss options and strategies. As a man of action, Gianni liked nothing better than to solve problems for her.

Olivia Rose longed to feel that she and Gianni were developing a foundation for the romantic aspect of their relationship. However, she sensed that being a man of action did not stretch to include his ability to maintain romantic relationships, and more often than not, she ended phone calls feeling strangely frustrated that the conversation was not more personal and intimate.

At times he treated her like a little girl. A favored youngster. Precisely as he might have treated an endearing stepdaughter.

Olivia Rose was too shy to make many overt observations. This was her first relationship, and, after the initial seduction, she expected to continue to be wooed, to be pursued. Instead, she was confused about the very nature of the intimacy they had shared.

Subtle questions designed to elicit information about his travel plans or the routine of his work schedule were answered with evasions. "I'm in Spain," he admitted on one occasion. On another, "On my way to Portugal before traveling back to Spain."

The name or whereabouts of Antoinette never intruded on the conversation. Olivia Rose longed to know the truth of their relationship. She got the impression that they spent a lot of time apart. Was that purely because of business? Or was there some deeper reason?

Gianni was not a man who chose to answer too many questions. Olivia Rose sensed that he was very much his own man. Any woman who tried to tie him down soon found herself cut loose.

Olivia Rose wished she had someone with whom to share some of her questions. The situation between her and Gianni was complicated, but she was anxious to know what had been his intentions in pursuing her in the first place. Was she a one-night stand, a notch on a bedpost that she was sure was filled with the history of many such encounters?

The one man she might previously have chosen to share her dilemma with, her father, was way off limits. Not that he was a person with much personal experience of women, but he would have listened sympathetically and tried to guide his only daughter. His primary concern always was that he should try to guide her away from being hurt. He would not want her to have her heart broken as his had been all those years ago.

His current dilemma had reinforced his belief that he was a fool where women were concerned. To cover his disappointment, he had taken to following leads on the internet to try to identify the scammers who had stolen his money. He still found it hard to believe that he had been completely duped and Natalia had never existed.

At times he acted like a brokenhearted lover who had been jilted at the altar, asking himself what he had done wrong. On these occasions, he swore revenge. For himself and other lonely men and women who had been duped. Jason accepted that he would not get his money back, but somehow he wanted to save face and not believe that he was a victim of what was known as the Nigerian Business Model.

He firmly believed that he'd never have fallen for it if an unknown contact had claimed he'd won the lottery, or that someone had come into an inheritance and needed him to help them get their money out of the country. The fact was that he was lonely and a sitting duck when it came to a beautiful young woman stroking his ego and turning his head with promises of sex on demand.

The remark that Jason repeated over and over again as the one that led him to dream he was about to embark on the love affair of a lifetime was "I want to walk down the street in your village holding your hand and let the world know that we are in love."

Tracking down the perpetrators of the crime had become Jason's new cause célèbre, and he spent hours every night on the internet making his inquiries.

Olivia Rose joked with him that unlike Alice who had disappeared down the rabbit hole, he had disappeared into the dark web. "Don't give away any more money," she warned.

"Funny you should say that," said Jason, with no trace of a smile on his face. "Some websites that offer to track down scammers are actually scammers. They charge hefty fees to find the scammers."

Olivia Rose was sympathetic, but apart from heeding a lesson to be careful in the future, she knew there was nothing else to be done.

In explaining to Gianni why she had to review her plans and could not ask her father for money to invest in her business, she was careful not to reveal what had befallen him. "He's got other things on his mind," she explained.

Gianni replied, "I'm sorry to hear that. I thought he was happy with his new fiancé. Is she giving him the runaround?"

"What do you know about that?" she demanded.

Gianni laughed. "You are delightfully naïve, my dear," he said. "We are all friends now in the world of the internet."

Chapter Twenty-Six

G ianni consulted the GPS and entered the instructions for "curvy roads." The journey he planned
was five hundred miles, and he figured he could make
the distance in ten hours. Riding on his supercharged
Honda cbf 1000 motorcycle, he relished the chance to
reconnect with his younger self and re-experience the
passion of riding for days up and down mountain tracks,
crossing countries and borders.

A favorite journey was to navigate the Swiss Alps
and challenge himself on the mountainous roads and
snowy peaks to which riders from all over the world
traveled to experience. As a young rider, he had discovered the exhilarating freedom to travel immersed in
nature and experience unfiltered sensory pleasures of the
sky, clouds, air and atmosphere and direct connection
with the weather and a kaleidoscope of sights, sounds
and smells. Good and bad. Embedded deep in the environment, his senses reacted to the fragrance of blossoms,
birds singing, the air pulsating.

He learned at a young age that "the journey is the
purpose." Unlike driving a car where the purpose is

to get from A to Z, motorcycling needs no excuse to undertake journeys of hundreds or thousands of miles.

Often too excited to sleep the night before a ride, the alarm clock was redundant. When it rang at 6 a.m., he was already awake, alert and ready to embark on his trip. The previous evening he went through his technical checks: filled the bike with fuel and inspected the tires, brakes and lights. Charged up the phone and satellite navigation and made sure that all were stowed in easily accessible places.

Gianni meticulously laid his clothes in neat stacks on the motel bed from where he would set off after having collected his motorcycle from a winter storage facility. He packed with precision. He traveled light but was ready for all eventualities. One waterproof side case contained a backpack with enough casual clothes for a week; the other, extra cold weather clothing and rain gear for mountain passes, basic provisions of water and energy snacks and a set of tools, including a puncture kit with which he could make roadside tire repairs. On the back of the bike, he strapped the square case that held an artfully folded business suit, shirt (no tie), leather shoes and ankle socks.

He threw back the covers on the motel bed with all the enthusiasm of a child setting off on a long-anticipated outing and jumped from his bed at the first beep of the alarm, excited to start his latest adventure. Every journey, however carefully planned, held challenges and unexpected rewards. The thrill of the unexpected never failed to energize him.

He dressed in motorcycle leathers molded with extra cushioned pads to protect the limbs and vulnerable areas of hands, elbows, shoulders and knees. A heavy black leather jacket offered protection and warmth, and leather boots protected his ankles and wouldn't wear out quickly or come off if a collision made him fall off the bike.

Gianni swigged from a cup of coffee he had warmed up on the in-room coffee maker. The breakfast room was open, and he grabbed a croissant on his way to the parking lot.

He carried his prepacked cases to the bike and stowed them efficiently and safely with a method he had used innumerable times over the years. One small waterproof zipped purse, he stowed with extra care in the inside pocket of his leather jacket. He patted his inside pocket. A precious cargo.

Gianni ran a mental check in his head: bike, tools, luggage, keys, cell phone, sat nav, charger, credit cards, ID and passport. There was a slight chill in the air as he mounted the waiting machine, adjusted his helmet and goggles and pulled on heavy-duty riding gloves. "Time to hit the road," he concluded. "Let's roll."

Gianni prided himself on being an adventurous but highly controlled rider. He had been well taught and often quoted the adage, "There are risk-taking riders and there are old riders, but there are no risk-taking old riders."

Over the years he continued to update the technical and riding skills necessary to tame and maneuver a 600-pound bike capable of speeds comparable with those of a Ferrari. On the open road in the right conditions, his machine was built to touch speeds of 250 miles an hour, but he generally considered it safer, given the fact that he valued his life, to work with an upper speed of 150 miles an hour. There was no margin for error, he learned at an early age. Skill needed to be combined with judgment. Lower speeds allowed room for avoidance of problems.

Like a Zen master, his first teacher had impressed upon him the mental technique of hyper-focused awareness in a relaxed state of being. It was the closest thing to mediation that Gianni practiced. He was constantly conscious of his environment, eyes scanning to the front, the back and the sides, aware of the weather, road conditions and other riders. In the flow, and totally present.

It was a dance with nature and he shared his love of the ride. He waxed lyrical when asked to explain the attraction of riding: "A ballet, flowing with the curves, allowing the road to guide you, up, down, through the environment with nothing between you and ultimate reality. In that state of consciousness, you must be alert to every shift in temperature, change in weather conditions. Ready to react to an animal in your path, a patch of oil, grains of sand or gravel in the roadway.

"Panic is not an option," he stressed. "You are responsible. You make a split second decision to move through the obstacle or go around it. At all costs, you need to avoid it, and this you learn to do without impeding your progress."

Gianni planned to make his five-hundred-mile trip from Faro in the Algarve, Portugal, to the Costa Blanca, in ten hours. He was in no hurry, nice and steady.

At one hundred miles, he reached the first rest stop outside Seville. Behind the counter of a small roadside café, Gianni greeted a friend—and along with his coffee, dropped off a package.

As the sun rose higher in the sky and the day warmed, roads that started off clear of traffic began to get busier. All around, the villages he passed through came to life, people went about their business, and shops, stores and cafes opened up.

Roughly every one hundred miles or every two hours, he stopped for a rest break, a chance to drink, to eat a small snack and perform running maintenance. Dead bugs and insects needed to be removed from the protective windscreen, and his goggles required cleaning, though often a timely downpour did the job for him.

After two hundred miles, on the outskirts of Granada, he stopped in a rest area, and in the parking lot, he met a friend. They exchanged greetings—and a package changed hands.

Approaching the halfway mark, Gianni identified his upcoming stop but not in time to save him from riding into a deluge, a hail storm. The rain lashed his face and bounced off his protective clothing. The bike was washed clean in that one downpour.

As he exited from the main road at the speed limit, he hit a patch of standing water and the bike hydro-planed. As he skied on water, and thanks to his inbuilt caution, he loosened his grip on the handlebars, instead of tensing up, and brought the machine to a smooth and controlled stop.

At three hundred miles, after driving through Cordoba, a friend approached while he filled up with fuel—and a package exchanged hands.

From his starting point in the Algarve, Portugal, he had plotted his journey. There were deliveries to make along the way, but he never lost sight of where he was headed. To the seaside town of Altea on the Costa Blanca. He drove through Seville, Granada, Lorca, taking a route north of the coast and then dropping down to drive through picturesque towns and abundant countryside.

Gianni preferred to ride alone but when necessary would allow a passenger to ride along. He had one rule. Keep talking to a minimum. His Zen-like state was accomplished better without the sound of human voices, but from time to time, if traveling with other riders, he used a radio system to maintain a connection.

After four hundred miles, he arrived in Murcia—less than one hundred miles to go—another friend—another package.

Gianni challenged himself when he rode but did not often ride competitively. He embraced the freedom of a traveling man and the Romany race from whom he was descended; he carried his life with him; in possession of his gleaming machine, clothes to wear and access to money and phones, he could go anywhere he chose.

The setting on the GPS allowed him to make

diversions, change plans, stop and restart the journey any time he chose. Today the end of his journey was set for Altea. He was on a mission but had not told Antoinette he was heading her way.

She had long since given up questioning his movements. Over the years she had heard whispers that the respectable businessman in the olive-growing business was not the whole story. They both took the view that the less she knew, the better.

* * *

Antoinette took her mind off personal problems by overseeing her business, an elite boutique she had opened years earlier. She employed a manager whom she trusted, and, as the owner, she appeared at the exclusive establishment only when it suited her. She used the fashion store to keep her mind distracted from the unasked and unanswered questions concerning the whereabouts of Gianni. Their relationship had always been fragmented. She in one place, him in another. The absences had been caused by her family situation in the early days; over the years, she came to accept that Gianni was a lone wolf.

* * *

Balanced on top of a ladder outside the building that had become her pride and joy, Antoinette was pleased with her artistry. The dilapidated building on the seafront had risen like a phoenix from the ashes.

"Are you sure you don't want one of my men to paint that sign?" asked the foreman.

"Thanks, but no, I want to do it myself," Antoinette called, raising her voice above the sea breeze that threatened to whip her words away.

Antoinette's early vision came to life as she worked with a team of builders, architects and designers. The tattered canvas showing an earlier image to restore the structure had been removed and studied to see what aspects might be incorporated.

"The roof terrace is to be a showcase," said Antoinette. She had been supported in her project by a great team of experts, and Jan was the leading man in coordinating all aspects of the restoration.

"It's traditional to build from the ground up," he advised her. "The more secure we make the foundation, the stronger the building will rise from the ground."

Antoinette was conscious that she did not have the technical or practical expertise to make significant construction decisions, but she insisted on sitting in on every meeting, listening to the overall plans so that she was aware of the difficulties and options.

The team quickly moved on from seeing her only as the owner, the one who was responsible for funding the operation, to valuing her input and insight. In her working gear of Levis, sweaters, sturdy boots and a hard hat, most passersby would not have recognized that under the construction workers' uniform was a beautiful young woman.

Antoinette had never done any manual work, but

the first time she was handed a tool belt by one of the workers, she honestly felt she had arrived. To her friend and confidant, she explained her position. "The building has become a part of me," she told him. "As I restore and renew the derelict property, I feel I am restoring and renewing myself. Rewriting my life."

Jan nodded and, over the course of the project, believed the spiritual connections she made with the old house. Antoinette told him, "From the inside out, I feel the connection to all the people who have lived here. To the ancient passing procession of fishermen, workers, craftsmen who were the early custodians of the town of Altea."

Antoinette came to know the men onsite by name; she developed a fondness for their honest attitudes, good humor and their skills learned over generations. The men who worked for the contractor all knew each other. Many were related, and they told stories of how their father and grandfathers had been the original builders. They laid the bricks, plastered the walls, painted the doors and by hand placed every one of the cobblestones.

The day for the workers and Antoinette started early, as soon as the sun rose, and finished late. Not for love or money could she persuade the men to forgo their three-hour daytime break for food and rest. With a fresh burst of energy, they returned for the late afternoon–early evening shift. Antoinette had known from the start the color of the outside paintwork. Sky-blue windows, doors and shutters and a canopy on the ground floor of beige trimmed with sea green.

Concrete plant pots were placed on the patio, painted and planted with vibrant blue blooms, pansies, and daisies. From the upper windows and black iron-work balconies cascaded bougainvilles in pink, red and purple.

"The work is almost at an end," Jan and the contractor informed her. Antoinette was flush with success. Though not without its problems and challenges, they had completed the project in record time and even brought it in on budget.

"Do you mean to open a restaurant?" Jan asked.

"In time, maybe, but for now I plan to make this my sanctuary. A hideaway overlooking the sea. But there is one finishing touch. Let me complete it, and then I'll treat you all to a glass of champagne as we christen my new home." Antoinette balanced two pots of paint on top of the ladder. She drew the design on a large sheet of white drawing paper and this she taped to the flat platform at the top of the ladder.

She traced the outline of a five-pointed star and painted between the lines with vibrant blue and added a serene pale-blue background with twinkling stars.

In a scrolling freehand, she wrote the name she had received in a dream, *Casa Olivia Rose*.

Chapter Twenty-Seven

Champagne glasses chinked as the construction crew celebrated Antoinette's successful restoration of the seafront building. With her back to the sea, Antoinette raised her champagne flute and toasted the newly painted sign. "Here's to Casa Olivia Rose," she said.

She felt a hand on her shoulder.

"Don't I get a glass of champagne?" She could not fail to recognize the familiar male voice. Gianni smiled as she turned and in surprise faced him. Her own glass shaking in her hand.

"What are you doing here?"

He showed no emotion, but the words were clear. "Did you think you could keep all this secret from me, Antoinette? You underestimate me. I always know what is going on in my domain."

Antoinette hesitated, and then she laughed and hugged him, getting as close as she could through the heavy motorcycling gear. "You've spoiled the surprise," she said, "but you arrived right on time. The building is finished, and I have christened it. It's dedicated to my daughter, Casa Olivia Rose."

She handed him a glass of champagne.

Gianni looked up at the sign and frowned. "That does take me by surprise," he said. "You and Olivia have hardly been close over the years."

"I know, and the guilt I've felt about leaving her has been reignited since she and I met up again in Italy. I wanted to do something to show her how much she means to me."

The building team drifted away, calling out, "Thank you, Señora Antoinette. We hope to work for you again in the future."

Jan bid the team farewell and came across to shake Gianni's hand. "I was following instructions," he said, before Gianni could question him. "It was not my idea to keep this project from you. I and the bank manager who advanced the funds for the construction were sworn to secrecy. We were told it was to be a surprise for you. I hope you are pleased with the result."

Under no circumstances would Jan have gone behind Gianni's back on a business deal had Antoinette not assured him that the end would justify the means. "He will love it," she had promised. Jan looked for confirmation, anxious to make sure that was true.

"Good job, Jan," said Gianni and clapped Jan on the back. "I've learned over the years not to argue with Antoinette; she always gets her way."

Antoinette gathered up the disposable plastic champagne glasses and the empty bottle and walked inside the building to put them in a trash bag.

Gianni followed her in. He came up close, wrapped

his arms around her and whispered in her ear. "Let's go home," he said.

Antoinette could never refuse him. "Let me lock up," she said. "I'll meet you outside."

"The bike is on the seafront," he told her. "Leave your car. I'll have it picked up later."

Antoinette wanted to protest. She needed time to come up with the right words that would explain why she had bought and developed her building without consulting him.

Gianni was waiting, and he handed her a helmet. "Hold on tight," he told her as he accelerated up the narrow road off the seafront and onto the main road. "You and I need to have a long talk," he shouted against the wind. "You should know by now; I'm the driver in our relationship. You are the passenger."

Antoinette clung to Gianni, and even though she knew he was angry, it felt good to be so close to him. His robust and manly body protected her, and though she might not trust him in love, she knew she was completely safe with him on the back of a motorcycle.

The mist obscured the mountains, and there was a chill in the air as they rode in companionable silence along the highways and toll roads from Altea to their home an hour away up the coast toward Valencia.

Antoinette breathed in the smells from the abundant orange and lemon groves and delighted in the sight of olive trees in the roadside orchards.

The journey along well-maintained roads past rural farmland was peaceful, but on the horizon signs of industrialization were increasingly visible. Cranes stood sentinel over the small towns, and urbanization was expanding to declare the superiority of commercial interests over traditional open countryside. Red roofs, white houses and church steeples, this landscape had remained unchanged for hundreds of years.

Ten-foot high palm fronds waved in the breeze and were planted to block the noise from the highway. Still visible behind the makeshift fences were single-story, square farmhouses, many with religious icons painted on their sides.

Far in the distance, Antoinette recognized the industrial and technical parks on the outskirts of the city, the cranes and ship-lifting equipment of the Port of Valencia. In contrast to the working areas of the medieval city, she could make out the impressive modern museums and galleries, monuments to science, music and technology that declared the city a temple to cultural advancement. Almost as impressive was the magnificent villa that belonged to Gianni's family high up on the cliff top.

Gianni called over his shoulder, "Are you alright back there? Not cold? We're almost home."

Antoinette snuggled farther into the back of his warm jacket and wrapped her arms all the way around him.

"I've got a foolproof way to warm you up when we get home," said Gianni, as he covered her hands with his, the leather of his motorcycle gloves encasing and restraining her. He revved the motorcycle, and gravel sprayed up as he took the curve at high speed and skimmed the ground with the bike as he turned into a driveway guarded by ten-foot tall iron gates. The gates opened electronically, and Gianni sped up the driveway.

The columns of the white temple villa faced the top of the drive. Gianni swerved to the side and the back where he and Antoinette had private quarters in the family house. He parked the bike and handed the keys to a member of staff who had appeared as if from nowhere. "Garage it," he said. "I'm not going out again."

Antoinette walked on ahead and into the wing of the house where they shared an apartment. Across the terrace and up the grand staircase. In the bedroom, she sat on the bed to take off her shoes and then walked into the bathroom to freshen up.

Lucky that on the last day of construction, she was wearing Levis and a T-shirt, not her regular outfit of workingman's clothes. She dreaded to think what Gianni would have made of that. His background was privileged, and he'd grown up surrounded by household staff and would never have been able to see the attraction of her doing a builder's job. She took off her jeans, T-shirt and underwear and took a robe from the wardrobe.

Gianni entered the bedroom. "You won't need that," he said. He had already taken off his outer motorcycle clothing and wore only his leather trousers and a black T-shirt. "Come here, you gorgeous creature," he said as he took Antoinette in his strong arms and began to kiss her. The robe slipped to the floor and, naked, she stood in front of him.

Without ceremony, he threw her onto the double

bed and kissed her passionately, all the time murmuring words of love. The rough leather of his trousers scraped against her bare thighs, and he forced her legs apart. He grabbed her wrists and held them above her head as he thrust himself inside her. Antoinette cried out with pleasure and pain.

Gianni made love to her with a passion and intensity that she had almost forgotten they had found in each other. So often she steeled her heart against him, fearful that when he was making love to her, he was imagining another woman in his arms.

Holding nothing back, she gave herself to him and screamed out in ecstasy as they came together.

"I love you. I love you," he whispered in her ear. "I promise; I love you."

Lying in her lover's arms, Antoinette felt, at last, safe and secure. All the hurt and pain she experienced over the past months melted away. She held him close and stroked his face. "I was afraid I'd lost you," she said. "We're always apart. Tell me I was wrong."

Gianni held her close and traced the lines of her cheeks, lips and eyes with his powerful hands. "You are my woman," he said. "Don't you ever doubt it."

Antoinette let out a sigh of satisfaction and smiled with contentment. Gianni did not return her smile. His eyes were dark and his voice grave. "I warn you. Don't think you can betray me. I will always find out. You will pay for it. On that, you have my word."

Chapter Twenty-Eight

O n a cliff top terrace with a spectacular view of the Mediterranean, Antoinette and Gianni shared breakfast as they sat at a white wrought-iron table beside the infinity swimming pool. She filled his glass with freshly squeezed orange juice from fruit picked that morning and tore open fresh figs.

"Coffee," he said, without taking his eyes from the messages on his cell phone.

Antoinette regretted that the closeness of the previous evening was lost in the bright sunlight of the day. It was always business first with Gianni. "I plan to invite Olivia over to see the house I named for her," she said.

That captured Gianni's attention, and his reaction caught Antoinette by surprise. "Is that what this house business was all about?" he asked. "You don't see her for years; now you want her to live in your pocket. Your daughter has got a life and a business back in England; she doesn't want to be on a permanent holiday with you here in Spain."

Antoinette was on the verge of tears. "Why are being so mean? I thought you liked Olivia?"

Gianni threw his napkin on the table. "What is it you want from me, Antoinette?" he raised his voice. "You have a home here; you also have your own home back in Italy. Now you are going to play mommy with your grown-up daughter right on my doorstep in a house you didn't even tell me you were buying. Are you in a midlife crisis?"

She tried to explain, but Gianni picked up his phone and walked away from her and down the steps that led to the main house. "I'm away for a few days on business," he called over his shoulder. "Let me know which one of your many addresses I can find you at when I get back."

Antoinette had read once in a magazine that when engaged in an affair, men frequently react with anger toward their wives or partners. Women in the same situation, to assuage their guilt, tend to shower their partner with affection and extra attention.

Antoinette was left hurt and confused. Sun on her body would be a treat. She slipped off her robe and revealed the bikini she wore underneath. Leisurely, she stretched out on a chaise lounge and closed her eyes.

"What is my motivation?" she asked herself. "Why did I buy the house? Why did I feel the need to restore and renew myself? If I am honest, I have to admit that Olivia was not the driving force."

Reluctant to admit to the real reason for her restlessness, Antoinette was entrapped in a web of denial. She dialed Olivia's number. "How have you been?" she asked her daughter. "It would be great to see you, and

I've got a surprise for you. Can you take time off work and come to Spain for a few days?"

"I'd love to, but I'm about to leave for a trip to the Dominican Republic. If the invitation is still open for the end of the month, I'll come then. What's the surprise?"

Antoinette laughed. "If I told you, it wouldn't be a surprise. Of course, you can come any time it suits you. I want us to rebuild our relationship. We've wasted too many years. I feel I hardly know you, who you are, what you do, what music you like. I don't even know if you have a boyfriend."

Ignoring the one question that she had no intention of answering, Olivia Rose told her mother, "There's plenty of time to get to know each other again. We're not so dissimilar. Dad always says that I remind him of you, and I know for a fact, we have the same taste in lots of things."

Antoinette wished Olivia Rose a safe trip and told her, "Promise that you will come at the end of the month. Gianni is looking forward to seeing you again."

"Got to go," said Olivia Rose, "there's another call coming in. Bye, love you."

Antoinette couldn't relax or settle by the pool. The row with Gianni upset her, and she knew deep in her heart that things were not right between them. Maybe they never would be again. So determined was she to write the perfect love story of childhood sweethearts living happily ever after, she hated to acknowledge the flaws in their relationship.

All those years ago, during her marriage to Olivia Rose's father, Gianni lived an independent life. Their relationship was a holiday romance, short periods of time together and extended periods apart. Their romance was exciting and adventurous because she was a married woman. When she was at home with her daughter and husband, Gianni lived the life of a single man. It was difficult for her to question his lifestyle.

She was aware that, like the proverbial elephant in the room, both of them ignored the realities of their ongoing relationship. They had not had the opportunity to grow together and learn to accommodate each other. Gianni was so distant at times that she doubted she knew him at all.

Alone on the terrace, Antoinette stared into the distance and tried to make sense of her feelings. Gianni was so interwoven in her life; she never questioned whether she loved him or if the life they lived together was what she wanted. She was frightened to admit they had so little in common.

He refused to involve her in his business world. Gianni had big ambitions; he lived his life on the move, this business deal, that contact, this new opportunity. He was a restless soul, always chasing the next big chance. He long since moved on from the olive farms of his family and saw himself instead as an international businessman. A wheeler, dealer. Antoinette had no idea what he was up to most of the time. She convinced herself it was better she not know.

Now that her pet project was complete and the

house restored, Antoinette acknowledged she was desperately in need of a new adventure. She walked to the stone wall at the edge of the property and feasted her soul on the sights and sounds of nature and watched the activities below from way up at the top of the world.

A movement caught her eye and she watched a man jump from a cliff edge, hurl himself into the air and glide away on a multicolored parachute. Thoughts of Callum came unbidden into her mind. A daredevil, a risk-taker, thinking of him made her heart beat faster.

Against her will, she admitted the emptiness she felt before he came into her life. The aching inside that longed for a true connection. A relationship with a man who needed her, not one who took her for granted because she had become so much a fixture that he no longer saw her.

Callum was young, inexperienced in relationships, but he had reached out and promised her an experience unlike any she had known before. A small voice warned her. Your heart will be broken; are you willing to take the risk? There was no contest. She wanted to feel alive again. Feel valued, feel good enough. Not spend her life in regret. This might be the last opportunity to connect with herself and find out what would make her truly happy. Fulfilled. Callum needed her. She wanted to be desired, adored. Even if the price was high.

In a moment of blinding clarity, she knew why she had restored the house, why she was driven to restore herself. Callum offered an experience, unlike anything she had ever known before.

She looked again to where the paragliders jumped off the cliff and made a decision. *I'm willing to take the leap of faith.*

* * *

Callum wrote to Antoinette from prison. She was flattered but reluctant to reply, trying hard to avoid the inevitable consequences.

"Thoughts of you brighten up my gloomy existence," he wrote. "I think about you all the time. You make me believe that my life is not over. I have something left to offer. With you by my side, I can build a life that's worthwhile. I have to get away from this country and start anew.

"In prison, I have the advantage of being a known celebrity. In here people don't judge or condemn. I keep my head down and do the best I can to keep out of trouble and get the sentence over. Outside, it's different. My criminal record is a stigma. I think of you and Spain and a life in the sunshine."

Callum explained that his six-month sentence for assault meant three months of prison time. Then he was a free man.

She had refused to hold out false hope to him but now decided that she was going to take a chance. Gianni's warning rang in her ears. She did not doubt he meant what he said, but having made her decision, she was determined to see it through.

To Callum, she wrote, "There are no guarantees in

this life. I was filled with doubts and fears about whether you and I could sustain a life together.

"Now I believe we have as reasonable a chance as anyone else. I've come to the realization that I'll regret it for the rest of my life if I don't give us a chance. When you're released I will make arrangements. There are complications and these need to be dealt with, but if you're willing, I am. You make me feel alive again.

"You're unlike anyone I've met before. I'm fascinated by you, and I want to believe that I can help you come to terms with the demons that have made relationships so traumatic in the past. Who would have thought that a dog bite would have led us on this path? If this is what you want, I'm committed to following this through. Thanks for restoring my faith in myself—and giving me a belief in you. I watch the paragliders and think of you. Let's hold hands, and jump. Love A x."

Antoinette had never felt so sure of anything in her life. Of course, she could not deny that she should have been honest with Callum about the reality that she was in a long-term relationship. She had no explanation for the fact she had not owned up in the first place. Except, in her defense, she had not anticipated an unexpected encounter with a handsome young man to lead to talk of romance.

That he was so much younger than her worried her. That he was a criminal should have set warning bells ringing. His history of drinking and drug-taking was cause for concern. So why was she putting herself in the flames?

The answer shocked Antoinette. *I seek redemption. The guilt I feel for having run away from my life, my husband and my daughter are so profound that I want the chance to redeem myself. To save another human being. To answer the cry of his soul in pain. To plunge myself into the fire and be healed.*

To prepare herself for the challenges ahead, Antoinette knew there was one more thing she wanted to do. Unfinished business. She opened her laptop and wrote an email letter to her husband, Jason. "I've never said this before," she admitted. "I've been too busy blaming you, but I want to ask your forgiveness. You were a kind man, and I hurt you badly. You gave me a great gift, our daughter, Olivia, and I know you dedicated your life to her. You deserve more happiness than I was capable of providing.

"Olivia appears to have survived and thrived but to be abandoned by her mother must have left scars. I see no outward signs of her acting out, but it's possible I don't know the full story yet.

"The last time we discussed divorce, you said no. I hope you will now agree. I have accepted that it is time. Who knows, you may want to remarry one day."

Chapter Twenty-Nine

"Cancel my deliveries," Gianni shouted into his radio control system. He slammed his foot on the accelerator and pushed the Honda close to a death-defying maximum speed. News that his company offices were about to be searched by local police concentrated his mind. "Call the lawyer. I'm on my way. Half an hour max."

Gianni ran a tight ship. Only two people had access to his office and his files. His older brother, Xavier, and his trusted personal assistant, Consuelo, who had been with him for over twenty years.

Exporting premium olives and the finest olive oil all over the world was the family business built up over three generations. As traditional in Italian family businesses, the company was part of a wider "fraternity." An organization that offered protection and regulation to its members. A hierarchy of power operated and standards were reinforced at every level.

Gianni's delivery business was operating outside the rules. He knew the dangers of setting up an independent operation. However, the involvement of local police was unexpected. Matters of discipline were dealt with internally.

Gianni called the office. "Have they got a search warrant? Ask for identification. I'm almost there."

An unassuming fiberglass cabin in an industrial park served as his office. Gianni parked alongside an unmarked dark sedan and slowed down as he entered the building. *He was not about to appear to be in a rush or a panic.*

Consuelo met him at the door. "I explained that I had no keys for your office, no access to the files."

In the small reception area beside Consuelo's desk, two clean-shaven and smartly dressed men lounged in the worn-out armchairs. "Sorry. I'm sure they're not very comfortable. We don't get many visitors," Gianni apologized as he offered a handshake. "How can I help you?" With a wry smile he added, "Officers."

"Detectives," they corrected him. "Your name has come up in the questioning of a ring of small-time crooks based in various Spanish cities. We'd like to ask you a few questions to eliminate you from our inquiries."

Gianni asked Consuelo, "Is the lawyer on his way?"

"Yes," she answered, "but he was in court so it will be a while."

"Okay, we can take this down to the police station and tell him to come there," said the older of the detectives.

"Why don't we go into my office and try to resolve this?" asked Gianni. Consuelo took the keys Gianni held out and unlocked the door.

"Give me a second to open the shutters," she told them. As she walked past the whiteboard inside the door, she raised her hand and with the sleeve of her cardigan covering her hand, she wiped the surface clean. She pushed open the outer shutters and raised the inner blinds.

"Anyone for coffee or water?" she asked.

All three men shook their heads.

Gianni waved the detectives to two wooden chairs at the back of his small office. He walked behind the desk and opened a drawer with a key on his key ring. From the drawer he took a substantial bundle of 50 euro notes and placed them on the top of the desk. "Looks like the lawyer is delayed," he told the detectives. "Can we go ahead and settle the matter here and now?"

Careful not to offer any money, he instead walked over to the window and looked out at the parking lot, as if checking on his motorcycle.

When he turned back the notes were gone. "Will that be all?" he asked.

"Always a pleasure to do business with you," said the young detective as he and his colleague left the office.

Consuelo waited until they were clear of the premises and their unmarked vehicle had left the parking lot.

"The visits are getting more frequent," she warned Gianni. "Please be careful."

"Thanks for wiping the board clean," he laughed. "How stupid of me. I needed to go into the office for the cash, but I should have realized. You saved my sorry ass again. What would I do without you?"

Consuelo and Gianni had history. Over the course of their twenty-year working relationship, the boundaries crossed into personal on several occasions. Fortunately, mutual respect and affection ensured that they valued the working relationship and knew the personal was a pleasant diversion, not a true romance.

Gianni sank into the worn-out armchair; Consuelo sat behind her desk. "Do you think they're following leads, or following the money?" she asked. "You make easy pickings for them, but I don't know how much information they have on you."

Gianni shook his head. "I knew that last run was a risk. There are too many new kids on the block. They talk too much, to each other and to the authorities when they get caught."

Consuelo was concerned. They had lost several couriers lately. Recruiting and training new ones was a dangerous job.

It was known that undercover police infiltrated the criminal organizations. Operatives were often embedded for years.

"What's the solution?" she asked.

Gianni laughed. "Maybe I should go back to grow-ing olives."

"Not such a bad idea." Consuelo did not laugh. "It was because of your family's global export business that you got sucked into this 'sideline.' It's not too late to extricate yourself, Gianni."

"I hear you," said Gianni, "but it's not easy to walk away. I'm tied up with career criminals. They won't accept if I tell them I want to quit. No, I've got to find another way to handle the situation."

The office door was ajar. Gianni and Consuelo did not hear the lawyer arrive with Gianni's brother. "Sounds like all is well here," he said, "judging from all the laughter."

"Hi, Ramon," said Gianni. "Thanks for coming."

Ramon was used to being summoned by Gianni and other members of his family. They were among his best clients. Formally dressed from having come straight from court, Ramon was sweating.

"Cold beer? Or a glass of wine?" Consuelo asked.

"Beer," he told her.

"Nothing for me," said Gianni.

"What's the problem?" asked Ramon.

"Couple of detectives looking for a payday bonus," said Gianni. "Maybe following a few leads from little fish way down the food chain, but I don't think there's any danger. They're chasing rumors. They haven't got any evidence."

Ramone was not so sure. "I don't like you doing deliveries," he said. "Puts you too close to the action. I think it's time you took a break. Go away for a few weeks. The operation is running smoothly. Leave the details to me. The less you know, the better. You, too, Consuelo."

Gianni was all set to protest, but Ramone had another suggestion. "One of my clients wants to expand his internet business. I know you've been dabbling in the underground. You can help him get some traction. Introduce him around. Build up his reputation."

"What's his business?" asked Gianni.

"Usual dark web stuff," Ramone explained. "Drug dealing, money laundering, and fraud. The beauty of it is we keep your hands clean. No one knows who you are. You operate anonymously. All you need is a computer and a series of security passwords. My client supplies the technical know-how. Your role is as a middle man. A trusted associate. It's the way forward. The money to be made is astronomical. Can I tell him you're interested?"

"I've got nothing to lose," said Gianni. "I can make a fortune sitting in my pajamas in front of a computer screen. Deal me in."

* * *

Antoinette made a daring decision. She would bring Callum to live with her right under Gianni's nose. She rehearsed the story she planned to tell Gianni. The restored seafront building was destined to open the door to her freedom. Instead of escaping to her Italian home as she did so many times over the years, she'd be closer to Gianni's family home, but they would also have space that she judged to be beneficial to both of them.

"Come and give me your opinion, Jan," she urged her friend. "The whole house needs to be fitted out. I have decorating ideas, but I value your professional expertise."

Jan was happy to cooperate. "A day trip to Alicante is necessary. We'll hit all the best stores and retail outlets.

Locally we can source accessories and soft furnishings, but for a larger selection we need the city. Make a list of the rooms you mean to furnish. Internal construction we can discuss with the foreman who did your exteriors.

"The walls are plastered, ready to be repainted any color you choose, and the floors are concrete and ready to take tiles. When do you want to go?" he asked.

"Soon as you can make it," she said. "I'm anxious to finish the job and move in."

Jan could not help but observe that Gianni had looked none too happy at the celebration of the exterior completion. He wondered what he would make of Antoinette's plans to move in and live on the property.

Antoinette must never know, but he was informed that an executive at the bank let slip to Gianni about her construction project. "In all good faith," he had insisted, "Señor Gianni is a very influential customer of the bank. We didn't realize he didn't know."

Antoinette was in her element. She toured her property with an architect and the contractor whom she had come to trust after his excellent work on the restoration of the building. Together they advised and assigned a function to each of the spacious areas, taking into consideration Antoinette's preferences.

Antoinette considered all aspects, from light to shade, from hot to cold, from noise to silence; she paid special attention to the flow of smells associated with each space and reviewed the tactile surfaces underfoot. Her innate sense of grace guided her to contemplate an agreeable atmosphere that embraced the laws of harmony and beauty. Heat, air, light, color, sound, surface, space. Her new home would radiate the peace and security she craved.

Consulting her overflowing notebook, she shared her vision with the construction team she had come to know and trust. "The kitchen and utility room are to be on the ground floor," she decided, "and there will also be a cloakroom.

"Second floor is an open plan reception and dining area, and the third floor will have two bedrooms and en-suite bathrooms.

"The top floor with its spectacular views of the sea is a sun lounge with a terrace and roof garden running the length of the building."

Antoinette spent weeks making sketches, deciding on color schemes and consulting on finishes, flooring and options for fittings in the kitchen and bathrooms. She was involved with every aspect of the process and insisted on being consulted on all decisions.

"Tiled floors throughout," she instructed. "Italian tiles. I'll go direct to the factory and choose the designs myself. Each floor will have a different theme based on the four elements of fire, earth, air and water."

Two hundred years before, the structure was constructed in a stepping stone design with each floor leveled, as if built as four separate properties. "The ground floor represents the earth," said Antoinette. "The color scheme is to be brown and green and bronze. Second floor depicts fire, the heart of the home. Decorations need to be dynamic; red and orange and ruby to ignite energy and represent flames. The bedrooms and bathrooms are air, so we choose the colors of clouds, pristine white and yellow and cream. The sun lounge brings the ocean into the home so our color scheme reminds us of water and waves and rolling surf."

Antoinette and Jan were on a mission to find the best, most unique, luxurious, stylish furnishings and decorations. At all times, Antoinette carried in her pocket the polished blue stone that she had found on the beach, the one that started her on her renovation project.

"It was a message from the universe," she explained as she proudly showed the stone to those who worked with her on the seafront house. "The house is called Casa Olivia Rose and is dedicated to my daughter. From the ground up and embraced by all the elements: earth, fire, water and air. Our lives and relationship have been reborn."

Antoinette avoided telling Gianni too much about the purpose of the house. All she admitted was, "It's a scared space, a place where I can renew my spirit."

"What happens when your spirit is renewed?" he asked as they shared a rare meal up on the terrace of his cliff-top house. "Will there be a place in your heart for me?"

Antoinette lifted her gaze and watched the paragliders jump off a rocky ledge on the side of the cliff. She refused to lie and instead admitted, "I can't make any promises. Our future is in the lap of the Gods."

Chapter Thirty

Antoinette commanded Olivia Rose, "Keep your eyes shut till I tell you to open them." The pair had traveled from Alicante airport in Antoinette's red convertible, and after less than an hour on the highway, they stood together on the seafront at Altea.

Olivia Rose dreaded the visit and had delayed the dates of her trip until she ran out of excuses. She wrestled with her conscience and knew deep in heart that her mother did not deserve the pain she was ready to inflict on her. She wanted to punish her mother for a separation that she had prolonged by refusing to visit or even answer the constant letters that her mother sent.

The familiar blue border of an airmail envelope would drop into the letter box at their family home in England at least once a week and Olivia Rose was defiant that she would not read what her mother had written.

"You hurt yourself by ignoring her," her father tried to break through the barrier. "At least find out what she has to say."

He had no way of knowing that, when he was out, in secret Olivia Rose often steamed open the envelopes over a boiling kettle and avidly read the words of love from her mother. Olivia Rose knew, without doubt, that her mother loved her and, as much as she put on a brave face, she could not deny that she returned Antoinette's love. On the one hand, she wanted to hurt her; on the other, she longed to be with her.

Antoinette continued to press her to name a date to come to visit. She was persuasive and so eager to share her surprise that eventually Olivia Rose gave in.

On the journey, Antoinette quizzed her daughter about her business. "How is your company, White Roses Wedding Services?" She raised her voice above the noise of the motorway traffic. "Sounds like it's doing well. Your diary is always jam-packed. I hear you're building up a great reputation. I check out the website and see the photos of the weddings in the local paper."

"I accepted an offer to partner with the Vineyard. You know the place—on the main road out of town. A country estate that stretches for miles on the foothills, it has a restaurant, an excellent event facility and grapes as far as the eyes can see. They do tours and wine tastings. We had lunch there many times when you lived with us. You used to collect me from the riding stables."

Olivia Rose stopped and looked across at Antoinette who seemed close to tears. "Sorry, I didn't mean to bring that up. It's awkward talking about our life together. It sounds like I'm blaming you for leaving us, but I remember plenty of good things about our relationship."

Antoinette responded, "You must be able to say what you think. I'm sensitive enough to know that there must have been many times when you were angry with me."

The honesty of Olivia Rose's answer took her by surprise. "I still am. Often, I lie awake at night thinking about how I can hurt you for the pain you inflicted on me—and dad. You abandoned me. To get over that will take a lifetime."

Olivia Rose stared at the passing scenery, the mountains, the ocean and the citrus groves.

Antoinette drove and remained silent as she allowed Olivia time with her thoughts. When she was ready, Olivia Rose resumed the conversation. Like an eager child, she chatted as naturally as if she had not, a few minutes earlier, taken a knife to Antoinette's heart. "The Vineyard is a great opportunity, and they've agreed I can still run my own business. Dad insisted on that, and I was glad to follow his advice.

"Promoting the business takes up a lot of my time and energy. My trip to the Dominican Republic was a great success. The location and five-star resort is out of this world. I've had several inquiries from potential clients for the Indian Wedding on the Beach. No wonder. Even the photographs can't do justice to the full spectrum of color and elegance. The ceremony is a spectacular orchestrated theatrical event. Talk about making memories. It speaks volumes that Beyoncé and Jay Z spent their second wedding anniversary at the hotel; they had a private bungalow on the beach. I'm putting together a whole section on my website of wedding venues with celebrity connections."

"Is George and Amal Clooney's Venetian Palace still at the top of brides' wish list?" asked Antoinette, keen to re-establish friendly relations and distance herself from the painful truths.

"Yes, but you can't beat a royal wedding for sending bridal expectations sky high. Prince Harry and, before him, Prince William set brides dreaming of castles and carriages. The Cinderella story never gets old. Even modern women dream of marrying a prince and living happily ever after," answered Olivia Rose.

"Do you buy into the fairy tale?" her mother wanted to know.

Olivia Rose diverted her attention to look for a lipstick in the handbag that was open on her lap. "I haven't found the man of my dreams yet," she said. "I'll let you know when I do."

Antoinette sensed that the conversation was closed.

"Are we there yet?" Olivia Rose asked, and they both laughed.

Antoinette pulled up on the seafront half a block from her property. "We'll come back for your overnight bag," she told Olivia as she took her daughter's arm and steered her toward the promenade. The sun was warm on their faces and they were immediately above the spot where she found her talisman; she instructed Olivia Rose to face the sea and the mountains and close her eyes.

"Turn around, Olivia Rose," she whispered in her ear. "You're home. Mi casa es tu casa."

Olivia Rose turned slowly and opened her eyes.

Gleaming in the sunlight, the stonewashed building with blue shutters and rose bougainvillea cascading from the balconies stood proudly and rejoiced in its reincarnation. As if to draw attention to itself, the hand-painted sign creaked a little as it swung in the breeze and declared, "Look at me."

Casa Olivia Rose, it proclaimed for all to see.

For a moment, the home's namesake, Olivia Rose, was startled. Her eyes grew wider, and her hands covered her mouth.

Antoinette watched the smile spread across Olivia Rose's face and reached out to hug her daughter. "My home is your home," she said, "and this one is named for you."

Olivia Rose took a photograph of the sign and the house and then a selfie of her and her mother. "To send to Dad," she said.

"Do you want a tour?" asked Antoinette.

"You bet," answered Olivia Rose. "Casa Olivia Rose is gorgeous. Thank you for naming it after me."

"The house is a symbol of my desire to rebuild and restore our relationship." She smiled at Olivia Rose. "I hope you'll let me. You have an open invitation to stay here whenever you choose. The house is ours—yours and mine."

Olivia Rose followed Antoinette from room to room and floor to floor and became more enchanted by each revelation. She wasted no time in letting her know how impressed she was by what her mother had achieved. The elegance and vision of the whole project was a perfect reflection of her.

"There's no doubting where I inherited my love of beauty, style and symmetry," she told her mother and took her hand.

"Who sent the memo to say that today's outfit should be blue with white accessories?" Antoinette teased her. "Again, we are wearing almost identical dresses."

Olivia Rose wanted to make restitution for her previous hurtful remarks. "Matching titian tresses complete the picture," she observed. "Instead of mother and daughter, we look like sisters."

Antoinette was pleased but not convinced by the compliment. Youth always has the edge in the beauty stakes. "Let's go get your bag from the car and put it in your room."

At the front door, Antoinette crossed the threshold first. "Age before beauty," she reminded her daughter.

★ ★ ★

Anxious to show Olivia Rose around her town, Antoinette proposed that before dinner they walk along the whole length of the promenade as far to the east as the beach at Cap Negret and back toward the mountain overlooking the Port of Altea.

"Tomorrow I'll drive you up to the iconic blue-domed church. You'll enjoy exploring the old town with its narrow cobbled streets and fashionable galleries, boutiques and artisan stores. You'll see why Altea is called the Town of Artists."

"Tonight, we can stop anywhere along the bay if you see somewhere you'd like to try out or if we make it all the way to the Port, we can eat at my favorite Italian restaurant."

Olivia Rose was desperate to ask one question, but she held back. She fought an inner battle. One the one hand, she appreciated all her mother had done for her and could see that she did have the best of intentions. It would be cruel to inflict further hurt deliberately. Unfortunately, a desire to be a loyal daughter did not stop her desire to ask if Gianni was to join them for dinner.

No promises. Business first, as usual, he wrote in the text he sent before she boarded her flight from London. I'll get there if I can. Tomorrow no chance—I'm out of town.

Olivia Rose felt a stab of guilt as she acknowledged that, if not for a chance to see Gianni, she might have continued to refuse her mother's invitation to visit her in Spain.

Confusion and anger bubbled to the surface. Surely Gianni should have made an effort to see her. Business or no business. They texted and skyped regularly.

"You are an extraordinary girl," he told her. "Of course I want to see you again. How could I forget the night we spent together? But, it's complicated. My behavior was not honorable. You deserve better."

Olivia knew she was acting like a lovesick teenager, and truth be known, because she was so inexperienced, her emotional age was probably about sixteen. It did not escape her perception that it was almost exactly the same age her mother walked away from her family home.

Antoinette and Olivia Rose walked and talked on the palm tree-lined promenade. Both insisted on wearing their high heels even though flats would have been more comfortable.

Night-time eliminated the day as mother and daughter, arm in arm, engrossed in conversation, headed for Il Timone restaurant at the picturesque port opposite Club Nautico. A full moon reflected on the peaceful sea, and the white globes that illuminated the curve of the bay were alight. They accepted an outside table sheltered behind a plate glass window and under a hot air heater.

"Italian food is my favorite," said Olivia Rose happily.

"Mine, too," said Antoinette. "Guess it's in the genes."

Olivia Rose choose a traditional spaghetti Bolognese and Antoinette ordered salmon carbonara.

The waiter brought hot bread accompanied by tangy olive oil and wine vinegar.

"Shall we have a bottle of wine to celebrate your homecoming?" asked Antoinette.

"That would be a treat, but would we have red to go with my spaghetti or white to compliment your carbonara?"

"Neither." Antoinette called over the waiter. "We'll have a bottle of rosé," she said.

"Cheers." They clicked their glasses of rosé wine.

"By the way," said Antoinette, "according to the text I received a few minutes ago, Gianni is planning to join us for dessert."

Olivia Rose tried to hide her delight. "That's nice," she said. "I was hoping I'd see him."

Antoinette laughed. "He was under orders to make an effort to get here for our family dinner," she said. "I suppose dessert is better than a no-show."

Dinner was served, and the women thanked the waiter for the plates of steaming pasta he delivered to the table on brightly painted platters.

"Before he gets here, I want to ask you a question," said Antoinette. Olivia Rose stopped mid-twirl as she was wrapping her spaghetti around her fork.

Worried that she'd drop the cutlery, she put the fork on the side of the platter and picked up her glass.

"Go ahead," she said and took a slow sip.

"Did you father tell you I sent an email and asked him for a divorce?"

Olivia Rose could not hide the sigh of relief that escaped from her tense body. "Yes," she said. "You must be psychic because he has considered getting married again."

Antoinette steadied her hand and balanced her fork on the side of her plate, as Olivia had done a moment before. "How extraordinary. What timing. Well, I'm pleased for him," she said.

"Don't be," said Olivia Rose. "It's all gone wrong. I'll tell you the whole story, but not now."

She looked over Antoinette's shoulder as Gianni

entered the restaurant. He winked at Olivia Rose and walked to the table, kisses all round, on both cheeks for Antoinette and on the hand for Olivia Rose.

"Trust me to find the two most beautiful women in the restaurant," he said, taking his place at the table between the two of them. "A glass of house red," he told the waiter. "I'll leave the rosé to the ladies. For dessert, tiramisu."

Gianni flashed one of his winning smiles and asked, "Are we all up to date with the family news?"

Antoinette did not like his tone.

"Tell me, Olivia," he said, "how do you like the Casa Olivia Rose?"

"I love it, she told him.

Gianni fixed his gaze on Antoinette and addressed Olivia Rose. "Did your mother tell you that she plans to leave me and live there?" he asked.

"Take no notice," she reassured Olivia Rose. "He's joking. Casa Olivia Rose is to be a family home. We can all live there happily together."

* * *

The three of them linked arms and Gianni escorted Antoinette and Olivia Rose the short distance back along the seafront to Casa Olivia Rose.

"Enjoy your stay," he said politely to Olivia Rose, and as he leaned in to brush her cheek with a kiss, whispered, "I'll call you."

Antoinette turned away as he reached to kiss her

good night and with her back to him unlocked the front door. "Let me know if you need anything," she told her daughter as she showed her upstairs to the bedrooms. "I'm an early riser, so I expect to be awake before you. If not, you'll find everything you need in the kitchen downstairs."

Olivia Rose knew her mother was upset but didn't know what to say to make the situation better.

"Good night. Sleep well, darling," said Antoinette.

"Night, night, thank you for inviting me. I love the Casa O.," Olivia Rose replied. "Not many daughters are lucky enough to have a building named in their honor."

She turned her phone to vibrate and locked the door of her bedroom before heading to the bathroom. She slipped between the silky sheets and waited. More than an hour passed before Gianni kept his promise to call.

"You looked beautiful this evening," he told her. "I wanted to wrap you in my arms and hold you close to me. In fact, I wish I were with you now in your comfy bed to show you how much I've missed you. But I have to admit; you probably wouldn't get much sleep."

Olivia Rose sighed. No one had ever love-talked her in this way before. Gianni knew all the right things to say. His terms of endearment imprinted themselves on her heart and mind. "I wish I could see you," she said. "I mean you and me, without my mother."

"I've already told you I'm out of town tomorrow," he emphasized what he had told her before. "Anyway,

Antoinette is not going to leave you on your own. She's in seventh heaven to have you here with her."

"Olivia," he said, and his voice became serious. "Your mother loves you very much; you don't know how much she regrets that she walked out on you. I must take my part in the blame for that. She has been so desperately sad over the years. Now all she wants is to have a relationship with you. I've broken her heart too many times. I'm not proud of it, but I care too much about her to allow it to happen again. I promise you she would never get over it."

Gianni tried to make Olivia Rose see reason, but he was fighting a losing battle. He had not realized how impressionable and unsophisticated she was when he started the dangerous game of pursuing her.

"Does that mean we'll never be together again?" she asked in a small, sad voice.

"It's for the best," said Gianni, relieved that she seemed to have got the message. "Now let's say good-bye and we can be friends but, sadly, not lovers."

Olivia Rose was not ready to give up. In a demanding tone, she threatened, "I'll tell her. I'll tell her what happened in Florence."

Gianni froze, unsure how to handle the situation. He had walked away from many love affairs, but the women were generally grown-up about the inevitability of the ending. "Olivia," he pleaded, desperate to keep control of the situation, "what do you think that will achieve?"

"It will make me feel better," she said in a sulky

little girl voice. "You used me. I want to get my own back."

"When do you leave?" asked Gianni, buying time.

"Sunday lunchtime," said Olivia Rose.

"I guess your mother is taking you to the airport."

Determined not to lose a possible chance to see him, Olivia Rose said, "No, she asked if I would mind taking a taxi. She's going to church. I didn't know she was still religious."

Gianni ignored the remark. Of course Antoinette was religious; wasn't she an Italian Catholic woman?

"Text me the time of your flight; I'll meet you at Alicante airport."

Olivia Rose went to bed with a smile on her face. She knew how to get her way; she'd used her manipulative tactics on her father all through the years they had lived alone together. Deep in her heart, she felt guilty about betraying her mother, who was trying so hard to make up for the past, but more than that, Olivia Rose felt the need to avenge the wrong done to her.

She wasn't about to let Gianni abandon her and walk away. He had to be punished.

Chapter Thirty-One

"I promised to show you Altea's famous blue-domed church," said Antoinette to Olivia Rose as they prepared a breakfast of fresh orange juice, hot croissants with fruit jam and local cheese in the downstairs kitchen. "Dedicated to Saint Consuelo. You can see the domes for miles along the coast."

"Weddings are my business, so I visit many churches," Olivia Rose replied. "Even though lots of special venues hold licenses to marry, church weddings are still very popular in England, and I'm sure even more so in Spain."

"Our church is superb for weddings," Antoinette explained as she carried a tray up the stone staircase to the roof terrace. "The Chapel of Christ is built on the ruins of an ancient church, and was dedicated more than a one hundred years ago. It's so ornate; it sometimes feels like being inside a great big piece of wedding cake."

They both laughed.

Antoinette was not exaggerating about the ostentation display of the church on Plaza Iglesia high above the town. An awesome sight high on the hill overlooking the ocean. The highlights, the iconic blue domes and bell tower grace the square and sanctify the cobbled embattlements. Blue pottery tiles are decorated with dragon figures and curved spines while an elegant cross reaches to the sky.

Olivia Rose stood perfectly still to absorb the sight as she stood at the large wooden doors of the church on the threshold of the interior of the dome. Her eyes widened and she appeared over-awed by all the ornamentation.

"I've never seen so much pink marble, golden plating and alabaster," she said. "It does remind me of the icing on a wedding cake."

Statues of gold and an entire flower shop of white lilies paid homage to the Virgin Consuelo. "You worship here?" she asked her mother, as they sat on a polished wooden pew gazing at the gold encased altar.

"Yes, frequently. I love the theatricality of the setting and the bells and smells of incense and candles. This church knows how to do pageantry. I take part in the community events whenever possible. It fills my soul."

"I stopped going to church after you left," said Olivia Rose in a quiet voice. "I blamed God for taking my mum away."

Antoinette felt a stab in her heart at the overt criticism and the obvious intention of the guilt trip to wound, but could not blame Olivia Rose. If she had three wishes, Antoinette knew she would give them all to turn back the clock. Only now was she learning of the devastating affect her leaving had on her only daughter.

"I'm dreading asking the next question," she admitted. "Did you keep up your piano studies, or the ballet classes?"

"No," Olivia Rose shook her head. "Dad was too busy to take me and I didn't want to face the other pupils. Girls can be very cruel."

Antoinette reached out and took her daughter's hand. "I'm sorry for the pain you were caused. You didn't deserve that to happen. Will you light a candle with me here, and see if you can start to heal? If we can both start to heal."

Olivia Rose remained reluctant. "I don't believe," she said. "But you can go ahead and light one."

"I've lit a thousand," Antoinette confessed as tears poured from her eyes.

As they left the church and walked back toward the car, Antoinette asked, "Do you like macarons? I know the best place ever. The macrons are ice cream, frozen and gigantic as cartwheels."

"Macarons we can agree on," said Olivia Rose.

"Great, that's one thing we can do together; the other suggestions you may not like so much. I have tickets for a Chopin recital this afternoon at a concert venue in the town next to Altea on the coast, Albir. The pianist is a friend of mine. A very accomplished Italian musician, the artistic director of an International Classical Music Festival I attend every year. We don't need to go if you'd rather not."

"Let's go," said Olivia Rose. "We can find out if I do have a soul that can be stirred by beautiful music."

The handsome young musician acknowledged Antoinette as he walked out on to the stage and sat on a black leather stool at the Steinway grand piano. A selection of some of Chopin's most famous works resonated throughout the concert venue, and the elite audience of classical music aficionados rewarded the musician with a standing ovation.

"They're serving wine and tapas," Antoinette told Olivia Rose. "Do want to come and meet Alfredo?" Antoinette beamed as she introduced her daughter to her friend.

"Bella, bella," Alfredo exclaimed. "Your daughter is very beautiful," he complimented Antoinette.

"Do you play the piano?" he asked Olivia Rose.

Olivia Rose laughed and replied graciously, "If I did, it wouldn't sound remotely like your virtuoso performance. You were magnificent. I hope to hear you again one day."

Alfredo responded, "Then I insist your mother bring you to my International Classical Festival this year. You will both be my VIP guests."

"Thank you, that's a date," said Olivia Rose.

"Thank you, Alfredo," said Antoinette. "We look forward to attending. It's always magnificent."

He bestowed double kisses on both ladies.

On the short drive home, Antoinette complimented Olivia Rose, "Thank you, you were so charming."

"I can be." Olivia Rose grimaced. "I'm not always a brat."

"Okay, what would you like to do now?" Antoinette asked.

"I'd like to go and lie on the beach for an hour or two."

"Your wish is my command," said Antoinette. "I know a secret spot just a few miles down the coast at l'Olla, a soft, sandy beach. I'll drop you there, and, when you're ready, we can go eat at one of the little beach *chiringuitos*. They're not fancy, but the food is home-cooked and the fish is fresh-caught on the beach. We can have dinner at a creaky outdoor restaurant with the waves splashing around the rocks."

"That will be perfect," Olivia Rose agreed. "I already have my bikini in my bag."

"And I put a couple of large towels and bottled water in the trunk," her mother told her.

"By the way, is there anything else you'd like to do before we go to the airport in the morning?"

"I thought I was to get a taxi," said Olivia Rose.

"Not at all," said Antoinette. "When you suggested a taxi, I said I wouldn't dream of letting you go to the airport without me. I want to be there to wave good-bye to you."

Alone on the beach, Olivia Rose texted Gianni, No change to plans. I'm going to the airport by taxi. Mum won't be there. Can't wait to see you.

Chapter Thirty-Two

"You look like a fashion model," said Gianni, as he approached Olivia Rose who sat on a high stool at the gleaming white open plan bar in Alicante airport, drinking champagne.

Antoinette had commented on her choice of traveling outfit. "You're certainly dressed to impress."

Olivia Rose wore a figure-hugging one-piece trouser suit with a shoestring halter top in a trademark Versace gold chain print. A fitted white jacket and white stilettos completed the outfit. It was Olivia Rose's private joke. Versace for Gianni.

"You never know who you might meet at an airport or on the plane," Olivia Rose told her mother. "I always have my eyes open for potential clients. I got an upgrade to Business Class with the money you sent me."

Antoinette insisted on driving Olivia Rose to the airport and agreed to park in the short-term drop-off space for fifteen minutes, leaving Olivia Rose to go through to the gate on her own.

Olivia Rose put her plan into action. First, she needed to ensure that Gianni was inside the airport and her mother was outside. Where are you? she texted Gianni.

At Starbucks by the departure gates.

Okay, meet me at the Champagne Bar in ten minutes.

She texted Antoinette. Sorry, Mum. Before you drive off, I left a makeup bag in your car. Can you bring it to me in the terminal?

Okay, I've already left the airport. Not a problem. I'll circle around and come back. What color is your makeup bag?

Olivia Rose ignored the question. To her knowledge there was only one makeup bag in the car. She hid it at the back of the driver's seat.

Gianni sat beside her at the elegant counter and ordered a glass of Moët & Chandon. Olivia Rose acted for all the world like they were a loving couple on a date. She smiled into his eyes and moved her body close to him. If she noticed his discomfort, it did not stop her. She had waited a long time for the moment when she would exact her revenge on those who had caused her excruciating pain. Gianni deserved no mercy; he was as bad as her mother. Totally narcissistic, they each put their own needs first.

"You do understand your mother must never know we have been more than friends. From now on, you must promise me, we are family. We are friends. No one must get hurt. Let's be adult about the situation."

Olivia Rose smiled. "Excuse me, I need to send a text," she told him.

There were three texts from Antoinette. Can't find it. It's not here. Okay, got it. Where shall I meet you?

Olivia Rose replied. By the Champagne Bar.

Not much time. Antoinette was on her way.

"Gianni, I need to ask you a question. Please tell me the truth," said Olivia Rose. "Did you have anything to do with the 'fake bride' who stole my father's money?"

He looked as if he might laugh but instead shook his head. "No, not directly. I know people, not very nice people I will admit, who run those scams. Some of their targets are random, others have a personal connection. I heard something, but I was not responsible. I won't insult you by saying 'I'm sorry.' But I am sorry. I'm not proud of myself."

Olivia Rose pushed her body closer to his and rubbed her shoe against his trouser leg. Gianni stroked her cheek by way of an apology, and Olivia Rose reached over to kiss him.

Embarrassed, Gianni twisted on his stool and attempted to move away. He was not quick enough.

Antoinette had the pair in her sights as she marched across the concourse. She stepped in to separate the two of them. Her eyes blazed as she slapped Gianni across the face.

She threw Olivia Rose's makeup bag at her, and it landed on the floor. The customers at the Champagne Bar fell silent as they watched the furious scene.

"Are you satisfied?" she shouted at Olivia Rose. "Have I been punished enough?" In tears she turned and ran through the crowds in the busy airport terminal and toward the exit.

Gianni gave Olivia Rose a look of complete disdain. "How stupid of me. I underestimated you," he said. "Now your mother's heart is truly broken." Onto the shiny marble counter beside his untouched glass of champagne, he threw a fifty euro note. With no good-bye, he walked quickly to catch up with Antoinette.

Olivia Rose stooped to pick up the makeup bag from the floor under the bar, calmly walked over to a rubbish bin and dumped it. There was nothing in the bag that she wanted or needed; it had served its purpose. She felt proud of herself, except for when she had seen the pain in her mother's eyes. In that moment, she hated herself and wished she could turn back the clock. If revenge was meant to be sweet, this feeling was as bitter as acid.

Gianni caught up with Antoinette in the parking lot. She leaned against the car and wiped her eyes with a handkerchief.

"Let me talk to you," he said.

"The time for that is long past," she told him. "I've been a bloody fool. But it's finally over."

The red mark on his face showed where she hit him. "Stay away from me if you don't want me to hit you again. I couldn't trust myself to stop."

Antoinette unlocked the car door, and Gianni held it open for her while she got into the driver's seat.

"Let me drive you home," he said. She shook her head. "Will you be okay?" he asked.

"Gianni, I may never be okay again, but there's nothing you can do to help. Close the door. Don't try to contact me. I'll send for my things. Stay away from me."

"When can I call you?" he persisted.

In disbelief, she asked, "Are you crazy? I don't want to hear from you ever again. What part of 'never' do you not understand?"

Olivia Rose settled in her window seat in Business Class on the flight to London. *Revenge is sweet*, she tried again to convince herself, but the taste in her mouth was metallic. She knew the pain in her mother's eyes would haunt her for a long time. *She did worse to me,* she told herself in an attempt to justify her actions.

After Antoinette left, for the sake of her father, Olivia Rose put on a brave face, but she cried herself to sleep every night. Rage filled her, and she vowed that one day she would avenge the wrong that had been done to her. She blamed Antoinette for stealing her future and shattering a dream of happy ever after.

"Champagne, please." She smiled through her tears at the male cabin steward. "I'm celebrating the completion of unfinished business."

★ ★ ★

Jason was waiting to collect Olivia Rose at the airport. "How was your mother?" he asked when they were motoring along the highway on their way back home.

Olivia Rose had no intention of telling him even half the story, but she did want to share what she considered her greatest triumph: the fact that Gianni admitted that he had a part in scamming her father. "I repaid some old debts," she said. "The score is settled. We can all start afresh."

"Funny you should say that," Jason told her, "because I've met someone."

"Oh, no, Dad," said Olivia Rose with genuine horror.

"Not on the internet. At the local library. I went to sign up for a computer class and met this lady who was enrolling for the same course. It's synchronicity."

Olivia Rose gave him a sharp look. "I hope she's not after your money."

"She'd be out of luck, wouldn't she?" laughed Jason.

"We must never shut the door on the possibility that romance is waiting just around the corner. Or at the local library. Where would your business be if we all stopped believing in happy ever after?"

* * *

Antoinette locked her front door, unplugged the phone, pulled the duvet over her head and cried bitter tears into her pillow. She raged at the pain of her double betrayal and wallowed in the well of self-pity reserved for a woman wronged and alone.

She treated her depression with long walks on the beach, ate chocolate and ice cream, watched sad movies and listened to melancholic music that released yet more floods of tears.

Day by day, week by week, she felt herself come back to life. When she judged that she had cried and suffered enough, she considered her options. She could abandon herself and remain burned up with resentment, or she could seize the fresh start she had promised herself.

Callum's letter arrived as she surfaced from her trauma.

"I've served my sentence," he wrote. "I'm about to be released. Thoughts of you have kept me going. Am I kidding myself? Do we have a chance? Are you willing to believe in me?"

Antoinette felt a mixture of emotions: fear, excitement and anticipation. "Are you allowed to travel?" she wrote to him.

"Yes," he answered. "The justice system has decided that I've completely paid my debt to society. There are no restrictions on my release. My passport will be returned, my lawyer has confirmed."

"Then all I need to know is when you will arrive," she assured him. "I'll pick you up at the airport. Don't fly into Alicante; that place holds bad memories for me. Book a ticket to Valencia."

Callum had family matters to take care of before he left. "My mother is looking after my daughter," he wrote. "I'll stay with them for a few days and then head to Spain. I hope you don't mind, but I told my mother about you. She was worried and wanted to know where I was headed. She didn't want me getting into trouble. I told her I'd met a lady, not a girl. A person I respected and wanted to spend some quality time with in the sunshine. She laughed when I told her that you reminded me of her. In a good way. Who knows where this will lead, but after what I've been through, I promise you, I don't need drama. For once I want to work at a relationship, build it up together. Let someone see the real me. You know I'm no hero, but I will try to behave myself."

Antoinette was touched by his sincerity and obvious insecurity. She warned herself that this was not necessarily the greatest romance, but it might be the special friendship they both needed to make them feel whole.

Strange that all this should have happened when she was so alone and had no one to answer to about her actions. She had not heard from Olivia Rose and ignored all approaches from Gianni. Finally, he seemed to be getting the message.

Casa Olivia Rose would be a retreat, a home to nurse Callum back to wellness, give him tender loving care after the harshness of prison. He had entrusted her to show him the way to mental and physical health. His damaged psyche was crying out to be healed. If only she had realized earlier that her daughter was suffering, had carried the burden of abandonment for years. Perhaps it would not have erupted in so destructive a manner. Callum had admitted that the shame he felt about his stepmother, the way she made her living and the secrets he was forced to keep blighted his life. He was isolated and never felt good enough. The same thing had happened to her daughter.

Antoinette prayed that she may be allowed to help heal this damaged young man. If there was not an intervention, she felt sure his life was on a downward path. Could she save him from himself? She made a commitment that she would give it her best shot.

At Casa Olivia Rose she prepared the room Olivia Rose had used during her brief visit. She filled the bedroom with sweet smelling lavender, the bathroom with scented candles and stocked the fridge with good wholesome food.

Antoinette believed herself to be on a mission. She was seeking redemption. The restoration and renovation of her home had transformed it into the sanctuary she craved. She let her mind drift out over the rolling waves of the Mediterranean Sea and prayed for the strength to accept whatever challenges lay ahead.

Chapter Thirty-Three

Callum was the first person off the plane. He was pursued by a group of young soccer fans who were on their way to an international game. His soccer fame when he was a regular on the field and on the sports channels was eclipsed now by the news stories since his release from prison.

The fans wanted "selfies." Callum declined. "What do you want a photo of me for?" He teased them, "To make a WANTED poster?"

Casually dressed in a pressed blue button-down shirt, untucked, dark navy denims and the black and gold sneakers, of which he had several pairs, he looked every inch the athlete he had been in a previous life. Heading straight for Antoinette, he grabbed her in a bear hug and lifted her off her feet. "You look gorgeous, even better than I remembered," he said.

Antoinette smiled, there was no denying she had put extra effort into her appearance for his arrival. A couple of the fans whistled when they saw her.

She wore a red Santiago Sanchez mini dress and black Jimmy Choo sandals. Long, burnished-auburn hair fell free around her shoulders, and she wore one small diamond side clip.

In the long weeks of depression after the emotional fallout with Olivia Rose and Gianni, Antoinette had lost weight. A bonus of her misery. She adhered to the adage that "You can never be too rich or too thin."

Callum carried all his belongings in a black backpack. "Travel light, ready for flight," he joked, or at least Antoinette chose to believe it was a joke.

Her red convertible was parked in the airport parking lot. She had no intention of returning it to Gianni; she figured she was due compensation for all the years she had devoted to their relationship and for the heartache she endured. The pain was not completely erased, but an adventure with Callum might help heal the wounds.

He threw his backpack on the rear seat and climbed into the passenger seat. "I like your style," he told her. The drive from the airport to Altea always made Antoinette feel like she had come home. The mountain ranges and the dramatic views of the ocean made her feel secure, protected and enclosed.

She braced herself for the drive past her former cliff top home. A white columned temple, seen for miles around, was indeed magnificent, but she never felt at home there. It was perched atop the mountain range, which reflected shades of brown, orange, green and black and identified the ages of the rocks. Gianni was master of all he surveyed. She wouldn't put it past him to be able to identify her car from way up there on the terrace.

Antoinette pointed out to Callum examples of the idiosyncrasies she loved about Spain. The religious paintings on the sides of walls; the dried up river beds; conical trees, standing straight as sentries; metal sculptures of black bulls; and in the distance, flesh-and-blood black bulls roaming the fields.

"I got a great view of the coastline from my paragliding trip," he reminded her.

"There's a paragliding center up there near that white house," she told him.

"Perhaps I'll jump from there one day," he said.

Antoinette laughed. "Yes, and perhaps I'll jump from there one day."

Bringing him up to date on her life, she told him, "I'm pretty much settled in Altea now. There are a lot of great towns on the Costa Blanca, but Altea is special. A lot of Spanish families have holiday homes in Altea, and the visitors tend to be British, Dutch, Belgian and Russian. The atmosphere is laid back and quite refined. For one thing, we have restaurants and very few bars so the tendency of some tourists to drink themselves silly is not as apparent. Also, the beach is mostly pebbles, and we have little sand, so that deters sun worshipers and families.

"Altea is known as 'The Town of Artists,' and there is an amazing variety of art, culture and concerts. It's a great reason to live here."

"I wouldn't expect any less of you," he told her. "You're a class act, which is why I am so attracted to you."

He had told Antoinette about his mother on the

previous visit when he parasailed onto the beach at Altea. "Funnily enough, my mum is also very stylish and cultured. Before my dad left her and she had to find a way to support three kids, she'd had a very traditional middle-class upbringing. Gone to high school and expected to go to university, but got married instead.

"My dad was a successful businessman, and she stayed at home raising us kids until the day he went on a business trip and didn't come back. He sent money for a while, then the money dried up. After a while, we found out he'd been having an affair for years with the woman who became my stepmother. Mum was devastated. She and the woman she'd been left for couldn't have been more different.

"Mum started to help out at catering events for a friend and then learned that the business was really a cover for an escort agency. The money was better. Mum always insisted that her job was to man the office and she was never an escort. I didn't dare tell her that my stepmother owned the business. It was the largest agency in our area.

"'Running the office was the perfect job,' she told me when I questioned her why she stayed in that business instead of finding another job. 'With three kids at home, I could work when they were in bed.'

"The escort agency had a great reputation and after a couple of years, my mum bought my stepmother out. That was her revenge: to *make the agency the best*. It was all down to Mum. She was a great organizer and she treated the girls' right. They all wanted to work for her.

"'I've got daughters of my own, and so I work hard to keep the girls safe,' she used to say. 'I put the clients who want an escort with suitable young ladies. The girls have to make contact and arrange the dates. What they do on that date is their business. I take money up front on a credit card payment. Our service is to offer company, not sex.'"

Callum rolled his eyes. Apparently he had heard this justification all his life.

"Did you resent what she did for money?" Antoinette asked.

"I'd like to say no because she did it for us and we all got the benefit of money for anything we wanted. She was generous and a great mum. I see now that she didn't have a life outside her spare bedroom where she ran the office. She never had boyfriends, and she wasn't a party animal. She's not a drinker either. She says I get that from my dad.

"I wish, though, that she'd been in a different business, and we could still have had all the financial advantages. I'd lie awake at night hearing the phone going, but though no business was done at our house, occasionally a driver would come by to collect something. I was always worried that my friends would find out about our business. I lived two lives. I never tell her how I feel, but I know the resentment is buried deep inside me."

Antoinette listened to his story and imagined how much resentment her daughter Olivia Rose must have felt at being left alone and forced to face the condemnation of her school friends. "Callum, I think we may have more in common than you realize. I have a daughter who is still resentful of me for the life choices I made. I don't know if I'll ever be able to heal the rift with her. Perhaps you and I can help each other on the road to recovery."

★ ★ ★

Casa Olivia Rose never failed to impress. Callum was no exception. He quickly identified the place he had landed on Altea Bay but could not recall seeing the building.

"It's been totally transformed," said Antoinette. "I bought it just before your visit; it was utterly dilapidated."

Diamond-tipped waves danced on the rolling sea and crashed into the rocks on the beach.

With a hand up to his forehead to shade the sun, Callum let his gaze wander over the whole Bay. "Perfect choice," he told Antoinette, "and I haven't even crossed the threshold of the house yet. Who is Olivia Rose?"

"That's my daughter. I named the house after her, and I was trying to make restitution for being a lousy mum. It didn't work. We're estranged. But I can't take all the blame. It hurts too much to talk about yet. Come on; I'm so excited for you to see the house."

Antoinette opened the front door and led the way into the house through the kitchen, upstairs to the living room, and onward to the two bedrooms. She stepped back at the door to his bedroom and allowed him to pass.

Like stepping into a room that radiated sunshine and celebrated the great outdoors, the furnishings were a subtle blend of lemon, beige and misty green. "What a contrast. Sure beats spending twenty-three hours a day locked in a cell," he said. "Thank you for welcoming me into your home."

"Do you want to freshen up while I put the kettle on? Tea or coffee for you?"

Callum grabbed her by the waist and kissed her. "Ever since I saw you at the airport I've wanted to do that," he admitted. "I promise I won't overstep the mark. Your house, your rules,"

The kiss was long and satisfying, and Antoinette's heart did a happy dance that finally they could be together. "My bedroom is across the hall," she said. "I wanted to ensure that there was no pressure on either on us."

Callum laughed the loudest she had ever heard him. "Thank you, ma'am," he said. "I'm grateful. I wouldn't want to feel pressured by a gorgeous lady who I've flown across continents to get to and have been thinking about every day for months."

The irony did not escape Antoinette, but she was desperate not to make assumptions. The fact that he was so much younger than her was never far from her mind. She wanted to let their relationship develop, but now that he was here holding her in his arms, she was convinced she wouldn't be able to resist for long. Not when he kissed her with such intensity and looked at her with a longing she had almost forgotten existed.

She disentangled herself. "You didn't answer my question. Tea or coffee?"

"Coffee, please," he said. "But I know you're a tea drinker. That's why I brought you a pack of PG Tips from England; I didn't know if you could get them here."

"The one thing all Brits miss about home: a proper cup of tea," said Antoinette, as she accepted the square green and white box and turned to go downstairs.

"I also got you this," he said holding out another smaller package. "My mum said you sounded like a Chanel No. 5 lady. Was she right?"

"Thank you. Your mum knows her perfume." She leaned in to give him a thank-you kiss and then had to disentangle herself all over again.

"Our adventure should start now," said Callum when he came downstairs for his coffee and tapas. "Are you game for a ride on a Jet Ski?"

Determined to wrest as much enjoyment as possible from their relationship, Antoinette agreed.

"Okay, let's go. I told you I have friends who own the water sports center just south of here."

"I'm game," said Antoinette. "Will they provide a wetsuit?"

"If you insist, but I prefer to ski naked." Callum laughed one of his deep down laughs and said, "The look on your face is priceless. I'm joking. I take it you've never ridden a Jet Ski before?"

"A couple of times, long ago but I kept falling off."

Callum was enjoying the joke. "I'm not talking about being up on skis, but on a Jet Ski where I drive, you ride pillion and wrap your arms around me, so you don't fall off. I'll keep you safe."

Antoinette drove to the water sport center, and Callum hired a Jet Ski plus a wetsuit for her. She was relieved to note that he wore boarding shorts.

They took off at a furious speed, kicking up spray and foam. Her nervousness disappeared, and with the throbbing kick of the vehicle, the commanding presence of Callum as she pressed her face into his powerful back, the pounding foam and the wind whipping her hair around her face, Antoinette was soon squealing like a child on a roller coaster.

"Again," she shouted every time they finished their circuit. "Wow, this is the most fun you can have with your clothes on," she cried. "I can't believe I've denied myself the pleasure all this time."

Happy that he had found a sport to delight her, Callum suggested that next time they try paragliding.

"Don't think that's going to happen," said Antoinette. "Even flying in a regular plane gives me palpitations. But you are welcome to drop in on me anytime you like. You know where I live."

Home in the evening, they ate at the dining room table in the sun lounge and gazed out at sea. "It's different every hour of the day," she said. "I could never tire of this view."

"I could never tire of you," Callum told her. "I've come back to life." He took her by the hand and led her to the love seat in the terrace window. Sitting side by side, with classical music in the background competing with the screeching of the seagulls, they kissed and held each other.

"Nothing is going to happen that you don't want," he said. "For once I'm willing to take this slowly. I've waited long enough. A few more days or weeks or months are not going to change my mind about you."

Grateful there was no pressure, Antoinette told Callum, "You shared with me about the demons that have driven you and perhaps helped destroy your life and career. I know all about deep, dark secrets. One day I'll tell you mine, but for the time being, we start with a clean slate."

"Thank you for a wonderful time today. I felt completely liberated, even more than when they unlocked that cell door and let me out. I'm a grown man. I can't go on blaming other people for my mistakes. I always loved my mum, she's great, but now I see that she did nothing wrong. She loved me and I'm grateful for that. I've got to let go of the past. My debt to society is paid. From now on I want us to live every day feeling genuine excitement and spontaneity."

Chapter Thirty-Four

"Do you want me to scrub your back?" Callum asked as he walked into her bedroom and called from the other side of the bathroom door.

"Thanks, I'm capable of doing it myself," she answered.

"There must be a service I can perform for you," said Callum. "Let me know what it is. You may be surprised to hear that I'm a dab hand at polishing toenails. With two stepsisters, various cousins and a mother and all their friends hanging around the house, I was forced to paint their toenails so they wouldn't smudge their fingernails. I tell you, *those girls bullied me.*"

Antoinette came out of the bathroom wearing a colorful silk caftan. She sat on the bed and put her toes up for inspection. "I'll be sure to let you know the next time they need doing. But I don't know what my beautician will say about my getting a new therapist."

In his large, strong hands he held her feet and massaged them, then he kissed them and proceeded to work up her legs to her thighs. Physically they had quickly developed a close, loving relationship. Living together it seemed they were never far from each others presence.

In the kitchen performing a hundred culinary tasks, they invaded each others space and touched and stroked limbs and traded casual kisses. "How come you are always right alongside me?" she asked. "It's a big house."

"It's a tactic we use on the soccer field to intimidate our opponents. I'm a big guy. I keep getting in the other guy's way and never let him forget I'm marking him. I want you to get used to the fact that I'm marking you. I'm not going anywhere. I'm sticking like glue to you."

In the sun lounge overlooking the sea, they sat side by side and read, listened to music, watched television. Antoinette was constantly aware of Callum's athletic physique on show in sports T-shirts and figure-hugging shorts. His masculine smells pervaded her house, and in every room, she inhaled the overpowering psychic energy of his body.

Strong muscled arms caressed her, and with one foot stroking her thigh and his hips and torso pressed against her, she waited for the moment when the physical need would envelope them, and they would kiss and remain locked in an embrace for hours.

For such a robust and commanding presence, Callum was surprisingly tender. He never rushed Antoinette. "I'm like a cat," he told her. "I have infinite patience. I watch and wait and then pounce."

This scenario excited but also scared Antoinette. Having invited a young man, one she hardly knew and a jailbird at that, into her house, she could not claim to be unaware of his intentions. Or her own. An internal clock was ticking, and she imposed on herself certain boundaries until she felt the time was right to let go, give in and accept the inevitable.

Like a comfy old married couple, they settled into a daily routine. Fresh food shopping every day was a must for Antoinette. The gym was a must for Callum.

"Come to the gym with me," he asked. "Then I'll come to the market with you."

"My body doesn't like being pushed and pulled and juggled about. Sorry, I'm not a gym bunny. Now dancing, that is my thing. I'll dance till dawn. I love tango and waltz and salsa."

He backed away. "I can only dance on my own, disco style," he admitted, "and then only when I'm drunk."

"Okay, compromise," said Antoinette. "I'll do my dance fitness class and meet you afterward to go food shopping."

He strode off down the promenade, and as she watched him go, Antoinette felt a glow of satisfaction. She could never have believed during the grieving time of her pain over Gianni and Olivia Rose that one day she would be this happy. She felt proud, protective and purposeful. For all his bravado, Callum had the wound of the loss of his career to cause him disgrace and humiliation. No longer could he tell people he was a professional athlete. He was not allowed to work in any athletic capacity that paid money.

"Charity events were always a favorite for me," he told her. "I wanted to give back, but it's not the same now. I don't even feel good enough to be around those worthy people. I'm branded as an athlete who brought the game into disrepute. The most fun I've had lately was in prison when they made me captain of the prison soccer team.

"The governor talked to me about coaching youngsters. He thought I could find it very rewarding and be an example. 'Yes, a bad one,' I told him. He tried to persuade me that everyone makes mistakes and that it takes a big man to admit his and give back to those who may be in danger of going off the rails. I'm going to have to do something with the rest of my life, but I'm not sure I'm ready for youth club soccer."

Callum's prison sentence was not directly linked to his taking of a banned substance or the lifetime ban from professional sports. The offense for which he was jailed was an assault on his ex-wife's boss while drunk, on the day he learned of the ban.

"My head spins with it all," he admitted. "It was bad enough to be banned, but in my opinion, I could hold my head up because I knew I was made a scapegoat. The coach gave me the drug and said it wasn't detectable. To ensure I didn't make that public, I was given a big pay-off. It could all have been swept under the carpet. A four-year ban, or, who knows, I may even have been able to play again. Not at the same level I was, but in a junior league somewhere. But now I'm a jailbird; no one is going to take a chance on me."

"Is there no way you can get the ban reduced or lifted?" asked Antoinette.

"Don't even think about it," he said. "I'm more likely to fly to the moon."

* * *

For all her adult life Antoinette had been making daily trips to the market. Now, with Callum alongside her, she rediscovered a joy in the sights, sounds and smells of the farmers' market. A vast array of every kind of fruit and vegetables made up a kaleidoscope of goodness and freshness. Red tomatoes alongside yellow peppers with green and white cabbages, firm asparagus stalks, ten varieties of potatoes, lettuce, carrots, parsnips. Every imaginable vegetable displayed like works of art, and each stall competing with the one alongside it.

Callum loved to flirt with the matronly lady stall holders.

"I need help," he'd tell them. "Which apple should I buy?" he'd ask while holding two or three in his big hands.

The ladies simpered under his smile and went into lengthy explanations about which apple was best. "To eat, to cook, for the family, for digestion?" they'd ask. He'd weigh up their answers and make his selection. Both sides enjoyed the transaction.

Sweet cherries, chunks of pineapple, delicious coconut, all were offered for a personally recommended taste test. These interchanges continued all around the market. "Does this orange have seeds? Which strawberries are the sweetest? Which plums are best to make a pie? Did you burn these almonds?"

Every new day provided a new adventure.

Fresh salmon, chicken, prawns passed the test and

made their way into his shopping basket. Back home, Antoinette drew up the menu, and with Callum's help, they prepped the meal together.

"Call me when you're ready for a walk," he shouted as he left the kitchen and climbed the stairs. An evening promenade always saw them return to the house with hearty appetites.

Dressed in skinny white jeans, a sports T-shirt that showed off her figure and a pair of lace-up gold boots, Antoinette grabbed a light jacket and called up the stairs that she was ready to go.

Callum came down the stairs, and his face turned bright red as he saw her standing at the front door. "What the hell are you playing at?" he shouted.

Completely confused, Antoinette burst into tears. "What? I mean, I don't know, what is it?"

Like a rabbit frozen in the headlights, Callum stared at her. "My trademark. My golden boots. Everybody knows I wear golden boots."

Antoinette regained her composure. "Everybody may know back in England, at least those people who follow soccer. I have never heard of this."

Slumping against the wall, Callum began to cry. "Of course you don't know," he said. "I'm a jerk. I'm sorry. There are still things that trigger the anger and regret. My gold boots are one of those. I couldn't look at them after I was banned from the game. It seemed like hubris. I'd flown too high, and the gods sent me crashing back to earth."

"Give me a minute. I'll go change," said Antoinette.

"They're new; I only just bought them. They're very fashionable. I'll exchange them tomorrow."

"Thanks," said Callum. He was still shaking as they left Casa Olivia Rose for their evening stroll.

They held hands as they walked and talked. Callum explained to Antoinette the brooding, dark feelings that still lay buried in him. "I work hard to make sure I don't unleash my uncontrollable anger. I always had a temper, but I saved the aggression for the sports field.

"My job was to be out there pumping it up, doing battle for all the thousands of guys in the stadium and thousands more at home. I was a warrior. Now I've got nothing left to fight. I've still got the anger though. Sorry, about the gold boots. It was a shock."

Antoinette knew from their first meeting that Callum had the fire of the demons deep inside. She felt them in his bodily vibrations, pulsating energy that threatened to break out like the Incredible Hulk. She admired the fact that he kept them so contained but did not fool herself that somewhere inside her gentle giant lay the seeds of destruction.

They slowed their steps as they reached a secluded rocky inlet alongside granite caves. The rocks were unstable underfoot, and Callum lifted Antoinette and carried her the last few yards.

Wearing his black leather jacket, which protected him from the jagged shingle, Callum leaned against the cave entrance and pulled Antoinette to him. He held her with all his might and almost squeezed the breath out of her. "Easy, tiger," she told him. "I'm here; I'm not going away. You're not alone. You have someone who loves and understands you."

As if giving her the kiss of life, he pressed his mouth roughly into hers. His kisses were passionate, demanding and unrelenting. His hand gripped her neck, and she clung to him as if her very life depended on it.

Above the sound of the rushing waves and the water trails that fell from the cave roof and splashed her face, Antoinette let Callum know that the time had come. No more holding back; she wanted him as much as he wanted her.

"Let's take this home," she said.

Casa Olivia Rosa was the setting she had imagined for their first lovemaking. She held his hand and led the way up the stairs, all the way to her bedroom. The shining rays of the evening sun made patterns on the bedspread. A sea breeze gently rattled the window frame and made its entry to the room trailing the smell of nighttime jasmine and orange blossom.

Callum undressed first and helped her to remove her clothes, which were damp from the sea and surf. He gathered them in one hand and threw them straight through the open door onto the tiled bathroom floor. "Laundry is not my department," he said.

All the fears that Antoinette had tortured herself with about whether her body would meet his approval, faded away.

"Finally, I get to see you naked," he told her in a tone of reverence. "It was worth waiting for."

Antoinette stood before him and allowed herself to

be scrutinized. "You have a figure like Venus," he said. "Spotless skin, full breasts, curvy hips and long, slim legs. All woman."

Antoinette giggled. She delighted in having received his seal of approval.

Callum reached out for her and slowly, sensuously ran his hands all over her body. His touch was enough to fire her passion. "I've never waited to make love to a woman before," he told her. "Most girls these days are pretty easy to get out of their clothes, and then I lose interest. All the mystery is gone. With you I've jumped through hoops.

"I knew the first day I met you on that ferry to Ibiza that I wanted to get you into bed. Who could have dreamt it would take so long?"

"Now I think you've kept ME waiting long enough," she said and reached for him.

Callum obliged by picking her up and positioning her on the bed. He pinned her hands above her head, spread-eagled her legs and placed himself on top of her. The full weight of his masculine body took her by surprise. She was anchored. Secured. Unable to move.

His lips pressed hard against hers, and his tongue moved urgently inside her mouth. Antoinette felt her whole body embraced, engulfed, enveloped. Every sense was on fire. Her body temperature soared, she heard the wretched seagulls circling the building and smelled the glorious fusion of sex ignited between a man and a woman.

Callum raised himself above her and with one

mighty thrust penetrated her. If there is such a thing as a born-again virgin, she would have vowed she was one at that moment. The bittersweet pain and pleasure, the feeling of being taken. She responded with a fervor that burst from her soul, releasing emotions she had not allowed herself to feel for decades. Antoinette gave herself to Callum, rejoiced in their lovemaking and allowed herself to be led deep down to an eternal place of passion and fever and decadence.

Joyfully they rode the wave of possession and power. Antoinette was taken back to the first time they rode a Jet Ski. This time the vehicle driving the fury was Callum, not a machine. They became one. They rocked their world together and climaxed together on a huge rolling ocean of spray and foam.

The anticipation of the wait ensured that they savored every moment and glorified the love they had discovered for each other.

"The great romance doesn't have to last forever," Antoinette told Callum as they lay together exhausted and satisfied. "But, it does have to be true. Love is too precious to be a game."

Chapter Thirty-Five

"This is the third time I've asked. Are you coming home for dinner, Callum?" Antoinette was fast learning that after living as a single man for all his teenage and adult life, Callum Lavelle did not appreciate having his movements questioned. Alone in England as a schoolboy trainee when he signed a contract with his first English soccer club, his family remained home in Ireland. Only later would they follow him, when he was rich enough to buy them all houses.

He answered angrily, "I told you. Don't wait for me."

Antoinette made a concerted effort to not wait for him for all of the next two hours. She decided to go ahead and eat, but, even sitting in her favorite sea watching chair, she discovered she had no appetite. The television news program she liked to watch with her meal held no attraction.

The words of the book she was reading, blurred. She stared out to sea. Furious and frightened. Gianni had put her through this a thousand times. But there was a major difference. Gianni was always true to his basic character. Predictably unpredictable.

Callum was a horse of a different color, a Jekyll and Hyde character. Of course, Antoinette knew that he had previously had a drinking problem. Naively she thought it was in the past.

"I got sober in prison," he told her. "Promised myself I would never drink again."

Antoinette did not know when he had started drinking again, but it became a more and more frequent occurrence.

"I'll have a small beer," he told her when they stopped for tapas at a seafront cafe. A Spanish guitarist played love songs and walked around the tables soliciting donations. One stare from Callum soon saw him off.

"I thought you didn't drink," she challenged him.

"Well, a small beer is hardly drinking, is it?" he answered. There was an edge of anger in his voice, and the conversation ended there.

A few nights later, the situation was repeated but this time Callum did not stop at one beer. He gulped down several bottles of the local San Miguel beer, and Antoinette detected a discernible relief in him as he stretched back and relaxed into an evening's drinking.

Antoinette raised her eyebrows as he ordered yet another, and Callum turned nasty. "Don't count and don't look at me like that," he warned her.

Though his behavior changed when he drank, Antoinette observed that he did not slur his words or stagger as they walked home. He obviously was used to consuming large amounts of alcohol.

Within a few weeks he was insisting on adding bottles of liquor to their supermarket shopping. The carefree lifestyle they had developed over the months when he was not drinking was gradually eroded.

Misunderstanding and rows erupted between them. Usually when Antoinette suggested that Callum should not drink—or at least not drink so much.

His outbursts of temper grew more frequent and many nights they slept in separate beds as Antoinette could not stand the smell of alcohol on his breath.

After rows, there always followed the apologies. "I'm sorry, please forgive me," Callum pleaded, close to tears. "I don't mean to take it out on you. I love you. I don't want to destroy what we've built up. I'll stop drinking, I promise."

For a while he was on his best behavior and to prove his good intentions, one evening he surprised her with a special treat. Served in a tall-stemmed sugar-rimmed crystal glass on a silver tray as if by magic, having said he would prepare dessert, he presented her with an exotic dish of homemade ice cream.

"I made it myself from an ancient Persian recipe I found in one of your oriental cookbooks." He glowed with pride. "Saffron and rosewater ice cream sprinkled with gold-tipped rose petals."

Antoinette declared it the most delicious ice cream she had ever tasted. Never before had she felt so spoiled.

With Callum seemingly genuinely contrite, Antoinette eagerly believed that he meant to stop drinking, and she took her chance to suggest he get help.

"You could go to a doctor or Alcoholics Anonymous or a treatment center," she suggested.

"Yes, yes, I'll think about it," he said, "if I get bad enough."

Day after day, the life they had together as a couple began to unravel. Antoinette hated the woman she had become. She behaved like a nagging wife, a worried mother, a jealous girlfriend.

"What a fool I've been," she berated herself but still she went on caring. *"I lose everyone I love. Olivia, Gianni, now Callum. None of them want to be with me. I must be the worst person in the world."*

"What time will you be home?" she called after Callum as he bounded down the stairs and out the front door. "Where are you going? Who are you going with?"

Making his way home always seemed the furthest thing from his mind.

Do you want a ride? she texted Callum. She had no idea where he was. He had been out as usual since lunchtime. He'd taken to indulging in dangerous sports at his friend's water sports center.

After she had refused several invitations to join him at the sports center, for perfectly legitimate reasons, he stopped asking if she wanted to go. He refused to accept she had commitments; he had none.

No thanks. No ride, he texted some twenty minutes after she sent the message. Then a PS, I'm not a kid.

To hell with you, she thought, but the ride was not about him, it was about her. What he called her need to control him. Maybe he was right. When Callum first moved in some months previous, he was dependent on her. He had no life in Altea, no friends, no contacts, just her. Gradually he became connected with guys at the gym and those who ran the water sports center.

In many ways, he was as loving and kind as he had been in the beginning of their relationship. He seemed intuitively to know what was acceptable in their situation.

They breakfasted together, went to the market together and ate dinner together, most nights. More important, as far as Antoinette was concerned, they slept together. More or less. They maintained separate bedrooms. Callum was often up and out to the gym at 6 a.m., and he claimed he didn't want to disturb her.

Her mind tortured her. Every aspect of their life together became suspect. Was he making phone calls to someone when he was alone in his room? Had he found himself a gym bunny—one who liked to work out at 6 a.m.?

Callum claimed he wanted to work at their relationship, build it slowly, learn to love and trust the other. Become a true partnership. That grand plan had gone out of the window. How quickly he appeared to have tired of her.

What do I do wrong? she asked over and over in her mind. *What is wrong with me?* She despised how pitifully she had turned from a happy, self-confident woman who had learned to deal with her problems to this emotional wreck who was beginning to regret ever having met Callum Lavelle.

She heard his key turn in the door. There was never a way to know what to expect. He might be charm itself and stagger off amiably to bed, taking her with him even though she loathed the smell of alcohol on his breath. Alternatively, he was frequently in a talkative mood.

Antoinette disappeared into the cloakroom, checked that her eyes showed no sign of crying and reapplied her lipstick. Standing in the hallway, she noticed he was being held up by the wall and his breath stank of booze.

"You got home okay?" she asked.

"Yes, thanks for the offer of a lift. Sorry if I was rude, but I do know the taxi number."

Now started a gentle dance of words. To ask, "Where have you been?" would be taken as an accusation. Antoinette counted the beats. Where was he headed, upstairs to bed or to the kitchen? Kitchen was the usual euphemism for a drink.

Callum sat at the breakfast bar and patted a stool next to him. "Come and sit down and talk to me. I've had an exciting afternoon and want to tell you my plans."

Pleased to have a positive response, Antoinette sat beside him and waited. "Do you have any champagne?" he asked.

Warning bells rang. There was not much in the way of wine, beer or spirits that Antoinette didn't have in her well-stocked larder.

"I won't have any, thanks," she said. "I've got a bottle of wine opened in the fridge."

He rolled his eyes. "Okay, you don't want to hear my good news?"

"Of course, I do," she said, "but it's late to be opening a bottle of champagne."

The atmosphere in the kitchen dropped a few degrees.

"Are you telling me when and what I can drink?" asked Callum.

"I'm excited to hear your news," she said in an attempt to deflect the row she sensed was coming. Antoinette made herself busy taking out glasses and ice and coasters and cutting up lemons. Into a wine glass for her, she poured sparkling water and added ice and lemon.

"Callum?" she asked holding up the opened bottle of wine.

He nodded and added another roll of the eyes to show his disdain. He was acquiescing, but he wasn't happy.

Antoinette judged that for reasons that would become clear, he needed to get her on his side.

"Tell me," she said, handing him the glass of wine.

Glass in hand, Callum visibly relaxed. She had begun to observe that once he started drinking he had an uncontrollable urge to keep topped off. She would top off the glass as slowly as possible, but she had no control over how fast he drank.

"My friends at the water sports center, you know the guys—they also own one of the extreme sports franchises for paragliding, jeeps, off-road vehicles, sky-diving—have made me a business proposition. They want me to join with them on one of their operations. That's where I've been tonight. We were working out the details. Honest, it's a great opportunity. You know I love all the sports, and now I'd get to take part while I'm showing the tourists around, and I'd have my own business."

"That's wonderful," said Antoinette, but she didn't think it. Spending even more time with his mates, drinking, hanging out and calling it business was not, in her opinion, a recipe for success.

"You think so?" asked Callum, and she wished with all her heart that she could see this opportunity as a challenge, not a disaster. Callum looked so sincere and so in need of her approval that Antoinette knew she would concede and give him the benefit of the doubt. She could see advantages, and it was the perfect business for him. Boy toys.

He held his glass out for another drink. Antoinette stifled a yawn. "Explain to me how it will work," she said. "Are you a partner or an employee? Is it a franchise or a limited company? Who owns what and who is legally responsible?"

Callum's eyes darkened. "I didn't ask for an inquisition,"

"Spain is a very bureaucratic country," she reminded him, "full of red tape and you are not a citizen, not even a resident. You don't have a bank account; how will you transact business?"

He looked daggers at her.

"Oh, I see," said Antoinette. "I thought I might have a role to play in this scheme."

"Don't act so bloody superior. You know I've got the money; I need help to transfer it."

"That's called money laundering," she told him.

"Not if we're partners," he said.

"You've been giving this serious thought. Are we talking personal or business partners?" she wanted to know. "Let's leave it till morning. It's far too late at night for this conversation."

Callum gave a howl of pain. "Here we go again. I can't believe you said that. Exactly like my mother. You could have added, 'You've got school tomorrow.' I was never allowed to question her or anything she did. I'd hear her running her business and talking on the phone at all hours of the night.

"How dumb was I that I'd believe she was talking to a friend. I was ignored. Be quiet, and you'll get more pocket money. You're only a kid; it's none of your business."

Antoinette anticipated the meltdown, the tears and the remorse that would be on him next day like a tiger.

"You're just like her," he challenged. "Domineering, controlling, always right."

"I'm sorry," said Antoinette. "I've had a long day. I really need to go to bed. We'll talk about your business plans in the morning. I can see it's a great proposition, we only have to see if it's workable."

Callum smashed his empty glass into the sink. "Yes, Mum," he said.

Antoinette knew better than to go too close when he was in this mood, but she did want to try to make things right. "Give me a good-night kiss," she said.

"Get away from me," he yelled, and the force of the push propelled her into the top kitchen cupboards. One of the doors handles hit her in the right eye and within minutes a bruise began to appear.

"Oh, God," said Callum. "I'm sorry. I didn't mean to do that. You know I didn't mean to do that. Let me get you ice and help you to bed."

Lying on her double bed with an ice pack covering her eyes, Antoinette was in no mood for forgiveness.

"This only happens when I've been drinking," said Callum, as if that were an excuse.

"Pardon me; I thought you had given up drinking before you came here. You told me you got sober in prison. Why did you start again?"

"I wish I knew," said Callum, as if the decision to put alcohol into his system was way out of his control. "Please give me one more chance; I promise it won't happen again."

Antoinette took away the icepack and made him look directly into her bloodied and bruised eye. "You're damn right, it won't happen again. I make my decisions sober," she told him, "and I carry them through. This is not the first time. But it will be the last."

Chapter Thirty-Six

Antoinette stood her ground. Gianni was the enemy. She refused to allow him back into her life. He tried every way imaginable to make her relent. Phone calls, texts, letters, emails, deliveries of bouquets, even a diamond bracelet in a red velvet lined box. She threw it in a drawer. Out of sight, out of mind. Like the man himself.

Except she knew he observed her and her house. Sometimes from the parking lot opposite, sometimes from a vantage point on the street behind.

Going about her daily business, he attempted to approach her. She turned her back and walked the other way.

"I love you," he pleaded as they waited side by side for the traffic lights to change.

"You have a funny way of showing it," she shot back.

"Please, listen to me. I'm going crazy. I don't know how to get through to you."

"It should have been easy; I was right by your side."

Preparing to drive out of the supermarket underground parking garage late one evening, Antoinette was abducted.

"Do as I say, and you won't get hurt," said a voice from the back seat as she got into her car. She could make out a shadowy figure crouched down in the rear behind the driver's seat. "Drive, and I'll tell you when to stop." The voice was indistinct.

"To the seafront and make a left at the lights opposite the international flags and fountains. Take the first right off the main road, the sports ground is on the left, stay to the right and drive down the gravel road. Pull up."

The darkness was falling, and she could see no one else around. She turned her lights up brighter. All of her instincts told her that the person in the back seat of the car was Gianni. But what if she were wrong? Antoinette was finding it difficult to breathe. She reached for a bottle of water in her car door. Her hands trembled, and her foot on the gas pedal threatened to cramp.

"Please, stop this game, whatever it is you're playing. What do you want from me?"

There was no answering sound from the silence. Antoinette wanted to turn around but was scared.

"You know I'm not going to hurt you," said a voice she did recognize. "Did you think I wouldn't keep a key for my car? I could have driven it away anytime I wanted."

Antoinette whirled on Gianni like a mad thing. "I'm going to kill you," she screamed. "How dare you do that to me? I was frightened out of my skin. Get out of the car. NOW," she said.

"Annie, Antoinette," he said. "Let me talk to you.

Please, let me talk to you. I need to try to explain. What you saw at the airport was not real. Your daughter staged the whole thing. From some sick place in her mind, she wanted to destroy the relationship between you and me. I was an innocent party. Honest. She texted and asked me to meet her at Alicante on the day she was leaving for London. I presumed you would be there. I didn't know what was happening. I don't know if she was drunk. Was that why she chose the Champagne Bar? Is she on drugs?"

Antoinette ignored the question. "I'm supposed to believe you?" she asked.

"Please, Antoinette, can I come into the front seat?" asked Gianni.

"Yes, if you want to risk me driving off and leaving you stranded."

"Okay, I'll stay where I am. I don't have anything else to say. That's what happened. I was tricked. Nothing happened between us. Honest. Cross my heart and swear to God."

Antoinette put her head down on the steering wheel and cried. Gianni leaned forward as far as his arms could reach to try to touch her and comfort her. "I don't know what to believe," she sobbed. "I've been hurt enough. Let me get on with my life."

"Your life with Mr. Muscles, you mean?" asked Gianni.

"What do you know about my life with Callum?"

"You underestimate me if you don't think I know; I know everything. I wanted to go in and kick him out the first day. I was furious that you moved a man into your house. And," he hesitated, "I was hurt. I was being blamed for something I hadn't done, and you wouldn't answer my calls. I tell you I've been going crazy."

Antoinette felt sympathy for him. "If, and it's a big if, you are telling the truth about you and Olivia Rose, I'm sorry. My daughter had no right to treat you in that manner."

Gianni knew that only by throwing all the blame onto Olivia Rose did he stand any chance of making Antoinette see the problem as hers, not his. Her daughter. Not his. Swearing to God? Not his problem. He lapsed years before. "Antoinette," he said, "promise me one thing. You will take care. If he ever hurts you, you must call me immediately. I'm always here for you. 24/7. I hear he drinks too much, and he's been involved in a couple of stand-offs with some of my associates. Don't put yourself in danger. Call me. And when you're ready to ask him to leave and invite me back into your home, I'll be there quicker than you can say GIANNI."

"Thank you, Gianni," she said. "I'll remember what you said, but hopefully it won't be necessary. Where shall I drop you?"

* * *

Now she was in need of a protector, but pride stopped her from calling him. However, she did need a contingency plan, and Gianni was pivotal to that plan.

It saddened her to realize she had begun to consider Callum a naughty schoolboy who so often acted out.

Her dream had been to rehabilitate him, to heal him, to walk with him to the dark places where his demons resided and set him free. She smiled at her naivety. If only it were so easy. Sober, he was one of the most polite, charming, thoughtful young men she could hope to meet. He was funny, intelligent and loving. On good days, he made her heart sing. On bad days, he broke her heart into a million pieces.

His rampant sexuality opened her whole being to a depth of lovemaking she hadn't previously experienced. Having had only two men in her life, Gianni and Jason, she was no expert. Jason was a conservative English gentleman not given to great physical or emotional displays. Gianni was a keen, robust young lion who thrived on the thrill of the hunt and plentiful supplies of fresh meat. Always on the prowl, always on the move.

Enough is enough, she admitted. *Callum has to go.* Antoinette hid her bruises behind makeup and dark glasses, but when she ran into Gianni as he parked his motorcycle on the promenade a few days later, she was wearing a bandage.

"What happened?" he asked, pointing at her eye. Antoinette cursed her misfortune in running into him tonight of all nights. "It was an accident. I hit myself in the face with a kitchen cupboard door. Honest, Gianni. I'd tell you if it was anything else."

Gianni glared at her. "You can't lie to me, Antoinette."

"Gianni." She grabbed his arm. "Don't make this worse. I'm okay. I don't need your help. Why don't you believe me? Everything is fine. You'll be the first to know if I need your help."

She crossed the parking lot, headed up the ramp, weaved between the evening traffic on the sea road and walked the few yards to her house. Outside she stopped and slowed down her breathing. Her heat was pumping. She composed herself and breathed in the smell of nighttime jasmine. The Casa Olivia Rose sign, still creaking, swung gently backward and forward in the breeze. She remembered how happy she was the day she'd painted the sign and decided to name the house for her daughter.

Life plays cruel tricks. She sighed. Her romance with Callum started off with such promise. Now a black cloud hung over their relationship and any possible future. Fingering the set of rosary beads she always carried in her pocket, Antoinette said three Hail Marys in quick succession. She opened the front door and called up the stairs, "I'm home." No reply, but she knew Callum was upstairs.

On the way past the bedroom, she dropped her handbag on a small ottoman beneath her jewelry table, hung her jacket in the closet and changed out of her outdoor shoes.

Up in the sun lounge, Callum watched sports on television.

There was a bottle of beer on the table in front of him, and he wore his workout clothes from the gym that morning. Or possibly from riding a Jet Ski in the afternoon.

Antoinette had given up asking him to change out of his sweaty clothes before sitting on her custom-made sofas. That was nagging woman talk. "Have you had a good day?" she asked while removing her dark glasses. The bandage was in place.

"Still wearing your badge of honor, I see. Good days, bad days, they're all pretty much the same." He shrugged. "Who were you talking to in the parking lot?"

Of course, perhaps she should have realized, he would be able to see her in conversation with Gianni.

"Friend of mine," she said and walked over to look out the terrace windows.

"Looked like you had a row."

"No, but you know the Italians. They get pretty heated about things."

"He's Italian?"

"Yes, he's Italian. There are a lot of us!"

"I've never seen you talking to him before."

Antoinette slumped into a chair. "Why would you? You don't know my friends. You don't go to mass or the spa."

"He goes to the spa?"

"No, he doesn't go to the spa. Well, I don't know if he goes to the spa. He's a friend of mine. An old friend of mine."

"An old boyfriend?"

Antoinette exploded, "What difference does it make,

he's a friend of mine." She stood up and made her way to the stairs. "Have you eaten? I'll make us something."

Callum's eyes blazed. "I want to know who he is."

There was an insistent knocking on the front door. Antoinette took the opportunity to make her escape down the stairs. "You soon will know who he is," she called up to Callum.

"He's at the front door."

Antoinette answered the door.

"Tell him I want to see him," demanded Gianni.

Callum walked down the stairs and asked, "Who wants to see me?"

"I do," said Gianni. "Let's take this outside."

Antoinette raced back upstairs to the sun lounge and watched the two men walk across the road, across the parking lot and down the stairs to the small rocky stretch of beach.

She wished she could stop what was about to happen. She had never meant for it to go this far. Why on earth did they choose to settle their differences on her special patch of the beach? Right where she found her lucky star rock.

In horrified fascination, she saw Gianni remove his motorcycle jacket. Callum wore a sports hoodie that he kept on. Scuffling and pushing and pulling, the two men challenged each other. A bumped shoulder, raised knee, a kicked foot, grappling with fingers and hands and arms. Gianni threw the first punch, and Callum responded by gripping his head in an arm lock. He punched Gianni in the face and Antoinette looked away; it was too horrible to watch. She started to beat her fists on the glass of the roof terrace doors, shouting at them to stop. She yanked open the full-length door and ran onto the roof terrace, shouting at the top of her lungs, "Stop. Please stop."

The promenade was deserted, and there was no one to hear her pitiful cries. Certainly not the two brawling men on the beach far down below. Antoinette sank to her knees. Her face and body felt every blow. One powerful punch put Callum on his knees, and she saw Gianni help steady him before he fell backward onto the rocks. The darkness obscured the fighters, and with both dressed in black clothes, she had trouble seeing who was doing what to who.

Antoinette grabbed her phone and ran. Tripping over the steps, she kicked off her flimsy indoor ballet pumps and ran down four flights of stairs. Toward the beach she ran dreading what she would find. Barefoot, her feet slapping onto the smooth paving stones on the box tree shaded sidewalk, she ran over the crosswalk, the blue painted cycle path and through the parked cars in the bays on the one track road. She watched in horror as Gianni roared on his black motorcycle up the side ramp toward the main road. At lightning speed, he accelerated through the traffic lights and was gone.

On the stony beach, she found Callum, bloody, bruised and dead. In her arms, she cradled his body and rested his head on Gianni's leather jacket, which was lying close by.

"Callum, I'm sorry," she told him over and over

again. "112 emergency," she screamed into her cell phone to make herself heard over the sound of the pounding waves. "Quick, I need an ambulance and police. On the beach by the seafront parking lot."

"We've got it. The emergency services are on their way."

Seconds later she heard sirens enter the seafront road. The vehicles screeched to a halt beside the rocky beach.

Antoinette was guided away from Callum's body by the paramedics. "I'll come to the hospital with him," The paramedic looked sympathetic look as he realized that she had not understood. "He's dead. He's in a body bag heading for the morgue. You may be required to identify him."

An evening rain started to fall, and Antoinette's tears flowed with the rain and formed a torrent. Her clothes, her hair and her face became engulfed. "We'll need his details and yours," said a young police officer who followed her to the brown-lacquered bench where she sat, head in hands on the promenade.

"Can you tell us what happened, ma'am, and your relationship to the deceased?"

She gave all the information she had, and when asked for the name of the man Callum was fighting, she gave Gianni's details.

"Have you spoken to him since he left the scene of the incident?" the officer asked.

"No," she said.

"We'll need to talk to you again, but it'll hold till tomorrow."

"Do you want me to call Gianni?" she asked.

"Are you his next of kin?" She shook her head,

"No, we're not married. His father is head of the family."

"Then I can't give you any information," said the officer.

"What do you mean? What's happened?" She looked into the policeman's eyes.

"Please, please. Tell me what's happened."

Perhaps because he was inexperienced or he saw the fear in her eyes. The officer looked away and said so quietly she almost did not hear, "There was a motor-cycle accident up on the mountain road."

"No," she screamed, "no. Not Gianni, not Callum. Please, God, don't take both of them." Soaked, bare-foot and distraught, she was in a state of near collapse. Gianni's number was on her speed dial. The signal was dead.

Chapter Thirty-Seven

The family closed ranks and took care of arrangements for Gianni, whose body was found beside his crashed motorcycle on the treacherous cliffside road. The British Consul helped Callum's family repatriate his body to Ireland. Both families excluded Antoinette and erased her from the lives of their menfolk.

Antoinette sunk into such a depth of depression she hardly knew or cared about funerals, coroners' reports or police investigations.

Two warriors fighting on the sand. Both sacrificed their lives. Antoinette's spirit drained from her and her soul died that day. Casa Olivia Rose was plunged into a period of mourning.

Windows and shutters and drapes remained closed. Antoinette's bright, sun-filled master bedroom disappeared under a sea of dark covers, shades and cloaks. Every chink of light was eliminated.

Antoinette had no desire to see or feel anything. A favorite gold-framed oil painting of her beloved Altea church and a golden starburst mirror were covered up. Blackness descended. No sights, no sounds, no essences. Her mind closed down. Life was draining from her.

Every morning she climbed the stairs down to the front door and collected her supplies for the day. A blue plastic beach chair, blanket, towel and an ice pack with water and grapes.

Dressed in a full-length black velvet dress with a woolen long-sleeve cardigan, she hid her tangled, red hair under a black hat. Heavy framed sunglasses shaded her eyes, and her bare feet showed the chipped and worn nail varnish that once had been scarlet.

On the pebble beach opposite her home on the spot Callum died, she sat from morning to evening. Grief engulfed her. Her eyes focused on the far horizon, and intermittently, she threw a pebble into the sea. At 6 p.m. she gathered her belongings, walked back across the road, deposited the chair and icebox inside her front door and after some menial personal maintenance and the consumption of minimal food, she headed to the Convento Plaza yards from Casa Olivia Rose.

She attended mass at the impressive sandstone church, which displayed a plain crucifix carved smoothly into the high wall of the centuries-old holy place, and stopped to pray at the statue of the kneeling girl in the tree-lined courtyard. Inside the ornate church, she attended mass and excommunicated herself from communion but attended confession. She lit candles. Daily devotion was the only practice she followed, and the young Spanish Catholic priest became her confidant.

Once she visited her lawyer in the town to amend her will and establish business formalities. Otherwise, Antoinette withdrew from life. She saw no one, went nowhere and rarely, if ever, answered her phone. Her email and television services were allowed to lapse. On her way home from church in the evening, she shopped for essential commodities that barely held body and soul together.

Her world had ended on the day Gianni and Callum died. Daughter Olivia Rose tried to reach out to reestablish contact. Antoinette ignored her messages.

To the parish priest, Antoinette unburdened her soul. In the small seating area behind the altar, she made her confession to the Father. On her knees in the sanctity of that divine space with the holy man she had grown to trust and respect, she told the story of her baby boy Salvatore.

Her palms clasped in prayer, she began, "Father, forgive me, for I have sinned." Her voice broke, and she struggled to hold back the tears. "Twenty years ago as a young married woman I had an affair with a boy whom I had known before my marriage. On a visit to my Italian village from my married home in England, he and I were intimate." She took a large gulp of air. This was the first time she had said the words out loud.

"Take your time," said the priest kindly.

"Back in England, I discovered I was pregnant. I already had a five-year-old daughter by my husband. Alone in a foreign country, I was distraught. I didn't want to tell my husband of the pregnancy even though I questioned whether I might be able to pretend the baby was his. For weeks I struggled with a decision, getting more and more scared as the time was passed. I hadn't been to see a doctor and only completed a test I'd bought from the pharmacy. Then one day, when I was going frantic with indecision, I read a women's magazine article about . . . it was about," she faltered, and lowered her eyes as she said the shocking word, "abortion."

Antoinette dreaded the look of shock she had anticipated would appear on the priest's face. She was mortified. This was the secret that shamed her, which she dreaded anyone discovering. Her mouth was dry; the priest handed her a small plastic cup of water. She sipped and wetted her lips.

"The article gave lots of information. I realized years later that I was not the only one. There must have been many young women in my position. There was an address and telephone number for a clinic in London. I had two appointments. I paid a few hundred pounds and made an appointment for a termination. I told my husband that a childhood friend was visiting and I planned to spend a few days with her in London. There was no reason for him to question the story. I didn't make a habit of keeping things from him."

The priest held out his hands. "Please, child, get up off your knees. Sit in the chair."

Antoinette refused. "I went to the clinic and had the procedure. A doctor asked if I wanted to know the sex of the fetus they removed. I said yes and was told it was a boy. I stayed alone in a hotel room for two days, though the clinic insisted I should have someone with me at least for the first forty-eight hours."

The silence in the room was deafening. Antoinette could hear every beat of her heart. She wiped away tears and admitted, "I never told anyone. Not my husband and not Gianni, the father of the child. No one.

"My heart was broken and, although I continued to go to church, I went to light candles for my dead son. The only place I revealed my secret was in a locked diary. I performed rituals for my son. He and I lived a secret life. I lit candles, gave him a birth date and named him Salvatore by drinking water from the baptismal fount. In my secret place I imagined that Saint Salvatore was taking care of my son in heaven.

"Every year on what I calculated would have been his birthday, I bought a card and baked a small cake with candles. I tried to make sure I was at my family home in the hills outside Siena so I could devote time to him. All through the years, I kept the cards and candles in my secret box in the attic above my bedroom."

Antoinette's chest heaved with deep sobs and tears streamed down her face. The priest lifted her to her feet and guided her to the armchair. A beam of light struck the crucifix he wore over his vestments, and she felt a moment of divine release.

"Did you ever ask forgiveness for the sin you committed?"

"I prayed and begged God but was frightened to tell the priest, even at confession, in case I was excommunicated. I thought everyone would know what I had done."

"You have suffered a heavy penance," he said softly.

"God would not have withheld from you his mercy. What of the husband and the father of the child?"

"Many years later I left the husband. The father of the child was Gianni, the man who died in the motorcycle accident. He never knew of Salvatore. To burden him with my guilt would not have helped either of us."

"Let's pray together," said the priest. Taking her hands, he clasped them around his heavy iron crucifix from which the beam of light glinted and enfolded his hands around hers.

"You are forgiven," he said and the light reflected in her eyes.

Antoinette felt the unbearable burden of decades of guilt lift from her shoulders. She experienced a new depth of breathing as anxiety and fear were released from her body.

"Your penances will be one hundred Hail Marys. Our Blessed Mother will help heal you. Go, in peace," he told her, "to love and serve the Lord."

"Thank you, Father," said Antoinette. "Thank you."

Together they entered the church, genuflected at the altar and walked down the aisle to the main door. At the candle stand, Antoinette paused. "I've made a new will and set up a foundation in the name of my son, Salvatore, An Eternal Flame for Salvatore. My home in Italy will be gifted to the charity and the nuns at my local church, many of whom I have known from childhood. They have agreed to administer the house and use it as they see fit in the service of girls or women in need of solace. Women like me will be able to light an eternal fame for their babies. May I add you as a trustee?"

"It would be an honor," he assured her.

"There's one more request. I promise it will be the last," said Antoinette grasping his hand. "In the event of my death, go to my house in Italy and make sure that no one is allowed to open my sealed box."

"Your wishes will be carried out, but let us hope that the day our Lord calls you home will be a long time coming. Good night, Antoinette."

Evening had become night, and night had become midnight as the priest heard Antoinette's confession. In the cloudless painted night above the church, a cloak of stars glittered and showed Antoinette her way home.

Chapter Thirty-Eight

At the taxi stand by the church, very early the next morning, Antoinette hailed a cab and told him to take her to the paragliding center in the mountains above Calpe. The one she observed from Gianni's house.

Today she dressed in white and abandoned her black clothing. A floor-sweeping white gown hid her bare feet. With no hat, her hair, once her pride and joy but now neglected, hung free.

"Thank you, God, I have my redemption," she said as she prayed at the statue of the kneeling girl.

The journey took less than an hour and heading out of Altea on the coast road at such an early hour, the roads were deserted. The taxi made the journey, farther and farther up into the mountains. The road became almost impassable and when she saw the paragliders she had observed so many times from an optimum viewing spot across the mountain, she paid off the driver.

"Do you want me to collect you to drive back to Altea?" he asked.

"No, thank you." She averted her eyes from the white temple at the top of the cliff. Like her, the family would never recover from the loss of their son. "Forgive me, Gianni," she said in a whisper as she prayed, a million times a day. "Forgive me, Callum."

Antoinette's feet were dirty, cut and bruised from endless days of walking without shoes. On a smooth rock, she sat down, wrapped her voluminous skirt around her knees and watched the gliders. They jumped, pulled cords and bright-colored canopies opened across the sky. Then they sailed off on a breeze into the wild, blue yonder.

Antoinette watched fascinated. Freedom. Liberation.

The sun climbed high above the mountains, clouds chased each other all over the sky and the ocean danced with snow-capped peaks on the waves that rushed to shore.

Through the scrubby grass and over the jagged rocks she walked, as if in a dream. In her mind's eye, the words of the psalm formed an image: "Angels will hold you up lest you dash your foot against a rock."

Antoinette walked to the edge of the cliff. Balanced her toes on a rock and raised her arms. The breeze fluttered around her diaphanous white dress. Her whole being transmuted with light. On the wings of angels, Antoinette flew home.

Chapter Thirty-Nine

"How do you feel about going back to the church where you two were married?" Olivia Rose asked her father, Jason, as their British Airways jet landed in Siena.

Jason was not one to deny his duty, and he insisted on accompanying Olivia Rose to Siena for Antoinette's funeral. Her remains were to be transported from Altea to her local church. "Your mother and I are still married," he reminded her. "She did mention divorce in one letter but neither of us pursued it."

Jason had answered the phone call that came from the priest in Altea. The priest's voice was hesitant and his English stumbling. "I regret to inform you," he said, "Señora Antoinette has passed away. It is my duty as her parish priest to make arrangements for the funeral. She requested to me that it be in Italy. Sorry, my English is poor. I may be able to put someone in touch who can tell you more details."

Olivia Rose refused to believe the news. "Dead?" she screamed when Jason told her. "Had she been ill? Was it an accident? When is the funeral?"

"I don't have the answers to the questions," admitted

Jason, "but I'm sure we will hear more details soon. Of course, we will both travel to Italy."

"Would you like me to call Gianni to ask for information?" asked Olivia Rose. "I can't sit here not knowing, not doing anything. I need to talk to him."

Jason couldn't put his finger on it, but her demeanor was strange. She appeared to be angry and afraid. Two days later she still had not cried. At least not in front of him. Perhaps she was in shock. "Gianni must know how to get in touch with us," said Jason. "Let's wait."

The phone call to answer all questions did not happen. Only another hesitant call from the priest who gave the date and time of the internment. One week away.

Brevity seemed to be the Spanish way, at least when dealing with people who did not speak their language.

The lawyer left a short message on Jason's, the next of kin's, home answering machine. "The will is to be read after the internment. You will be told where to go. Questions can be dealt with then."

Olivia Rose was beside herself, but whether with grief or frustration was not clear. "It all feels disorganized, and we still don't know where or when mum died."

"This is one of the hardest things you will ever have to deal with," said Jason. "It doesn't help that you and she have had a disjointed relationship for years. Perhaps you can put some of your guilt and regrets to rest when you are in her home village. Then we will get the full story."

"Don't torture yourself," he said, anxious to calm Olivia Rose's anxiety. "I'm sure there was nothing you could have done to stop this happening."

Olivia Rose wasn't so sure. She was haunted by the pain she could not avoid in her mother's eyes as she fled from the airport and her mother's tearful cry, "Have I been punished enough now?"

As if performing a ritual, a walking meditation, Olivia Rose trudged constantly from room to room in the house and round and round the garden. "I'm sorry, mother. Please forgive me," she whispered an anguished prayer.

"I'll get it," she insisted every time the phone rang. She was desperate to know the cause of her mother's death and whether she was responsible for it. *Why didn't Gianni call? He would know the story.*

Frustrated and scared, she called the lawyer who explained that any information they were supposed to have was in her mother's will. He planned to travel with her local priest to Italy with the body.

No arrangements had been made to collect Jason and Olivia Rose at the airport. They arranged a taxi, and Olivia Rose provided the address. She Googled and discovered a small pension near the church and booked them in for two nights. She had expected Gianni to collect them at the airport. *Where the hell was he?*

Father and daughter arrived late the evening before the morning of Antoinette's funeral. "I'll go by the church and see what arrangements are in place," said Jason. "Are you sure you don't want to come with me?"

Olivia Rose shook her head. She was behaving badly, and her fear had led her to pick up a resentment. "Why can't we stay at mother's home?" she asked petulantly. Antoinette had told her that the house would be left to her only daughter.

The day of the funeral was clear, sunny and mild. Olivia Rose had ascertained that in Italy funeral wear was formal and she wore a D&G designer fitted coat dress with black patent stilettos and a black net fascinator veil hat.

Jason and Olivia Rose were amazed by how many people turned out for Antoinette's funeral. They all talked of her with affection. Many had been friends since primary school. Antoinette was definitely a star of the village. The girl who had it all.

One person was missing. Gianni did not appear.

Olivia Rose inquired, the local people shrugged and said, "Gianni moved on from here many years ago. His home is in Spain with his family."

After the internment, a friend of Antoinette drove them the short distance to the restaurant where an official lunch was held, and the reading of the will took place after the meal. A handful of friends came from Altea, including Antoinette's development contractor, Jan.

Jan refused to divulge any information about her mother's death. The official version included the fact that her fall happened on the cliffside close to the extreme sports center. "*Accidente*" was the only answer given to her question.

"Why is Gianni not here?" Olivia Rose demanded to know.

Jan was a man who played his cards close to his chest. He was reluctant to be the one to break the news. "Gianni also had an accident. A road accident. He is dead. It's a tragedy. There are some dark forces at work. Better to not question. The less we talk about it the better."

Olivia Rose stared straight ahead, tears streaming down her face. Jan worried that she was going to cause a scene. "Here, take this," he said, and handed her a napkin to dry her face and blow her nose. "Today is about your mother. We must respect her memory."

A primitive instinct warned Olivia Rose to keep her feelings to herself. It really was none of her business. As far as anyone knew, Gianni was a relative stranger to her. The lover of her dead mother. Maybe at a later stage she would be granted insight. For now, she had to accept that Gianni, along with her mother, really had gone from her life. In death they were together.

* * *

Sitting at the head of a circular polished wooden table, the lawyer formally read the will.

I, Antoinette Marianne Frederica, do hereby state that the property at this my family home, the land surrounding it which I own and all furniture and furnishings are, on the occasion of my death, to pass to the administration of the nuns of San Savior's church, and be held in trust by them for the

Foundation to be set up and named for my son, Salvatore. The Foundation shall be known as Eternal Flame Foundation for Salvatore.

There was complete silence in the room. Shell-shocked, Jason sat bolt upright in his straight-backed seat. Olivia Rose gasped and slumped forward. Neither knew what was going on or had the remotest idea what might come next.

The lawyer paused and asked if there were any questions. Jason and Olivia Rose were too dumbstruck to think straight; questions would come later. Jason briefly closed his eyes and sighed. He shook his head when it looked as if Olivia Rose might be about to intervene. "Leave it," he warned her in a stage whisper.

The lawyer continued, *To my daughter, Olivia Rose, I leave the house already endowed in her name at Altea, Casa Olivia Rose. Furniture, furnishings and title are hers for life.*

To my husband, Jason, I leave my red Alpha Romeo convertible. Title and keys are now his. I wish him enjoyment to drive it.

The lawyer had checked, at Antoinette's insistence, whether Gianni's family wanted her to return the car. They did not. In response to the request their lawyer had sent the title, spare keys and also a letter stating that property Gianni gifted to Antoinette during their relationship remained in her ownership for her to dispose of as she saw fit.

There was little else in the will that impacted the English visitors.

Jason had questions galore about the son, Salvatore,

but in a brief conversation with the priest he was assured there was no actual person holding title to Antoinette's property. "It is her private business. Best please to leave alone," the priest cautioned.

Antoinette's intention was to set up a charitable foundation with very clear and specific objectives. This she had achieved.

All mourners were invited back to the house later that afternoon to meet the nuns who would act as administrators for the Eternal Flame Foundation.

Olivia Rose had questions about her Altea property and Jan promised to meet with her at a later date, give her a tour of the property and take care of any questions about real estate or development. "There are many loyal craftsmen who have worked on the building. They will be happy to provide any service or advice you require," he assured her.

"Do you want to go to this party back at the house?" Olivia Rose asked Jason.

"I do," he said. "I've no idea what it all means but it's a most generous gesture on your mother's part to leave the house to the church. You are more likely to get use out of your house in that lovely town of Altea. And I can't wait to zoom down the Surrey lanes in my Italian Stallion boy toy."

Olivia Rose gave a nervous laugh. "Let's walk there together and I can apologize for being such a nightmare daughter. Mum was always apologizing for being a lousy mum. I see now that I was a terrible daughter."

"She would never have said that," he told her and

patted her cheek. "You're headstrong and determined. Like her."

"I suppose now you're a free man—and one with a red convertible—you will propose to the Library Lady. She's moved into our house so I'm taking the hint it's time for me to move out. Altea has come at the perfect time. I have a seafront home in Spain and I can make a life there, without moving permanently.

"I can keep my job and fly back and forth to my weekend home. Thanks to mum. I owe her such a lot. I'll try to make her proud of me, and I'll honor her home in Altea and her memory. I may even start going to church."

Jason smiled. He knew his daughter was difficult, especially when she was frightened, but she was really a caring young lady. They had been through a great deal together and he loved her unconditionally. "As you've guessed, I may be requiring the services of White Roses Weddings. At least one of us deserves a happy ever after."

Olivia Rose looked shocked. "Don't rule me out. I'll have you know I have a date later today with a very handsome Italian male. He was a friend of mum's. A young friend. He told me, 'Every time she came to visit the church, she asked me to cut her a bouquet of white roses to put in her home.' Today he promised to cut a bouquet of white roses for me."

Chapter Forty

The party at the house was in full swing, and guests roamed freely all over Antoinette's house. Father Manuel heard a commotion upstairs in the attic. He climbed the rickety wooden staircase. Two middle-aged ladies, most likely school friends of Antoinette from three decades before, having had too much wine and emboldened to misbehave, were hacking at her private red box with a knife.

Father Manuel watched and waited. When he judged the moment was right, his voice of authority boomed across the small timbered attic. "Can you read what it says on that box?"

His white dog collar gleamed in the dim light.

The women looked embarrassed. Like naughty children caught doing wrong—and by a priest. Albeit one from a different parish. A different country.

"Read it to me."

Their voices were small and frightened as together they read aloud, "Personal—in the event of my death, destroy unopened. Antoinette."

"Thank you, bring down the box and put it in the trunk of my rental car. That box will accompany me back to Altea. The instruction means what it says, *Destroy Unopened*. I take full responsibility for making sure that is exactly what happens. Antoinette can rest in peace."

The End

Acknowledgments

Thanks to the excellent creative team whose experience and expertise helped make this novel a reality.

Gary Rosenberg of The Book Couple has been the designer and production team leader of all my books. Thank you, Gary, for always bringing the solution.

My editorial assistant, Michelle Ruger, excelled herself by providing the original inspiration for this work. Throughout the summer, she studied for the finals of her PhD, and as I wrote the last page of the story, she was awarded her doctorate. Dr. Ruger, you are a true gift in my life.

To my brother, Billy, congratulations. You cheated death twice this year. You are my Superhero.

To Mary, the best sister in the world, and the family and friends who loved and supported us all.

Today is Thanksgiving Day—for my abundant blessings, I give thanks.

Ellen Frazer-Jameson,
November 22, 2018

About the Author

Ellen Frazer-Jameson is a professional communicator working in media, print, and theater. A former BBC broadcaster and Fleet Street journalist, Ellen is a published author, producer, theater director, and performer. She co-presented the largest late-night audience show in Europe on BBC Radio 2. Ellen lives in London and Miami Beach and to relax dances Argentine tango.

Ellen's other novels include:

Love Trilogy:

The story begins with *Love Mother Love Daughter;* the love affair continues with *Love Refuses to Die,* and reaches its exciting conclusion in *Love Kills with a Kiss.*

Dark Hole in My Soul, the first edition of the retitled *Flame Island.*

Travels with Otto and *Slim with the Stars* are now available for the first time on Amazon.com.

You can contact Ellen through her website at
www.ellenfrazerjameson.com

Author photo courtesy of international photographer Dora Franco
www.dorafrancophoto.com

If you have enjoyed this novel,
or any of my other books,
please leave a review at
www.amazon.com

For more information,
I invite you to visit my website:
www.ellenfrazerjameson.com